T0043160

RIVER OF WRATH

By the Multi-Award-Winning Duo
Alexandrea Weis with Lucas Astor

Young Adult Novels
Death by the River

Adult Novels
The St. Benedict Series
River of Ashes (St. Benedict, Book 1)

The Magnus Blackwell Series
Blackwell: The Prequel (A Magnus Blackwell Novel, Book 1)
Damned (A Magnus Blackwell Novel, Book 2)
Bound (A Magnus Blackwell Novel, Book 3)
Seize (A Magnus Blackwell Novel, Book 4)

By Alexandrea Weis

Young Adult Novels
Realm
Sisters of the Moon
Have You Seen Me?

Adult Novels
The Secret Brokers

Forthcoming by Alexandrea Weis and Lucas Astor
River of Ghosts (St. Benedict, Book 3)
The Secret Salt Society

Forthcoming by Alexandrea Weis
The Christmas Spirit (Spirit of Elkmont, Book 1)

Praise for *River of Ashes* (Book 1)

One of Apple's Most Anticipated Books for Summer in Mysteries & Thrillers

"A psychological portrait akin to *Lord of the Flies*."
~Midwest Book Review

"Hooked from the first page, *River of Ashes* is dark, rough, and has a smorgasbord of twists and turns. Highly recommend."
~ The Strand Magazine

"If Gillian Flynn and Bret Easton Ellis had a book baby, it would be *River of Ashes*." ***~Booktrib***

"Despite its ghosts and hauntings, this evocative tale presents an all-too-real terror that gets under your skin—and stays." ***~Rue Morgue***

"A twisty, page-turning thriller filled with tension and Southern Gothic vibes." ***~Best Magazine*** **(UK)**

"Beau Devereaux is every bit the "bad boy" our mothers warned us about. Think Mark Wahlberg from *Fear* but imagine if he crossed paths with Sidney Prescott." **~GothGirlOnTheTrain**

"Once in a while, you come across a book that owns your heart and soul. *River of Ashes* was that book for me." **~BookmarkedByShreya**

"Weis and Astor have created not only a spine-tingling story, but also one of the most loathsome, twisted, and believable villains I have ever read. It was fantastic." **~beachesandreads**

"Chilling and suspenseful, *River of Ashes* is a story that mimics real-life abuse and violence in today's youth. What seems like innocent high school shenanigans quickly turns evil in the path of a predator."
~San Francisco Book Review

"Disturbingly nostalgic with a modern twist, this dark and twisty psychological horror will leave you feeling more than a little unsettled."
Melanie McKnight, Founder of Twisted Retreat and Unplugged Book Box (named #1 by ***USA Today*** and a top 10 pick by ***OprahDaily***).

RIVER OF WRATH

ALEXANDREA WEIS · LUCAS ASTOR

River of Wrath
St. Benedict, Book 2

This is a work of fiction. Names, characters, places, and incidents either are the product of the author's imagination or are used fictitiously.
Any resemblance to actual persons, living or dead, or locales is entirely coincidental.

Copyright © 2023 Alexandrea Weis and Lucas Astor
All rights reserved.

Cover Art by Sam Shearon
MisterSamShearon.com

Cover design by Michael J. Canales
MJCImageWorks.com

Edited by Livia Loren and Liana Gardner

No part of this book may be reproduced or transmitted in any form or by any means, electronic or mechanical, including photocopying, recording, or by any information storage and retrieval system now known or to be invented, without written permission from the publisher, except where permitted by law.

The publisher is not responsible for websites (or their content) that are not owned by the publisher.

ISBN: 978-1-64548-017-4

Published by Vesuvian Books
www.VesuvianBooks.com

Printed in the United States
10 9 8 7 6 5 4 3 2 1

"Come not within the measure of my wrath."

~William Shakespeare

Chapter One

Sweat gathered under the brim of Kent Davis's Stetson as he walked the sandy beach along the Bogue Falaya River. He didn't feel the brisk January breeze or pay attention to the mutterings of the forensic team. The unease burning in his gut shut out all distractions. He rested his hand on his belt, brushing against his Louisiana sheriff's badge. The rub of metal reminded him of the oath he'd sworn to protect and serve, but on days like this, he hated his job.

Dispatch had initially deemed the early morning call from a frantic jogger a hoax. After an officer confirmed there was a body, Kent arrived at the scene to confront his worst nightmare—another murder. He already had three unsolved deaths weighing heavily on his department. Two high school students and a woman from out of town had died there in a matter of months. City leaders had been breathing down his neck for answers.

Kent studied the black body bag the technicians carried. This was only going to make his job harder.

His crew combed the beach, where receding floodwaters had exposed a young woman's grave. From the looks of her bleached bones, partially covered in the remnants of a red dress, she'd been there for quite some time. He doubted they'd find anything admissible. There would be trace evidence, but no footprints, no debris, no blood, and no signs of struggle.

He climbed the steep hill from the beach to the parking area, scanning for any clues. Everywhere was a potential crime scene. After years of being in law enforcement, he doubted he could see the world in any other way.

"I don't like this one bit, Bill," Kent said, approaching the heavyset coroner waiting by the open doors of his van.

"What's there to like. We got a dead girl who's been buried here a long time." Dr. Bill Broussard removed a pair of black-framed glasses from his egg-shaped head. "You might find a lead in old missing persons reports."

"I'll access the St. Tammany Parish database when I get to the station. Until then, she's a Jane Doe." Kent eyed the coroner's van. "How long will it take to know something?"

Bill cleaned his glasses and moved out of the way while a technician slammed the doors closed. He waited until the man climbed into the driver's side before responding. "You realize workin' with old bones makes it harder to identify the cause of death. Let me get her to the lab, then we'll see."

"I got enough going on with Beau Devereaux, Dawn Moore, and Andrea Harrison." Kent tipped back his hat. "This makes four bodies and no leads."

"As soon as people catch wind of this, the gossip mill will run wild." Bill motioned to the van. "We already got enough rumors flying around about serial killers and rapists on the loose."

"But at least we know this isn't a serial killer."

"Do we?" Bill flipped through a few pictures on his phone and showed Kent the screen.

Kent looked at the bloody mess that had comprised the remains of Beau Devereaux. The golden boy of St. Benedict had been a football star and heir to the Devereaux fortune. The day Kent found his mutilated body along the river had been one of the worst of his career. Beau's death, on the heels of the rape and grisly murder of Dawn Moore, had shattered his faith in their small town.

He squinted at the picture. "What am I missing?"

Bill pointed at Beau's bruised and bloody neck. "Trachea isn't midline. It's in two pieces. In the autopsy, I discovered his neck had been broken."

Kent thought of the murder cases that cluttered his desk. "Same as the Harrison girl. Her neck was broken. Any chance wild dogs could have done this?"

Bill's meaty lips thinned into a line. "Harrison had no bite marks. Only Beau suffered extensive puncture wounds. For a dog to snap someone's neck, it would have to be big and have impressive jaw strength. Until your men find me an animal like that, I'm leaving Beau's death a homicide." He wiped his damp brow. "What worries me is this woman's bones show there might be a break in her neck, too. If that's the case, someone around here could have a long history of murder."

Kent grew irate. He'd left the turmoil of working for the New Orleans Police Department to get away from the steady dose of homicides. Ten years ago, St. Benedict had been the answer to a prayer for him, his wife, and their two boys. He didn't want to think such horror could have remained hidden for so long in the idyllic town.

"Send me the preliminary results of the autopsy as soon as you get them." Kent pinched the bridge of his nose, fighting off a headache. "I want it in my hand when I tell Gage Devereaux what we found. He might recall someone who went missing. He's lived here all his life and is bound to have heard something."

Bill swatted at a passing fly. "He won't be happy to hear about another body. You know how protective he is of St. Benedict."

"Yep. I expect this will piss him off."

The patriarch and owner of the biggest employer, Benedict Brewery, Gage oversaw everything in the town. Some called him a control freak—a trait many had seen in his son, Beau—but to Kent, Gage was thorough, detail-oriented, and would have made a great detective if he hadn't taken over the family business.

"He's gonna ask you if this has anything to do with the investigation into Beau's death." Bill frowned. "What're you gonna tell him?"

Kent clenched his jaw. "We don't know if any of these deaths are related."

"Yet," Bill added. "Seems like an awfully big coincidence to me."

Kent pulled keys from the front pocket of his jeans. "There're too many coincidences going on around here, and they all seem to center on this damned river. When can you get me a DNA report?"

"Might take a while." Bill scratched his head. "Budget constraints and the backlog of cases clogging the system have slowed everything down."

"How long are we talking? A week?"

Bill snorted. "More like weeks. A long-dead Jane Doe isn't exactly a priority. Otherwise, we could get a rush on it."

"Then we'll just have to wait and see what we get back," Kent grumbled.

Bill went to the driver's side of the van and spoke to the technician. He then waved at Kent before walking away.

The sheriff waited as the van slowly eased onto the main road, with Bill's black SUV following close behind.

Alone, Kent removed his hat and gazed up at the tall pines rimming the parking lot. Cresting above the tallest of the trees was The Abbey's single charred limestone spire—its twin lost in the fire.

The serene place had witnessed so many atrocities—suicide, fire, and Dawn Moore's murder. Kent would never understand what the Benedictine monks who founded the seminary ever saw in that cursed land. Legends about the abandoned abbey and its wild dogs had floated around the community for as long as anyone could remember.

When the dogs appear, death is near.

He'd never believed any of the stories until now. Kent feared there might be some truth to the legend, after all.

And the worst was yet to come.

Chapter Two

The warm air blowing through the vents in Leslie's new car did little to offset the bite of winter. She was constantly freezing these days, no matter how bright the sunshine or how high the heat.

Kelly Norton sat in the passenger seat as Leslie drove along Devereaux Road. She'd offered her a ride to school and was thankful when she accepted.

"I'm glad my mother moved here," Kelly said while gazing out the window. "Having you guys around has helped. But it worked out well for all of us, huh? Now we have each other's backs."

Leslie tucked a loose lock of blonde hair behind her ear. "Yeah, even though how the four of us became close wasn't ... Well, it's behind us."

Kelly's gaze dropped to her hands. "Do you ever think about that night and what we did? No matter how hard I try, I can't get it out of my head."

Leslie was keenly aware of how Beau Devereaux still haunted his victims. Alone at night, she swore his shadow lingered in the corner of her room, the hatred in his eyes scorching her skin.

"*I killed the wrong Moore twin.*"

His voice would send Leslie bolting from bed, drenched in sweat. The nightly visit from the sinister son of a bitch who had murdered her sister kept her teetering on the edge. "We did what we had to." Leslie bit her lower lip, fighting to shut Beau out. "We paid him back for what he did to all of us."

"Yeah, but I still don't get it. He was alive when we left him at The Abbey. After you dropped us off at school, we all went home, figuring he'd spend the night tied to a chair. So what happened?" A line deepened across Kelly's brow. "I wonder if he had something to do with the girl they found at the river."

Leslie turned to her. "I heard the girl's been dead for ages. It couldn't have been Beau."

"But that means someone around here probably killed her. Makes me appreciate the extra security at our new condo. Mr. Devereaux insisted my mom take the place." Kelly patted the black dashboard. "I guess we should be grateful he's been so generous."

Leslie stiffened at the mention of Gage. He was the other Devereaux she'd never be free of. "Luckily, the launch of his national campaign provided a plausible explanation for the bonuses Gage gave our parents. It would be hard to explain away my car, Taylor's Jeep, Sara's truck, and your fancy condo without it."

Kelly rolled a ringlet of red hair between her fingers. "Have you talked to Derek, or are you still pretending it's over? The guy's so in love with you it's almost painful."

Leslie's heart ached. After losing her sister, pushing Derek away had been the hardest thing she'd ever done. "He was asking too many questions."

"How long do you think we have before everyone finds out what we did?" Kelly muttered as she peered out the window. "The one thing about secrets is they never stay hidden."

Guilt tightened Leslie's throat. She should be used to the sensation by now, but it still filled her with the same self-loathing. The person who mattered most was Derek, and he would despise her for taking part in Beau's death. She had distanced herself from him before the truth tore them apart. Leslie reasoned that was better than watching him walk away, hating her forever.

Shivering, Leslie ratcheted up the heat again.

"Are you sure about going this way?" Kelly asked.

For several weeks, Leslie had avoided the road leading to the river. Even having Kelly by her side couldn't stop the horrible feeling in her stomach, but a nagging compulsion drove her forward. "I want to see where they found the body."

Kelly's voice dropped to a whisper. "You're not afraid it will remind you of ..."

Leslie clenched the steering wheel. Every conversation, thought, and breath reminded her of Dawn's death. Her hate for Beau had been the armor getting her through the funeral and a future without her twin. It had initially driven her to meet with Gage Devereaux and demand justice. But her restlessness had not abated after Beau's demise. She still needed answers about why Dawn had died so senselessly. She once believed revenge would soothe her grief, but it only seemed to escalate it.

"I can't run away from what happened." She coughed to cover her welling emotions. "Dawn would want me to live my life as best I can."

Kelly put her hand over Leslie's forearm and gave her an encouraging squeeze. "I shouldn't have said anything. I can't imagine how hard going back to school after Christmas break is. Maybe you need more time."

Leslie wanted to laugh. "And miss my last semester of high school? No way. Besides, knowing the bastard who killed my sister is rotting in hell helps me go on."

Kelly's eyes narrowed into slits. "Beau deserved what he got."

"Look at that." Leslie slowed the car and pointed at a stretch of yellow caution tape. "This must be close to where they found her."

Kelly crossed her arms tightly over her chest. "Yeah, and everyone partying at the river has probably been walking over her grave."

A deputy in the parking lot carried equipment to a white evidence van.

Leslie pulled over to the side of the road. "No wonder this place always creeped me out."

Kelly kept her gaze pinned on the parking lot. "I wonder who she is. Too bad we can't ask the lady in white. I heard she was the seminary's gamekeeper and now haunts the area. I bet she knows all the ghosts hanging around the river."

"Where did you hear about the gamekeeper?"

Kelly glanced at Leslie. "After the fire, I searched the internet and found an article about the female gamekeeper and her dogs. Maybe the dogs that killed Beau are their descendants."

Leslie stifled a small smile. "Yeah, I heard he was pretty chewed up."

Kelly rolled down her window. "Aren't you hot?"

The rush of wintry air was a shock to her system. The aroma of pine trees and the distant rush of water clashed with her senses. The trees around the parking lot entrance swayed in the breeze, and she caught a glimpse of The Abbey's remaining charred spire.

The thought of what Dawn had endured in that place made Leslie sick. She'd gotten a whiff of scorched skin coming from the hospital room, but her parents had kept her from seeing the scope of Dawn's injuries. "Do you think the girl they found will haunt the river, too?"

"I guess if you believe people hang around where they—" Her mouth clamped shut. "She's not there. Dawn's in Heaven." Kelly took her hand. "You're like ice." She rolled up the window.

Leslie managed a faint smile, not wanting to appear indifferent. "I'd like to believe that. But I've heard some people in town whispering about seeing Dawn's ghost at The Abbey."

"You can't believe that. That's just bullshit started by idiots wanting attention." Kelly gave a dismissive wave of her hand. "Dawn would never haunt The Abbey."

"But what if she is? What if she's trapped there and looking for me?" Leslie's dread escalated at the thought of her sister alone and lost in such a horrid place. "I can't rest until I know for sure."

"What are you going to do? Spend nights at The Abbey chasing shadows?"

Leslie put the car into drive, wishing she'd never mentioned her fear to Kelly. "I don't know, but I'll figure something out."

Kelly frowned. "Don't you dare go there by yourself."

Leslie checked the road before pulling out. "Maybe this is something I need to do alone."

Kelly angrily pointed at Leslie. "There you go again with your, 'I need to be alone crap.' What's up with that? And don't tell me it has to do with Dawn or breaking up with Derek. Ever since you bailed on us after leaving The Abbey that night, you've been pulling away. I get that you want space, but this lone wolf shit has to end. What we did bound the four of us together forever. You can't run from the past."

The burden of hiding her role in Beau's death pressed on Leslie's chest like a barbell. It had been her choice to participate in Beau's end, but no one warned her about the repercussions—the sleepless nights, the nightmares, the guilt, and resentment. There were moments when Leslie questioned if she should've stayed away from Gage and left Beau to the cops. But she knew it was the right call, even if she found it hard to live with.

"I'm not running," she finally told Kelly while driving toward Main Street. "I've been trying to get my head straight." She kept her eyes on the road, choosing not to face her friend. "It's funny, when we were at The Abbey and had Beau where we wanted him, I was convinced my life would get better after that. But now I realize that wasn't the end of my grief. It was the beginning."

Kelly offered her an encouraging smile. "I'm here if you need me. We all are. Taylor and Sara are worried about you, too."

Leslie arched an eyebrow. "Sara doesn't worry about anyone but Sara."

"Boy, ain't that the truth." Kelly sat back in the leather seat. "All Sara talks about these days is her new clothes. That girl is obsessed with shopping."

The traffic lights of Main Street shone in the distance. Leslie had survived their trip to the river without breaking down. On the inside, her melee of emotions was, at times, staggering. Losing Derek had taken away the last guide rails to her sanity. No matter how much Kelly and the others tried to help, Leslie remained convinced that her descent into hopelessness was an absolute certainty.

Leslie pulled into the school parking lot. Confronting the daunting red brick walls of St. Benedict High after the long Christmas break wasn't going to be easy. She welcomed the distraction of school, but not the memories the familiar halls would awaken. Leslie doubted she'd ever feel comfortable there again. But, for Dawn's sake, she would force herself to embrace every experience. That was Leslie's promise to her sister—to accumulate enough happy, meaningful, and bizarre moments to fill two lifetimes.

Kelly got out of the car and gazed around the quiet parking lot. "Where is everybody?"

Leslie hit the lock on her remote and pulled her blue coat closer. "It's freezing. They're probably inside."

"You've been cold a lot lately. Are you getting sick?" Kelly asked, walking toward her.

"Maybe I need to load up on vitamin C or something."

Kelly remained close as they made their way to the entrance. Leslie was glad to have her there, but she missed walking into school with Derek. She'd battled with her feelings for him too many times to count, but today would be tough.

Only a few students lingered on the grassy quad outside the school. Like Leslie, everyone headed to the stone steps leading to the front doors, anxious to be out of the frigid breeze.

The moment she stepped inside, she sighed at the embrace of warm air. But her reprieve was short-lived. All the students gathered at the entrance turned her way, and an uncanny silence swept through the hall. Then the whispering began.

Kelly encouraged her along with a gentle nudge. "Ignore them."

After Dawn's death, Leslie had been too wrapped up in grief to give a damn about the stories circulating in town. But the dead girl at the river had sparked fresh gossip about her sister.

Leslie followed Kelly through a small crowd clogging the corridor. "You think they'd be terrified another body was found. I swear the people in this town are obsessed with death."

Kelly stared down a group of freshman girls huddled together. "Everyone believes it will never happen to them until it does."

Leslie gripped the strap of her bag, thinking of her sister's bouncy walk and swinging ponytail. "Some sooner than others."

"All right, bitches." The boisterous declaration came from behind the freshmen. "Get lost." Sara Bissell emerged from a flurry of girls scrambling for cover. Dressed in black from head to toe with matching goth-inspired makeup, Bondage Bissell, as she was known, had changed her look.

"What the hell, Sara?" Kelly said.

"It's Madame Sara now. I'm a medium." She placed a hand on her hip. "I discovered my gift when my parents took me to New Orleans over Christmas vacation. A fortune-teller in Jackson Square told me I could speak to the dead. God knows this town has more than its fair share." She grimaced as her attention fell on Leslie. "Damn, I'm sorry. I didn't mean to say Dawn was—"

"Did this fortune-teller say to dress like that?" Leslie interrupted, changing the subject.

Kelly motioned to Sara's outfit and chuckled. "You look more like a vampire than a medium."

"Fuck off." Sara tossed her long platinum-blonde hair over her shoulder.

Leslie stepped between them. "We're just surprised by the sudden change."

Sara pressed out a crease in her skirt, her devil-may-care expression showcasing her usual blithe attitude. "With all the crap goin' on, the last thing anyone would notice is little ol' me."

Kelly focused on Sara's tall black boots, seemingly transfixed. "Madame Sara does have a point."

"Careful, Norton. Someone might think you have an actual brain under all that red hair," Sara taunted.

A slender brunette scurried up to them with a packed bag weighing down her shoulder and carrying several books. Taylor's loose-fitting clothes and slightly disheveled appearance bothered Leslie. She'd encouraged her to get some help to cope with the aftermath of what Beau had done, but she feared Taylor had ignored her advice.

"Guys, guess what I found out?" The light in Taylor's eyes did little to offset the dark circles beneath. "Did you know the Devereaux family has a history of mental illness?"

Sara's glower sent the last of the students in the hallway back to their lockers. "Everyone in town knows that." She pointed at the books in Taylor's hands. "Are those new?"

Taylor hugged them close, her gaze guarded. "Yeah. I got them from an old bookstore over break. They have all kinds of information on families in the South. One has an entire chapter devoted to the Devereaux family."

Leslie gently touched Taylor's wrist. "You've been reading everything you can on Beau's family? Why?"

"She thinks she's gonna find an answer for why he was such an ass," Sara said.

Taylor raised her chin, appearing unusually defiant. "That's not it. There's something evil about them. I read the family line was cursed by a local chieftain after the tribe's land was stolen by a Gerard Frellson in the 1800s. The Devereauxs were Frellsons back then."

Kelly titled her head. "There were tribes in St. Benedict?"

Taylor nodded. "Tribes were all over St. Tammany Parish, including where The Abbey is."

Sara cocked a dubious eyebrow. "You got all this out of a book?"

"Several, plus old newspapers." Taylor shifted her bag.

Leslie flinched when the loud peal of a bell echoed through the hall.

A brooding guy with rugged good looks appeared from around the corner. Her heart dipped at the sight of Derek Foster in a new brown leather jacket. She wanted to rush to his side, but those days were over. It took every ounce of strength not to crumble when he leveled his icy gaze on her. She still loved Derek, but had to keep her distance to protect him.

He slowly walked by, keeping his attention on Leslie. The furor on Derek's face weakened her knees.

Kelly angled closer to her ear. "Are you okay?"

Leslie opened her mouth to speak, but nothing came out. She wished she could scream from the rooftop that she would survive without Derek, but her body betrayed her.

Sara smirked after Derek walked by. "I'm so glad you dumped him. He's not worth the risk of losin' all we've got."

Leslie shot Sara a dirty look as she noticed Derek glance back. She counted off the seconds, praying he wouldn't say anything.

Derek quickened his stride and hurried down the hall just as the second bell rang.

Leslie's shoulders sagged, already worn out before the day started. "Sara, you can't say something like that in front of people. What if Derek heard you?"

"You have to pull it together." Sara wrinkled her nose. "You're done with Derek, so stop fallin' apart when you see him. He'll ask questions you can't answer."

Kelly twirled a red strand of hair around her fingers. "What do I tell people when they want to know why I transferred here? Questions make me nervous."

"Tell them the truth." Leslie encouraged. "Gage Devereaux gave your mom a job at the brewery to help prepare for the national campaign."

Sara spun around to Taylor, her nostrils flaring. "You have to stop with the Devereaux family shit. No more research, no more books. I'll kill you if you screw this up for us."

Leslie bumped Sara's shoulder. "Hey, chill. Taylor doesn't mean any harm."

"Then she'd better start actin' like one of us." Sara gave Taylor a once over. "People are talkin' about her strange clothes and weird behavior."

Leslie coughed into her hand. "Says the *medium.*"

Taylor snorted. "Why are you acting so paranoid? We didn't kill Beau. Everybody knows the dogs did it."

"But we were the reason he was at The Abbey, you little idiot." Sara pinched Taylor's arm. "We swore to keep quiet about what happened. That means you need to be cool. Got it?" She snatched Taylor's phone from one of the outside pockets of her bag and started scrolling. "You didn't keep that video of Beau and Andrea in the cells, did you."

"Give that back." Taylor dropped her books on the floor and tried to grab for the phone, but Sara twisted away, evading her.

Sara remained fixated on the device, and then her jaw dropped. "You lyin' shit. You said you didn't send the video to Sheriff Davis, so why's it still on your phone where anyone could find it?" She stabbed the delete icon and then furiously flicked through the photo gallery until she sucked in a sharp breath. She shot Taylor a murderous glare. "Are you out of your fucking mind? You have a picture of Beau bound to a chair in The Abbey on here."

Taylor picked up her books. "So? I like looking at it."

Sara shook her head and deleted the picture before shoving the phone into Taylor's bag. "Something like that in the wrong hands would land us all in jail. If we aren't careful, we'll go down for killin' that worthless asshole."

Leslie spotted students hurrying out of the way of a woman in a vibrant green pantsuit closing in on their group. She loudly cleared her throat, wanting to warn the others.

"Ladies, is there a reason you're still standing here after the second bell?"

Ms. Greenbriar's screeching voice made everyone cringe.

Leslie hoped the middle-aged principal of St. Benedict High hadn't overheard their conversation.

"Ms. Moore, Ms. Haskins, you two need to get to English lit." Her beady eyes traveled the length of Sara's heavy makeup and black clothes. "Ms. Bissell, that isn't gonna fly. Go to the bathroom and wash your face, and please wear something more suitable tomorrow."

Sara's haughty smirk widened. "I'm a medium. I have to wear black to communicate with the dead."

Ms. Greenbriar, aka *Madbriar*, pursed her lips. "The dead don't attend St. Benedict High, so your services will not be needed on campus." She pointed at the girls' bathroom door. "Get to it." Her gaze settled on Kelly. "Who are you?"

The color drained from Kelly's cheeks. "Kelly Norton. I transferred from Covington High."

Ms. Greenbriar moved closer, twisting her lips as she inspected Kelly. "Ah, yes. Come with me to my office, and we'll get you situated."

Kelly shot Leslie a help-me look as she walked away with Madbriar. Leslie felt guilty for not rescuing her friend, but she didn't need the principal up her ass on the first day. She had enough to deal with.

Taylor tugged her arm. "Let's get to class."

Leslie turned toward English lit and saw a sudden flash of Dawn, alive and happy, strolling the hall in her cheerleading uniform. Leslie longed to curl into a ball and disappear.

No time for that. You must go on for Dawn.

Chapter Three

Gage Devereaux sat behind a massive desk as he stared out the wall of windows in his office. The morning light breaking over Benedict Brewery brought out the green rooftops and shimmered along the bricks of the smokestack atop the main building.

He'd devoted his life to this place, and Beau had almost brought it crashing to the ground. He should have known the boy would screw up. Years of hard work and a small fortune would've gone down the drain if his son's true nature had gotten out.

Now there would be different problems to deal with—the four girls who'd suffered at Beau's hands. He had to keep them quiet for the sake of the Devereaux name.

"Gage?"

Kent Davis stood in his office doorway.

The lean, scrappy man with his brown, sweat-stained uniform shirt and blue jeans seemed better suited for a job as a ranch hand than a law officer. But Kent's easygoing manner had won Gage over, and his tight rein on crime in their small town had put everyone at ease—until the first body had shown up at the river.

Gage suspected something was amiss by the way Kent held his Stetson, nervously thumbing the brim. Then he spotted the manila envelope under his arm. The sheriff was there on official business. Gage stilled the current of doubt surging through him. He had to appear calm and collected at all times. *Never let anyone see who you really are.*

"Kent, what can I do for you?"

The sheriff moved into the office, his gait slower than usual. "You need to be aware of what we found at the river."

Gage folded his hands, maintaining his unruffled persona. "Is this regarding the woman everyone's talking about?"

Kent stood before the desk, looking him in the eye. "The recent high water exposed her grave. Bill Broussard estimates she's been dead about twenty-five years."

Shock forced the air from Gage's lungs. *It can't be.* Then he quickly suppressed his reaction. "Any idea who she is?"

Kent's jaw muscles tightened. "I was going to ask you the same thing. No one shows up in my records, but I thought you might recall a missing person from when you were in high school."

Gage flexed his fingers. "That's a long time ago."

"I know, but was there any gossip about a missing girl? Maybe a tourist who disappeared?"

Gage remembered he was supposed to be a grieving father and had better act like one. He added a touch of fragility to his voice when he asked, "Are you going to let some dead girl who died in the nineties distract you from my son's case?"

The sheriff tossed the envelope on the desk. "This girl might have more to do with your son's death than you think. That's Bill's autopsy report. Cause of death was a broken neck. Andrea Harrison, the woman we found in the river, had a broken neck, too. So did your son."

Gage stood and picked up the envelope. He pulled out the document, scanned the report, then tossed it down. "You can't expect me to believe these are all related."

Kent tapped his hat against his thigh. "All I know for sure is this town hasn't had a murder since 1942. In a matter of months, I have what could be four. In my experience, when bodies start piling up, you have to look for a pattern."

The burn in the pit of Gage's stomach flared into a blaze. "Are you saying a serial killer has been hiding in St. Benedict for twenty-five years?"

"I'm saying these deaths have one obvious thing in common—they happened around The Abbey."

Anger brought back a flood of memories, mostly bad, about Beau and his obsession with the river. "It's a ruin. How can you think my son's death is related to any of this? He was killed by wild dogs."

Sheriff Davis hesitated as he studied Gage. "We know Beau was held at The Abbey. We found traces of his DNA, and there were zip tie burns on his wrists. But how he ended up at the river is a mystery. There's no evidence he was dragged or put up a struggle. And Bill said it would've taken one damn big dog to break Beau's neck. Until we find an animal like that, I'm not ruling out homicide."

Gage took a deep breath, fighting off a wave of panic. *Fuck.*

"If you ask me, this was done by pros, and the dogs helped cover their tracks." Kent raked his fingers through his hair. "You've got enemies, we both know it. I want to hand the investigation over to the St. Tammany Sheriff's Department. I just oversee St. Benedict and don't have their resources."

That irked the living shit out of Gage. If Kent brought in the parish investigators, things would move quickly on the case. "You seriously want to involve more people who'll ask me the same gut-wrenching questions about Beau? Do you know what this has done to my wife? My business?" Gage slammed his fist into a pile of papers on his desk. "Damn it, no outsiders. It won't bring Beau back. It won't heal his mother's broken heart, and it won't make my life any easier." Gage returned to his chair. "Let's give your team a while longer and wrap up this investigation. Elizabeth needs closure."

Kent picked up the envelope and stuffed the report inside. "Is there anything else you're not telling me? Were there any threats, unusual phone calls, strangers hanging out at your house or the brewery?"

"No. I would have come to you." Gage scowled.

"Look, I have to ask." Kent gave a frustrated sigh. "This girl's body being found at the river will bring up new questions about Beau's death and the others. You and Elizabeth should be prepared."

Gage summoned his restraint, putting on his stony, businesslike face. He still had a job to do—one pounded into him by his father and grandfather. "I appreciate the heads-up."

"There's one more thing. Bill said there was another set of bones in the midsection of the girl. She was over eight weeks pregnant. I just wanted to tell you first before others get wind of it and the gossip mill starts." Kent put on his hat and strolled out of the office.

His reserved cool impressed Gage, but he knew underneath that Kent was nervous as hell about another body.

Gage faced the wall of windows. He wanted to make sure the man returned to his patrol car—one of five that Benedict Brewery had donated to the force. He drummed his fingers on the windowsill, waiting for the car to pull out. Once Kent headed down the narrow road, Gage picked up his phone.

After three rings, a gravelly voice came through the cell's speaker. "Do we have a problem?"

Gage's attention stayed on the cruiser as it neared the security gate. "No problem. Just a nosy sheriff looking to put a feather in his Stetson. You're sure your man was thorough at The Abbey?"

"Yep. He gave Beau a head start into the woods and cleaned up the evidence at The Abbey. It was just dumb luck those wild dogs killed the boy on the beach before my guy got to him. There's no evidence because there was no crime."

Gage nodded. "That's what I needed to hear. Thank you again."

The raspy chuckle was unexpected.

"And I thought I was the cold bastard. You make me look like a pussycat."

Gage browsed the open folders on his desk. "No one would ever mistake you for that, Joe. Talk soon."

He hung up and grabbed the closest folder. Gage scanned the information on the brewery's projected sales for the coming year and liked what he saw. The national campaign introducing Benedict Beer to America was about to hit the ground running. If his accountants even came close to their projections, then everything Gage had done to protect his family would be worth it. He'd saved the brewery and kept the Devereaux name from scandal.

"*If you have a problem, get rid of it.*" His father's advice rolled through his mind. Whether dealing with enemies, friends, or family, Edward Devereaux had treated everyone with the same contempt—even Gage. He sometimes wondered if Beau's behavior was the result of all the years he'd been under Edward's influence. He wanted to blame his father, but deep inside, he knew the boy hadn't been right. Beau had been born with a venomous force controlling him, and no matter how hard he worked, Gage could not tame it.

There were moments when he missed his son, but the bad times far outweighed the good. He didn't have to worry anymore—Beau's evil had vanished forever. He could have more children. If not with Elizabeth, then someone else. Gage would find a way to carry on the family name, and just like his father had taught him, he would raise his heir to protect the Devereaux legacy at all costs.

The final bell of the day had Leslie scrambling for the door, desperate for fresh air. Her panic had mushroomed as the afternoon progressed. Everywhere she turned, she found herself looking for Dawn. Then the awful truth would stamp out her hope.

She reached her car and calmed a little. For the past few days, she'd searched online about dealing with panic attacks. The information helped, but the pressure constricting her chest today was worse than usual. Leslie wanted to chalk up her heightened agitation to the return to school, but she knew the real cause of her dread—the whisperings.

Everywhere she went, stares from the other students cut into her like razor blades. For a girl who once ignored what people thought of her, this new reality was like a slap in the face. The whispers she did hear were even more upsetting.

"*That's her. The girl whose twin was murdered,*" one freshman remarked to another in front of the lockers.

"*They say her sister haunts The Abbey,*" a student said quietly behind her in class.

The most hurtful of all? "*I heard she hated her sister.*"

She leaned against her car, drained.

"Hey, you okay?"

Zoe Harvey, a close friend of Dawn's, walked up to her. She wore a short, white cheerleading uniform that highlighted her deep brown skin. Seeing the outfit sent a jolt of anguish through Leslie.

Zoe put an arm around her. "You're shaking."

Leslie bristled at the gesture. She straightened and fought to contain her emotions. "I'm having a crappy day, and seeing you in ..." She gestured to Zoe's uniform.

Zoe glanced down at the red St. Benedict High dragon on her chest, and her face fell. "I didn't mean to upset you. I wanted to see how you were holding up."

Leslie waved off her apology and set the book bag on the hood. "I'm just tired."

"Dawn used to always talk about how strong you are." Zoe offered a reassuring smile. "I can see she was right."

Instead of bringing on more grief, Zoe's words comforted her. She and Dawn had battled like archenemies the year before she died, and it helped to hear her sister had expressed something positive during that tumultuous time. "Thank you for telling me. She always said I was too stubborn. I never imagined she admired me for anything."

Zoe put her hand on Leslie's shoulder. "She did, very much. Don't ever think she didn't."

Leslie fought back tears as she opened a pocket on the bag to retrieve her keys.

Kelly rushed toward them. "Everything okay?"

The strain in Kelly's voice worsened Leslie's guilt. She needed to get it together. "Fine," she told her.

"I've got to get to practice." Zoe gave Kelly a keep-an-eye-on-her look and hurried away.

"You don't seem *fine* to me." Kelly crossed her arms. "What happened?"

Leslie watched Zoe run across the grassy quad to the athletic field behind the school. The way Dawn had done so many times before. "I saw her cheerleading uniform, and it got to me. I should've been better prepared for that."

"Don't beat yourself up." Kelly brushed a strand of hair from Leslie's face. "No one expects you to bounce back overnight."

Leslie pressed the remote on her keychain and unlocked the doors. "Are you sure you want to hang out with me? I'm a mess."

"You're the most together person I know." Kelly opened the passenger door. "My mom says scars only cover the surface—they don't change who you are. Give yourself time."

Leslie questioned if her scars hadn't irrevocably erased her identity. A stranger stared back at her in the mirror every morning—one with the same blue eyes and blonde hair as her dead sister. For years, she'd cursed being born identical to Dawn. Now, it was all she had left of her.

Kelly looked at her over the roof of the car. "How about we stop by The Bogue for pizza, and then we can do homework. I have a lot." She grimaced.

Leslie wiped her eyes, feeling foolish. She wasn't the only one suffering. "I guess you have a lot of catching up to do, with it being your first day at St. Benedict High."

Kelly eyed the school's quad. "I knew transferring in the middle of the school year wouldn't be easy, but I never expected the drama."

Leslie's stomach rumbled as she considered returning to The Bogue Falaya Café. Everyone would be there, but the sooner she tackled the hurdles of revisiting the places she'd frequented before Dawn's murder, the easier life would be—or so she hoped.

"What is it?" Kelly's voice softened. "Are you worried about running into Derek?"

"I'm sure he won't be at The Bogue. He works after school with his mom at that law firm in Covington."

"Ambitious guy." Kelly raised her eyebrows. "Sounds like a keeper."

Leslie shook her head. "Stop pushing us back together. It's not happening."

"Because you won't let it." Kelly scowled. "You don't have to cut yourself off from Derek to keep us all safe. You know that."

An avalanche of regret stifled a snarky response. A flash of Gage Devereaux sitting at his office desk added to her unease. He'd executed the perfect plan to kill his son, and she'd been his willing accomplice.

Leslie dropped into the driver's seat, undone by the mistakes of her past. *Derek has no idea how ruthless I've become.*

Chapter Four

The late afternoon sun stretched over the rooftops of Main Street, sending crooked shadows across the blacktop road. The reassuring slow pace of the small town eased Leslie's anxiety. The businesses in the quaint, one-story shops lining the sidewalks had a steady stream of customers buying clothes, hardware, and groceries. Outside the Central Feed Store, trucks loaded with hay waited to head out to the surrounding farms. The normalcy of life reassured her. Nothing had changed, so why did she feel so different?

"Are you still going to LSU?" Kelly asked as she peered out at the shops.

Leslie tightened her grip on the wheel as she remembered the application for LSU sitting on her desk at home. Leslie had tried half a dozen times to fill it out, but something always stopped her. "I'm not sure. Derek and I planned to go together, but I'm thinking of applying to another school."

"Yeah, I get it." Kelly examined the dress in Dottie's Boutique window. "Out of state might be a good idea."

The coil of guilt in her belly wound tighter. "I don't want to go out of state."

"Why not?" Kelly faced her. "You could get away and forget about things."

"Leaving St. Benedict isn't going to make me forget what happened."

Kelly opened her mouth to say something else but quickly closed it. She sat back in her seat and stared ahead at the road. "Sorry. I was only trying to help."

How could she tell Kelly that leaving St. Benedict was impossible? There were still too many unanswered questions about Dawn's death—the major one being *why.* Why had she gone to confront Beau? Why had Dawn left her behind that night? Then there was the possibility of Dawn's ghost haunting The Abbey. Leslie could never walk away from her hometown knowing her sister remained trapped there.

The neon sign with *The Bogue Falaya Café* in green letters came into view, and she maneuvered the car into the parking lot. When she eased into a spot in front of the side entrance, Leslie saw several classmates filling the booths and tables. She shuddered at the prospect of confronting more inquisitive stares, but then something glinted across the lot, drawing her away from the restaurant.

A dark green 1966 Mustang GT, in pristine condition, caught the dying rays of the sun. The car roused her curiosity.

Kelly gathered their bags. "Are you sure you're ready? It looks pretty crowded in there."

Leslie was grateful for her friends during the funeral and mind-numbing days after, but their constant concern had grown tedious. "Stop worrying. I'm fine." She shoved open her car door and shivered in the biting breeze.

Kelly went around to her side. "When you start acting like you're fine, then I'll stop worrying."

Leslie clutched her bag and walked toward the glass door. Avoiding confrontation had developed into a defense mechanism. It kept her from speaking her mind and telling everyone to go to hell.

The warm, pepperoni-flavored air eased Leslie's shivering. Dozens of St. Benedict High students greeted them with prying stares. Leslie inspected the people crowding the tables, stools, and orange vinyl booths. She could almost hear their thoughts as she negotiated the narrow aisle.

"*There's Dawn Moore's sister. The twin that survived.*"

The aroma of cooking meat wafted by, and a wave of nausea almost buckled her knees. The intrusive gawking, the din of muttering, and the music's relentless pounding from the red, yellow, and green neon jukebox made her want to bolt.

Leslie walked with Kelly to the back of the dining room, passing a collection of faded posters of menu items. Ceiling fans spun while images of Coke floats and ice cream sundaes hung from the fluorescent light fixtures. It all felt so familiar, but to Leslie, it was an alien world.

She scooted into their booth and, slowly, the intensive observation turned into occasional glances. The rumbles of lively conversation and laughter returned.

Her shoulders sagged. Every store she entered, every classroom, every building in town, she'd gotten the same response, "That's the dead girl's sister." But with a new dead girl found at the river, she hoped the townsfolk would focus their fascination elsewhere.

Scanning the crowd of familiar faces, Leslie noticed a new server around the tables. He wore a red-stained apron over blue jeans and a white T-shirt. Despite the January chill, he seemed ready for summer with tanned skin, thick, toned arms, and sun-streaked light brown hair. He smiled at the customers as he cleared away plates and glasses. The girls were drawn to him. Giggling and longing looks followed as he walked away from a booth packed with girls from the school's volleyball team.

Leslie took in his square jaw, sharp, chiseled features, and green eyes. He was quick with a smile and to chat with the customers, but it was how he moved that held her interest. His muscular frame and the effortless way he weaved and skirted between the tables reminded her of someone—Beau.

An icy chill gripped her. She could still hear Beau's screams as she'd run from The Abbey, following Gage's instructions to get out of there before she saw something she'd regret.

The shadow began appearing in her bedroom not long after that night, eventually taking the shape of a man. The apparition would grin at her with all the savagery of a rabid wolf and say, "*I killed the wrong Moore twin.*" That was how she knew it was Beau.

But as she watched the captivating server, her nightmare faded.

"Oh, new eye candy." Sara licked her lips as she slid into the booth and settled next to Leslie.

"Keep a lid on it," Kelly insisted. "Someone will hear you."

"Who cares?" Sara slapped her bag on the table.

Taylor slinked into the spot next to Kelly.

"Did you know they were joining us?" Leslie asked.

"I might have texted them in the car." Kelly brushed a red tendril from her face. "You don't mind, do you?"

Taylor retrieved a book from her bag and opened it to an earmarked page. "Kelly said you needed cheering up. So here we are."

Leslie gave Kelly a faint *I'm sorry* smile, hoping it would make amends. She hated to admit it, but the girls did make her feel better. They helped insulate Leslie from the world.

"Does anybody know who he is?" Sara asked, her gaze glued to the new guy's ass.

Kelly scooted over to make more room for Taylor's overflowing book bag. "I'm sure we'll find out soon enough."

The handsome newcomer strolled up to their booth. He retrieved a pencil from behind his ear and removed a pad from his apron pocket. "What'll it be, ladies?"

His voice had the same smoky quality as Beau's. Leslie cringed. The sound brought back the torture she'd endured from his obsession.

"You're new in town," Sara said with her usual candor.

His smile instantly warmed Leslie. Any similarities to Beau ended there. No cruelty was hidden behind it, no pretense, no sick desire. It was genuine, warm, and instantly put her at ease.

"The name's Luke Cross, and yeah, I got here just before Christmas."

Sara's eyes widened as she looked him up and down. "Welcome to St. Benedict. I'm Sara Bissell." She swept her hand around, introducing everyone. When her focus returned to Luke, she asked, "Are you going to college around here?"

Luke shook his head. "I ditched college a few weeks back and decided to hit the road. Just me and Pearl."

"Pearl?" Leslie asked, more than intrigued.

He pointed out the window. "That 1966 Mustang GT is Pearl. We've been through a lot together."

The rays of the setting sun glistened on the iconic car. Then something in the shadows of the parking lot distracted her. An older blue pickup sat in a far corner—she recognized it right away. Derek's truck often appeared when she was in town. He'd been keeping an eye on her since she'd called things off, but this was the first time she'd noticed him skipping out on his after-school job.

The pickup sped from the lot and peeled onto Main Street, cutting off a few cars as it veered into traffic.

The childish act added to Leslie's frustration. She would have to talk to Derek before things went too far. He had to let go.

"But why St. Benedict?" Kelly asked.

Her bubbly, high-pitched manner of speaking urged Leslie away from the window.

The attractive redhead beamed at the handsome server. "What made you want to come here?"

Luke tilted his head. "I'm from Boston and always wanted to visit New Orleans. I prefer someplace quieter and safer, so I headed across Lake Pontchartrain and ended up here."

"Honey, we're far from safe." Sara scoffed. "St. Benedict's got bodies poppin' up all over the place."

Leslie glowered at her. "We don't know if the girl they found was murdered."

Sara snorted. "Then who buried her?"

Luke shifted his position, accentuating the taut abs beneath his thin white T-shirt. "Yeah, I heard about the body they found, as well as some others around here. Quite a mousetrap you guys got going."

"Mousetrap?" Sara's flirty giggle floated around the table. "What's that supposed to mean?"

Taylor stopped reading. "It's a reference for a murder mystery, dummy. It comes from Agatha Christie's play *The Mousetrap*. Don't you read our English lit assignments?"

Luke pointed his pencil at Taylor's book. "I can see you're the studious one."

"No, I just pay attention to things other people ignore." Taylor lifted the heavy tome. "This is research. I'm investigating the history of a local family."

Luke's eyebrows knitted together. "What local family?"

Leslie decided to sideline his interrogation before Taylor said something she shouldn't. "How did you end up working at The Bogue?"

Luke quickly scanned his other tables. "I came here when I hit town. Struck up a conversation with Carl, and before I left, he offered me a job. His old man's sick, so he needed someone extra to help out. After I agreed to take the job, he rented me an apartment not far from here."

Sara rested her elbow on the table, ogling his athletic build. "How long you plan on stayin'? I hope it's a while."

Luke shrugged his broad shoulders. "Not sure. If I'm lucky, maybe I can find a job restoring cars, building engines. Then I might make this place my permanent home."

"Marc Benning owns the garage on Main and Fifth Street." Leslie's stomach fluttered as his gaze stayed on her. "I'm sure he'd be willing to give you a chance. Let him know John Moore sent you. That's my dad." She sat back and folded her arms, pressing hard to make the uncomfortable sensation go away.

"If you're gonna stay, you've gotta check out the river." Sara moved into his line of sight, trying to attract his attention. "The Bogue Falaya River down by The Abbey. It's where everybody parties on the weekends."

Leslie's heart dropped. Sometimes Sara's audacity shocked even her. How could she bring up that place?

Luke twirled the pencil. "The Abbey? I've heard people say it's haunted."

Sara tossed her hair over her shoulder, batting her eyes. "You're in luck. I'm a medium and can make sure the ghosts never touch you."

Kelly kicked Sara under the table.

Luke chuckled when Sara winced.

He seemed friendly and likable, but an edginess simmered below the surface. Leslie silently chastised her suspicions. After Beau, strangers came across as threatening. He'd helped her see the worst in people.

She debated wanting to know more about him and then asked, "What about your family?"

He tapped his chin with the pencil tip. "None to speak of. I never knew my dad, and my grandparents raised me after my mom died. They passed two years ago. Car accident."

His story tugged at Leslie's heart. "That's a shame. Family is important."

An uncomfortable silence settled over the table and went on for longer than Leslie would've liked, but she couldn't think of anything to say. Somehow, he'd left her tongue-tied.

Leslie noticed the flour on his hands. She liked the strength she saw in his square palms.

Luke held the pencil to his pad. "So, what can I get you guys?"

"One large pizza with cheese and mushrooms." Sara pointed at Kelly.

"That's for us. And two iced teas."

Kelly scrunched her face. "I can't eat pizza anymore. Greasy things make me sick." She glanced up at Luke. "Can I get a salad?"

"A salad?" Sara rolled her eyes. "Are you kidding me?"

Luke chuckled again. "What kind of dressing?"

"No dressing, but extra croutons."

Leslie eyed Kelly with an inkling of concern. "You've been feeling bad a lot lately. Maybe you should get that checked."

Kelly slumped forward, leaning on the table. "It's just a bug."

Luke jotted a note on his pad and motioned his pencil toward Leslie. "And you?"

Leslie's stomach rumbled loudly, and a blush warmed her cheeks. "Ah, a small with mushrooms, jalapeños, and pepperoni. And a tea."

"Jalapeños?" Luke wrote it down. "You're brave. I love them on my pizza, too." He turned to Taylor. "What does the bookworm want?"

Taylor's face didn't show a hint of emotion. She didn't seem too impressed with Luke as she clung to her book. "I'm not hungry. I'll just have tea."

Luke's eyebrows raised. "Not hungry? Not in my diner. I'll bring you a slice of the double cheese pizza, just pulled out of the oven."

The pink in Taylor's cheeks faded. Her gaze darted about as if looking for someone to save her. "Okay," she uttered in a shaky voice.

Luke gave her one last curious stare and finished writing. "Be back in a few," he said before walking away.

Sara practically climbed over the table to watch Luke's butt.

Kelly shoved Sara back into her seat. "You're attracting attention."

Sara flopped onto the bench. "I wanna grab his ass."

Leslie shook her head. "Sara, what were you saying about playing it cool, earlier?"

Sara flashed her best sarcastic smirk. "Like you didn't almost jump out of your seat when he smiled at you."

"He didn't smile at me." Leslie clenched her hands in her lap. "He was being polite and trying to make friends in a new town."

Kelly tilted her head and squinted. "Who ends up in St. Benedict? It's not a big tourist town."

"Would you give it a break, Sherlock?" Sara's gaze burned into Kelly. "I'm grateful he ended up here. Sure will make The Bogue a lot more fun."

Taylor set her book aside. "He reminds me of Beau."

Kelly's jaw dropped. "Why would you say that? Luke's nothing like that animal."

Taylor glanced around the table. "We all thought Beau was quite the catch until we found out his true nature."

Leslie's chest tightened. The memories closing in triggered her need for fresh air. "Let's not talk about him ever again," she said, becoming jittery. "Beau's no longer our problem."

"We all know that ain't true," Sara muttered.

Taylor's fingertips brushed over her book's cover. "I wonder who the last person was to see him alive. Whatever happened, they know the truth."

The silence returned, and this time it was thick with tension. Leslie didn't like it. She'd promised Gage she'd keep the group under control. But Leslie had a feeling Luke Cross's arrival would make that a lot more difficult.

Chapter Five

The last rays of the setting sun filtered through Derek's windshield as he sat in his truck and stared at Leslie's two-story brick house. The inviting front porch, with a wooden swing, had once been a haven. Now a gnawing emptiness replaced the comfort.

He squeezed the steering wheel as he remembered standing on the porch when Leslie told him they were over.

"What do you mean?" he had begged. "You can't arbitrarily decide we're through. Not like this. Not now. Dawn hasn't even been gone—"

"This has nothing to do with Dawn," Leslie had snapped. "You need to stay away from me. I'm not good for you."

He'd attempted to touch her, but she recoiled.

"Leslie, please, tell me what I did wrong."

The flat, dull gaze in her blue eyes had devastated him.

"No. It's me. It's all my fault. If you ever knew—" Leslie had stormed into the house and slammed the door.

He'd been crushed, and the heaviness in his chest from that day remained.

Derek reached over to the passenger seat and grabbed Leslie's book—the one she'd been reading on life after death. She became obsessed with the subject after Dawn died. Derek believed it was a normal reaction to loss, and he'd waited for the bright, witty girl he loved to return. But that Leslie was buried beneath an angry young woman.

Derek sighed and got out. No matter how much he longed to be with Leslie, every passing day dulled his hope.

The old truck door creaked as he closed it. Derek approached the porch steps in the quiet, upper-middle-class neighborhood. The nip in the air felt good against his hot cheeks, giving him something to focus on besides his anger.

He cringed as the porch boards groaned under his weight. Derek was about to leave the book at the front door when he heard the click of the lock. He took a deep breath. Leslie wasn't home, but he dreaded running into her family's most caustic member.

"I should have known it was you."

Derek bristled at Shelley's acerbic tone. His grip on the book tightened as he stared into her bloodshot eyes. Still in her robe, with messy hair piled atop her head, Shelley Moore was nothing like the brash woman he'd known. He saw the old-fashioned glass in her hand, half-full of amber liquid, and cursed the tragedy that had sent the woman to seek solace in alcohol.

"Mrs. Moore." He kept any hint of emotion from his voice. "I wanted to return Leslie's book."

"She's not here," Shelley said with a toss of her hand. "She's probably hanging out with her friends."

He nodded, pinching the book's spine. "I know. She's at The Bogue. That's why I stopped by. I didn't think it was a good idea—"

"She told me you've been following her." The lines deepened around Shelley's mouth. "What's wrong with you? Can't you leave her alone?"

He didn't let her indignation get to him. "I'm just keeping an eye on her. We both know it's not safe in this town anymore."

Shelley propped her shoulder against the doorframe, cradling her drink. "She's better off without you. You were holding her back. All your talk of going to college together kept her from exploring other schools where she could become so much more. She needs to leave St. Benedict and start a new life."

The fire returned to his cheeks. "Leslie wanted us to be together. We had our future planned."

Shelley pushed away from the door, spilling some of her drink on the threshold. "I've only got one daughter left. I don't want to see her screw up her life by spending it with you."

Derek knew he should get in his truck and leave before he said something stupid, but he didn't give a damn what Shelley thought of him anymore. "You think you know your daughter, but you have no idea who she is. If Leslie leaves St. Benedict, it's because of you and how you made her feel second best to Dawn. You never were proud of Leslie. All you cared about was what others thought of your daughters and who they dated. Maybe if you'd paid more attention, Dawn wouldn't be dead."

Shelley's jaw slackened. She raised her hand to strike him, then hesitated and took a step back inside. Her face twisted into a roadmap of angry lines, and her eyes transformed into blue flames. "Stay away from my daughter, or I'll make sure you do. She's too good for you."

Derek set the book on the porch and when he stood, he stared Shelley down.

"Take a piece of advice, Mrs. Moore. Give Leslie the mother she's always wanted, not a drunk that she'll hate for the rest of her life."

Derek turned and strolled away. He could feel Shelley's eyes on him, stabbing his back like daggers, but he didn't quicken his stride. The moment his feet touched the walkway, the slam of the front door reverberated behind him.

He paused, letting the tension ease from his shoulders. That wasn't how he wanted to leave things with Shelley, but she'd driven him to speak his mind.

I'm never going to regret that.

Derek walked to his truck, keeping his head held high. The satisfaction from his confrontation didn't replace the pain of losing Leslie, but it did make amends for the months of suffering he'd endured thanks to Shelley's prejudices. He wasn't the boy from the wrong side of town anymore.

The dying red line along the horizon disappeared into the darkening sky just as Derek pulled into his driveway. The familiar yellow wooden house with its gleaming tin roof, bright white picket fence, and new brass mailbox wasn't like the rundown home he remembered.

Home. The word sounded foreign. Since his breakup with Leslie, everywhere felt empty. Derek focused on his after-school job at the law firm and preferred spending time in the school library instead of trapped inside his house. Every room bombarded him with memories. His grief seemed unshakable at times.

Will this ever end?

He parked behind his mother's new car, grabbed his book bag, and then stopped, trying to cool off.

Derek got out and slammed the truck door. The loud *smack* exasperated him even more. He pressed his bag to his chest, fighting an urge to run away.

Derek shoved the front door open and stepped inside.

Carol Foster stood next to the newly inlaid dark granite kitchen counter while peering over her coffee mug. "You're home from work early."

Already wearing sweats, Carol walked to the dining room table, appearing ready to camp out in front of her computer for the night. Since taking a job at the law firm in Covington, she spent every moment typing reports to make extra money. The work had paid for renovations and a new car, but Derek felt his mother traded one demanding position for another. The hours she put in reminded him of the long shifts she'd worked at Mo's Diner. Carol earned more money now, but he sensed her fear that it could all come to an end at any moment.

"I didn't go today." Derek dropped his book bag on the floor. "What's with girls, anyway?"

Carol lowered her mug. "Is this about girls in general, or are we talking about Leslie again?"

He approached the kitchen counter. "Since Dawn died, it's like she's a whole different person. She hangs out with girls she never considered friends before. Everywhere she goes, they're together."

Carol's eyebrows went up. "Is that why you didn't go to work? You were following her?"

"No, well, not exactly. I was keeping an eye on her. Considering everything that's happening in this town, can you blame me?"

"Derek, she ended your relationship. You can't let it consume you. I don't want you to repeat my mistakes."

Derek pounded the back of the dining room chair. "But what if she didn't really want to call it off? Leslie was keeping things from me before we split. I think it has something to do with the girls she hangs out with now."

Carol patted his shoulder. "They're just girls, honey. They're not plotting the downfall of St. Benedict. Leslie's probably with them because they're helping her. I felt the same camaraderie in high school with my friends. Gage used to tell me I spent too much time with them. He hated my friends."

"I hate the way they act." He held his head. "They were all over the new guy working at The Bogue."

"What new guy?"

"I met him the other day when I was picking up a pizza for dinner," Derek told her. "He's from Boston."

His mother's delicate features fell. "Boston?" She set her coffee mug next to her computer. "Not my favorite place."

Derek studied his mother's drawn lips. "What's wrong with it?"

She pulled out a chair. "Ever since Gage's family sent him away to college there, I've cared nothing for it."

Derek considered all he'd learned about the Devereaux family. He sat in the chair next to his mother. "Did you know Gage's family well?"

Carol shifted a few folders overflowing with paper. "How do you mean?"

He recalled overhearing something Taylor had mentioned. "Did you ever hear about mental illness in their family? Or see anything in Gage that gave you concern?"

She picked up a folder and then looked at her son. "Why are you asking me this?"

He noted the tense line between her brows. "We both know Beau wasn't right, and maybe his death had something to do with his family's past."

She lowered her gaze, then set the folder aside.

"Gage once made a passing comment about his unstable family. I laughed it off. But there were rumors around town about him and his father—that they were prone to fits of violence. I never saw it in Gage, but his father sure showed me his ugly side. When I went to their house after Gage returned from Boston, Edward Devereaux yelled at me and called me all kinds of names. Once he drew back like he would hit me, but then Gage's mother stepped in and ushered me out of the house. I've never been so frightened in my life. After that, I figured the rumors about Gage were true."

Derek sat back. "I'm sure whatever was wrong with Beau came from his father."

Carol returned her attention to the files. "Well, it's over now. Beau's gone, and he can't torment anyone anymore."

Derek stood, unease digging into his gut. "He can't, but the Devereaux family can. They always find a way to bounce back."

The first evening stars peeked through the oaks lining the street as Leslie drove through her quiet neighborhood known as The Elms. Many of the homes belonged to those who worked for the Devereaux family—either at the brewery or for their other ventures.

Her house wasn't far from the arched black gates of the Devereaux Estate. Before Beau's death, she'd avoided passing the entrance whenever she could, but now those wrought iron monsters held a peculiar fascination. They represented the secrets she worked so hard to protect.

Leslie hummed a familiar tune as she eased her car into the garage. She turned off the engine and realized she felt more optimistic than she had since ... She wasn't sure if it was relief over surviving her first day back at school or something else.

Luke?

He was cute, but her heart was still recovering from Derek.

She spotted her father's luxury sedan, and another trouble lifted from her shoulders—she wouldn't be alone with Shelley. Since Dawn's death, her mother had been a ghost. Occasional sightings did happen, usually in the morning before Leslie went to school. Shelley would hover over the coffee pot, downing two or three cups at a time. Leslie had given up speaking to her. Most conversations ended in crying or yelling, and John usually had to usher her mother back to her room.

"You have to make an effort," her father had whispered after a horrible shouting match.

For Leslie, their relationship was beyond repair. Beau had taken away more than her sister—he had destroyed their family.

Once through the back door, she listened for any movement, hoping Shelley wasn't downstairs.

Seconds ticked by, and she didn't detect a peep. Leslie tiptoed along the hall—something she did a lot lately.

When she rounded the corner, Leslie halted. Shelley stood in the kitchen, holding a partially filled, old-fashioned glass.

She's drinking already.

The bourbon usually appeared after Leslie retreated to her room.

"I hope you've eaten." Shelley peered into her drink. "I didn't prepare anything for dinner."

Home-cooked meals had become another rarity. Before Dawn's death, her mother practically lived in the kitchen.

Leslie hiked her bag onto the countertop, then remembered Shelley's rule.

"*Books on the floor, not on the counter.*"

Shelley didn't notice the transgression. Another side effect of grief. Her mother paid attention to little, these days. Leslie could walk through the house nine months pregnant and Shelley wouldn't bat an eye.

"I had pizza at The Bogue."

"Yeah, I heard you were there." Her voice was flat and emotionless.

Leslie approached her mother, more irritated than concerned. "What is it?"

Shelley swirled the bourbon in her glass. "That boy stopped by earlier and told me where you were." She motioned to the hall table. "He dropped off your book."

Leslie closed her eyes as refrains of "that boy" grated on her nerves. "What did you say to him?"

"I told him to leave you alone." Shelley took a sip of her drink. "Nothing good can come from that one."

The rage Leslie had held in finally exploded. "From the woman who thought something good would come from Beau, that's a laugh. You have no idea what that sick bastard was like. The things he did and—" She shut her mouth, afraid of saying too much.

Shelley's nostrils flared. "How dare you say such things about him. People looked up to Beau in this town. He would have amounted to a hell of a lot more than that sorry excuse you dated."

A lump formed in Leslie's throat, but she swallowed it back, determined to ignore the hurtful jab. "What else did you expect from me, Mother. I've never been good enough for you. I don't fit your definition of the perfect daughter, so no matter what I do, say, or who I date, I'll always be your biggest disappointment."

Shelley took a step forward, her face coming into the light. The hard lines in her forehead softened, and the constant dullness in her eyes faded. "Is that what you think? That I love you less than …" Her voice faltered. "I want the best for you—a family, a home, a loving husband. But I gave up thinking you had any interest in those things. I just can't stand by and watch you make a terrible mistake with someone like that boy."

Leslie recalled that night in The Abbey with Beau. "Derek's a better person than I'll ever be."

Her mother's cynical chuckle cut through Leslie.

"You sound just like your father. When I met him, he always saw the good in every low life he represented. I have never been that accepting. I guess that's why I always considered you his child. You have his mind and his love of a challenge. Your sister," she peered into her glass, "she was mine. As long as I had her to talk to, to share clothes and makeup tips with—all the girly things you despise—I was happy."

Leslie longed to rip the drink from her hand. "So now that all you have left is a daughter who doesn't want fancy clothes or a fancy husband, you have nothing to live for. Is that what you're saying?"

Shelley sipped her drink. "If I asked you to be more like her, would you?"

Leslie wanted to scream, to argue, but staring at Shelley's near-empty glass, she knew anything she said would be a foggy memory by morning.

The lines on Shelley's face were more pronounced, along with the dark circles rimming her eyes. She'd clipped back her messy hair, leaving several tufts out of place. Her mother had always taken pride in her appearance and fussed over the slightest flaw, but Shelley had given up on everything and become a broken shell. Leslie doubted any effort she made to comfort her mother could help. She wasn't Dawn and never would be.

"Where's Dad?" she asked, fed up with their conversation.

Shelley pointed her drink toward the darkened family room connected to the kitchen. "In his office."

Leslie eyed the bourbon bottle on the kitchen counter. "You always taught us that drinking would never make us popular, or better, or solve our problems."

"No, but it does make those problems a lot more bearable." Shelley put the glass down. "After hearing about the girl they found at the river, I needed something to take the edge off." She pushed away from the counter and stumbled toward the stairs.

Leslie listened for footfalls on the landing, waiting for Shelley to disappear into her room.

The optimism she'd celebrated on the drive home faded. Her mother's drinking and despondence made Leslie wish she'd stayed at The Bogue.

She touched the book on the kitchen counter. It was one she'd lent Derek shortly before ending things. She caressed the worn cover, recalling the hours she'd spent glued to the pages, desperate to find answers about her sister's death.

Derek's visit only added to her despair. He needed to stay away. One moment of weakness, and she would confess what she'd done. Then he would hate her forever.

With a heaviness pressing on her chest, she plodded across the family room toward John Moore's office. She stared at the floor, anxious to avoid the wall of family photos filled with Dawn.

Leslie knocked on the door, and it popped open. The lock never seemed to stay in place and was on her father's to-do list, but like so many other things in the house, he'd never gotten around to it.

She gingerly slipped inside.

A single lamp gave the office an eerie glow. A collection of papers cluttered her father's desk. John sat back in his chair, facing a shadowy wall, his profile barely detectable.

"Dad?"

John turned to her and smiled. "Hey, Leelee."

The nickname chased away her heartache and, for a split second, things were as they had been before that horrible night.

He clicked on another lamp. "How was school today?"

She moved closer, glad for the added light. Darkened rooms had become all too familiar.

Leslie rubbed her arms. "Everybody at school was talking about the girl they found at the river."

Deep lines indented the sides of John's mouth as his lips pressed together. She knew the look—it was the one he got when angry or frustrated.

He collected his glasses from the desk. "I hope you're not listening to the gossip. I'm sure Kent Davis is working hard to solve the case."

"Do you know anything about it?"

John assembled his papers, forcing them into a neat stack. "Only that the police have been sweeping the town and asking questions. They'll figure out who she is."

"I heard she's been buried for around twenty-five years. She must've died around the time you were at St. Benedict High." Leslie leaned across his desk. "Do you remember her?"

He never glanced up from his papers. "No, I don't remember anyone disappearing at that time."

"What about a stranger in—"

"Drop it, Leelee," he snapped. "Leave the dead girl to the authorities."

The curt tone was very unlike her father. He'd never been harsh with either her or Dawn. They used to joke that their dad was the one to go to when they were in trouble. He would protect them from Shelley's wrath.

Leslie stepped back, stunned. "I'm sorry."

He tossed his glasses to the desk. "I shouldn't have said that. I'm tired and not sleeping well. It's just that our family has been through enough. Please don't go around asking questions or looking for trouble."

"Sure, Dad." She wanted to laugh. If he only knew the truth.

Leslie spun around, in a hurry to get out of the office before saying something she would regret.

After closing the door, a shiver slithered down her spine. Her father's reaction meant only one thing—he knew more about the dead girl than he cared to admit.

That bothered the crap out of Leslie. John Moore didn't keep secrets, especially from her.

Chapter Six

The recessed lights reflecting off the ash paneling in Gage's office added to his throbbing headache. He ran his fingers across his temples, yearning to close his eyes, but the folders piled on the desk demanded attention. There never seemed to be any break from business. Lately, interruptions at the brewery required he spend more late nights playing catch up. He would need help one day.

He lifted his glass of scotch while rereading the latest PR analysis for the national campaign. The alcohol burned in his throat. It helped him focus, something he'd never needed before Beau.

A knock on the door intruded on the quiet.

Elizabeth entered his office, walking across the red rug to his desk. He liked her flowing light pink dress and was glad she'd not returned to her yellow robe. Her quick recovery from years of heavy drinking surprised him. He believed his fake grief had lasted longer than hers.

"To what do I owe the pleasure? You never come in here."

He'd considered her timid when they first married, but after Beau arrived, she became a fierce and protective mother. That was, until Beau attacked her with a knife. After Gage brought his wife home from the hospital, she'd stayed away from their son and retreated into her whiskey.

Elizabeth had a seat in one of the burgundy leather chairs in front of his massive desk.

He detected a whiff of perfume. The flowery scent seemed out of place in his distinctively masculine office, but he liked it. It reminded him of the fragrance she'd worn when they had met at a party hosted by his mother in New Orleans.

"I was wondering if Kent Davis spoke to you about the girl they found at the river." She folded her hands in her lap, the model of decorum.

He put his scotch aside and sat back in his chair. "The coroner thinks she's been buried twenty-five years or more. Her killer is probably dead or far away from here."

She eyed the glass on his desk. "Did you know her?"

He gave her an incredulous look. "There were no missing girls when I was growing up in St. Benedict."

"That's not what I'm asking."

Her harsh timbre awakened a sliver of anger. He folded his hands, settling in for a lengthy discussion. Elizabeth never spoke to him without a well-thought-out agenda. "What are you suggesting?"

Elizabeth eased closer to his desk, keeping her pink lips pursed. "I know Beau got his cruelty from you. He was a lot like you, keeping his hate lurking beneath the surface. I used to be afraid of you when we were first married."

Gage picked up a pen and rhythmically tapped it against the folders. "Why? I never hurt you like Beau."

"But you wanted to. Your father arranged our marriage, and you weren't happy about it." She stood, staring down at him. "Before the wedding, I was warned Devereaux men kept many secrets. I was so in love with you, I hoped the rumors weren't true."

He dropped the pen. "Why bring this up now?"

"Because Beau is gone, and I don't have to hide his sins anymore. I realize it makes me a shitty mother, but when he died, I was relieved. While we had our son, we had some semblance of a family. Without him, we're strangers living in this big house."

Gage fought the instinct to lash out. He had work to do. "What do you want. A divorce?"

She folded her arms, and her deep gray eyes—Beau's eyes—studied him. "No, I want my family back. I want another baby."

The admission knocked the air out of him. Gage quickly regrouped. "Do you want it to be mine, or is there someone else you had in mind for the father?"

She slapped her hands on his desk, shaking the lamp next to him. "There's no one else. There never has been. But you already knew that."

He gave her a curt nod. "And I'm grateful for your restraint."

"Then do this for me. I don't care if we make a baby ourselves or hire a surrogate, it will be our child."

He studied her Amazonian stance, debating if he should believe her. "What if it's another Beau?"

She stood back, shaking her head. "You pushed him too hard. You never so much as smiled at him, let alone offered any words of encouragement. I won't let that happen again."

"You know my family history. There's a chance any child of mine will end up like Beau." He stood and walked around the desk to her side. "Can you handle that, or will you just hide in your room and drink again?"

She patted his chest, a hint of a smirk on her lips. "I may regret marrying into this family, but I know what the Devereaux name means to you and everyone in this town. The child must be yours. You won't accept it, won't defend it, and won't protect it unless it's a true Devereaux."

He sat on the desk, waylaid by her harsh assessment. She was right, of course. Any child they raised had to have his blood. He would never tolerate another man's offspring.

Gage folded his arms, determined to treat this like any other business transaction. "How do you want to proceed?"

Elizabeth took a step back and dropped her gaze. "I spoke with a specialist in Covington. He says I'm still able to have children and suggested we try the old-fashioned way. If nothing comes of it, we can start treatment."

He suppressed a grin. She'd been planning this for a while. "After Beau was born, you found me repulsive, so I sought others to fill my needs. Am I no longer so distasteful?"

Elizabeth closed the distance between them, her perfume teasing him. "I'll do anything for another child. My door will remain unlocked from now on."

He felt the urge to pull her close, but shut it down. It had been years since he'd visited her bed. Nevertheless, the prospect of a child would cure a lot of ills in his life. Maybe this was their chance to start again.

He stood and went back to his paperwork. "I'll come by after I finish here."

He expected her to say something encouraging, something hopeful about their new plan, but Elizabeth exited the room the same way she'd entered—as a woman on a mission.

The early morning sun streaked across the hardwood floors as Gage, with a bounce in his step, jogged down the curved mahogany staircase of his home. He felt good, better than he had in a long time. His night with Elizabeth had proved entertaining. She wasn't the same uptight woman he'd married. A seductive hunger had replaced her repressed sexuality, and he found the change intoxicating.

He stopped at the base of the steps, his hand on the newel post shaped like a horse's head, and then glanced back up the stairs. Gage wouldn't call what he felt a reawakening of his marriage—more like a temporary fascination. He'd never met anyone who held his interest for long.

Except for Carol.

The inner voice might have his father's gritty resonance, but it was his. It amazed him, after all the years, how Carol still drifted into his thoughts. Probably the reason he'd avoided seeing her whenever possible. As a man who prized his self-control, he feared what would happen if they were ever alone.

Enough of that.

The old floor groaned as he headed along the hallway, tugging at the cuffs of his shirt. Another long day of meetings waited at the brewery. Then he had more paperwork to get through that evening before he could indulge some long-suppressed fantasies with Elizabeth.

Family portraits of the Devereaux men who had come before him stared with disdain as he strolled by. The weight of their gazes reminded him of his duty—to protect the family name and sire an heir. Before Elizabeth had approached him, he'd been plotting for a way to have another son. If she got pregnant, it would give him an easy resolution. If not, there were other women he could find to replace her.

At the end of the hall, he went to the door and punched in his alarm code on the keypad. The green light flashed, and he turned the brass doorknob. The invigorating air hit his freshly shaven face. He liked the cold, thrived in it. It was the suffocating Louisiana summers that wore him down.

Gage stepped out on the grand porch, listened to the chirping birds, and surveyed the wooded grounds. More than running the family businesses, the land he owned always gave him strength.

Something white on the red brick steps caught his attention. He picked up an envelope. Gage stood, scanning the trees, but found no trace of anyone.

There was nothing written on the outside, and the seal had been left open. Carefully, he removed the folded white paper left inside. When he read the hastily scrawled note, his mouth went dry.

I know about Eva. I know about your family's past. I will reveal all unless you pay.

The lively sounds of the woods evaporated. He shook, making the white paper quiver in his hand.

Who in the hell would do this?

The dozens of men and women he'd pissed off over the years rolled through his head. But none of them would know about Eva. No one knew about her. There would be some in St. Benedict who might recognize the name, but little else. Besides, no one living in his town would dare cross him.

Gage ducked back inside and slammed the front door. He marched to his office and snatched his phone from the desk. His hand twitching, he called Kent Davis.

"Gage, what can I do for you so early in the morning?"

Kent sounded as if he had just stumbled out of bed. Gage let the lack of professionalism slip, not because Kent was a great sheriff, but because he followed instructions. "Have you seen anyone new in town? Anyone suspicious?"

Kent cleared his throat, a habit Gage found aggravating.

"You know we don't get a lot of new people around here. There's Beth Norton and her daughter. They moved in a few weeks back."

Gage paced in front of his desk. "I know Beth. She's handled my Covington real estate property for years. Anyone else?"

"What's this about? You have a problem?"

He glanced at the note crumbled in his closed fist. "Nothing you have to worry about."

Gage grinned at the silence on the line. He was glad Kent knew his place and when to stay out of his business.

"There's one other new face," Kent's voice blared from the speaker. "New guy working at The Bogue. Carl told me about him."

"You got a name?" Gage tightened his grip on the phone during another excruciating pause.

"Luke something." Kent cleared his throat again. "I wrote down his name to do a background check since you like me to look into anyone new around here. I can call you with the details when I get to the station."

Gage summoned his self-control. "I'm pleased you're staying on top of everything. Call me with that name. I want to make sure we keep any bad elements out of our town. Can't have it turning into another warzone like New Orleans."

"I agree. I don't want to go back to those days with the NOPD. They were rough."

Gage relaxed the tension in his shoulders. "Thank you, Kent."

He was about to hang up when the sheriff stopped him.

"I remember it, now. The kid's last name," Kent said. "Cross. Luke Cross. He's from the Boston area."

Gage staggered back into his desk, thankful for something solid.

"Cross? You're sure?"

Kent chuckled. "I'm sure. It may have taken me a minute, but I remember now."

Gage hung up as his fury escalated. He wanted to punch something but tried to bury the violent urge and summon his self-control. Clenching his jaw, he threw his phone at the wall. It shattered into pieces and settled on his red rug.

"Fuck!"

Outside the black iron gates to the Devereaux estate, sitting in her new Jeep, Taylor stared down the long, winding road leading to the famous plantation house.

She eyed the rising sun and smiled. She used to hate those gates, but since Beau's death, they had become her solace.

Taylor turned to several newspaper articles fanned across the seat next to her, proud of what she'd uncovered. They were faded and yellow, but one headline stood out from the rest. It mentioned the Devereaux family and the death of a girl named Eva. The article praised her as the beloved daughter of Edward and Amelia Devereaux and the only sister of six-year-old Gage, heir to the family fortune.

Taylor couldn't wait to drop this bomb on her friends. Maybe then they would take her research—and the Devereaux curse—seriously.

Chapter Seven

The last bell echoed through St. Benedict High. The cheers and whistles of students quickly followed as they spilled into the hallway. Leslie maneuvered through the crowd to her locker, grateful the long first week back had come to an end. The stress of returning to school, compounded by the dead girl's discovery, had taken its toll, but she'd survived. It gave her hope that the following weeks would be better and soon she could fall into a routine—her new normal. This would be the way of things from this point on, negotiating life without Dawn.

She'd barely gotten the locker open when Sara bounded up, sporting a fresh coat of black lipstick.

"Ready to party this weekend?"

Leslie set her book bag on the floor. "You must be joking."

"Hell no!" Sara stood in front of her locker, blocking her way. "We need this, especially after the week we've had."

Leslie shoved her aside and stuffed her history book into the locker. "Where do you propose we party? The Bogue?"

Sara's *tsk* followed her overly dramatic eye roll. "No. The river, of course." She inched closer. "I know I sound crazy, but I've watched you all week, hidin' from everyone, hopin' not to be seen or whispered about. You can't live that way. You have to confront this head-on."

Leslie shuddered at the idea of returning to the river. "I can't go there."

Sara gripped her shoulders. "Yes, you can. You gotta face your fears. Otherwise, you'll spend your whole life runnin'."

Her first instinct was to let into Sara with a flurry of expletives. What did she know about losing a twin and the constant heaviness dragging her under. Then, she slowly reconsidered. Maybe she was right. Until she returned to the river, she would remain stuck in the limbo she'd created for herself. Leslie needed to see the place where Beau had died, where Dawn had lost her life, and then she might be able to banish Beau's ghost from her mind and move on.

"We should invite Luke, too." Sara twirled a platinum lock of hair around her finger. "He can get to know everybody."

"Luke?" A ribbon of warmth chased away Leslie's apprehension. "The guy from The Bogue? You want to invite him?"

"Why not?" Sara asked in a challenging tone. "He needs to make friends like anyone else, right? I'm gonna stop there after school and ask him. The guy doesn't even own a cell phone. How weird is that?"

Leslie's heart sped up. "How do you know he doesn't own a phone?"

Sara grinned. "I found out when I asked for his number."

She cringed, picturing Sara shoving her cleavage in Luke's face. "I can't believe you're going to ask a practical stranger to join us."

Leslie didn't want to admit it, but Luke going to the river excited her. She could get to know him. Why that appealed to her, she had no idea. Most people bored the hell out of her, but there was something comforting about Luke.

Sara stared at Leslie's clothes. "How many layers you got on?"

Leslie glanced at her sweater, wool vest, and hoodie jacket. "I'm freezing."

"You look dead," Sara said matter-of-factly. "You sure you're not sick? You've been white as a ghost, lately."

How could she explain? The emptiness she lived with was nothing next to the cold she constantly experienced.

Leslie shut her locker door. "I'm fine."

Sara cocked her head. "Those are your favorite words these days. *I'm fine.*"

Leslie glowered at her.

"I bet this weekend will put a little color in your cheeks," Sara said with a wink. "A bonfire, some booze, and a hot man will get your blood pumpin'."

"But aren't you afraid of going back ..." Leslie let the implication hang in the air.

"Yes, but things are different now," Sara insisted. "Beau's gone. And if we run into trouble, we'll have Luke to protect us."

Leslie frowned. "But we know nothing about him. He could be a psycho."

Sara limply lifted her hand in a half-hearted wave. "Nah. He's cool. And he's old enough to score beer."

Leslie rubbed her forehead, uncomfortable with the plan. "What if no one wants to go to the river? Since they found that girl there, the whole town is terrified of the place."

"So what?" Sara smirked at her. "If everyone thinks we're goin', they'll follow. Plus, I can try to contact a ghost."

An acrid taste filled Leslie's mouth. "Could you talk to Dawn?" slipped out before she could stop it.

Sara gave Leslie an encouraging nod. "If she's there, I can talk to her."

The thought of Dawn trapped in such a cold and despicable place sickened her. "I hope she's not there," Leslie murmured.

Sara nudged her with an elbow. "Maybe Dawn can answer some questions. Things you need to hear. The dead know stuff we don't. You gotta keep an open mind."

Leslie collected her book bag. "All right, I'll go, but I'm not keeping an open mind. I'm not optimistic about your chances of contacting my sister. She didn't like you very much."

"Like that matters." Sara held out her hand, admiring her black nail polish. "If Dawn wants to speak to you, she'll need a conduit to do it. That's my job. Let me work my magic, and you can ask your sister anything you want. Got it?"

Sara tossed her hair behind her shoulder and disappeared into the mass of students flocking toward the front doors.

Her abrupt retreat didn't surprise Leslie. Like the rest of the world, Sara didn't understand the toll Dawn's loss had taken on her. And how could she? There were no words to describe her abject isolation. Grief was a barren sea of still waters without the slightest breath of wind, and Leslie felt stranded in the middle of it.

Chapter Eight

The expanse of the familiar red buckeye bushes in Leslie's headlights brought back memories of that terrible night. She tapped the steering wheel while driving along the shelled road to the clearing hidden beyond the dense hedge. Thick pines and tall oaks surrounded the parking lot, and at the far end, down a steep embankment, was the dirt path to the river.

A few cars were there—not as many as in the past, but enough. It would seem that not everyone at St. Benedict High bought into the ghost stories surrounding the river.

Leslie pulled close to the path and could hear pounding music in the distance.

For a split second, she pictured Dawn parking in the same place that fateful Halloween, dressed as one of the Three Musketeers and hurrying to The Abbey. Since that night, only one question had haunted Leslie—why? Why had she gone to The Abbey to confront Beau without saying anything?

A hand slapped her window. Leslie jumped and was about to scream when Sara stuck her face in front of the windshield.

"Come on. Let's have some fun!"

Leslie got out and took a moment to appreciate the depths to which Sara's twisted mind had degenerated. She wore fishnet stockings beneath a leather skirt and a see-through blouse along with tall, chunky-heeled leather boots. Her lipstick was black, along with her thick eyeliner.

Kelly walked up and eased close to Sara. "Jeez. Are you trying to speak to the dead, or scare the shit out of 'em?"

Sara glanced at Leslie's thick coat, baggy jeans, and fuzzy winter boots. "At least I don't look like I'm about to climb Everest."

Kelly put her arm around Leslie's shoulders. "Lay off. She's here, ain't she?"

"Just sayin'." Sara shrugged.

"Ignore her," Kelly muttered to Leslie. "She's pissy because she couldn't fit into the black corset she ordered on eBay."

Leslie searched the parking lot. "I thought you guys were bringing Taylor."

"The bitch bailed," Sara griped in a whiny tone. "Probably has her nose buried in another book on the Devereaux family. I'm tellin' you, she's gonna get us all thrown in jail."

Leslie unbuttoned her coat, attempting to fit in. "Leave her alone. It's how Taylor copes."

Kelly stepped back. "But she's acting weird and unpredictable, which could spell trouble for us. She keeps asking where you disappeared to after dropping us off that night. She thinks you bailed because of some secret. The girl's a conspiracy nut."

Leslie was acutely aware of the changes happening to her friends. "Why hasn't Taylor come to me with any of this?" She might not have understood what Taylor was going through, but all the girls who participated in teaching Beau a lesson that night seemed to be slowly unraveling.

Kelly urged her to the dirt path. "Forget about Taylor. We've got our hands full with Sara."

Sara ran ahead as she shouted, "Let's party!"

Her heart hammering against her ribs, Leslie descended the steep path to the river.

When she stepped on the white sand, her gaze settled on the bonfire pit next to the shore. Students she recognized from school relaxed on green picnic benches close to the fire. A speaker blasted out a rock classic.

Stars twinkled above the trees, their limbs dipping into the water, while a gentle wind rippled the river's surface.

Nothing had changed except for the people. When she first went to the river, Beau had ruled. His interest in her had turned into a sick fascination that led to a year of hell.

Leslie glanced at Kelly. "This feels weird."

Sara climbed on top of one of the green tables and shouted, "Who brought the booze?"

Kelly snickered. "She's so out of control."

The comment hit Leslie with the force of a hammer. Since Beau's demise, Taylor had retreated into books, Kelly had grown more paranoid, and Leslie had become fearful. Only Sara had gone in the opposite direction and lost all her inhibitions.

Leslie had an unnerving, prickling sense of being watched. She scanned the crowd of partygoers, but no one seemed the slightest bit interested in her. Something shifted in the woods leading to The Abbey and her hair stood on end.

An arctic blast grabbed hold of her, making it hard to breathe. Leslie put her hand to her chest, convinced she was in the grips of a heart attack.

"Hope you guys didn't start without me."

The smoky voice rose behind her. Fear gripped Leslie. It sounded like Beau. When she spun around, Luke's friendly smile greeted her.

He wore a short-sleeved white T-shirt that showed off his muscular arms and broad chest. How he wasn't freezing to death amazed her. Leslie noticed the curve of the faded jeans over his tight, round butt and felt a balmy rush flow through her. Her muscles relaxed, and the crushing pain in her chest receded.

Luke held up two twelve-packs of Benedict Beer. "I thought we could use these."

A squeal erupted from the picnic benches, and a blur of black descended on Luke.

Sara tossed her arms around the unsuspecting man and nuzzled his cheek while she expertly maneuvered one of the packs of beer from his right hand.

Then she backed away, a sly smile on her lips. "You're late. You really need to get a phone."

He stared at her see-through top. "Yeah. It's on my list."

Sara's fake giggle was obvious to Leslie, but he seemed to eat it up. *How can men be so gullible?*

Convinced Luke would remain glued to Sara's side for the evening, Leslie turned back to the woods leading to The Abbey, waiting for the awful feeling to return.

"Glad you could make it," Luke said, settling in next to her.

Why is he talking to me? Why isn't he running after Sara?

Luke held up the remaining pack of beer. "You wanna drink?"

Cheers rose from the crowd on the benches as Sara passed around the alcohol. The scene awakened the memory of putting her drunk sister to bed after a night with Beau and his friends at the river.

Leslie nodded, wanting to chase away the image in her head. "Thanks, I'll have one."

"You're driving," Kelly said, her mouth ajar.

Leslie sighed. "It's just one beer."

Luke winked at Kelly. "That makes you the designated driver." He handed Leslie a can.

Their fingers touched, and a tingle ran through Leslie.

Kelly dipped her hand into Leslie's coat pocket. "I don't mind playing the grown-up tonight. Beer makes me sick anyway." She pulled out Leslie's car keys and jiggled them in front of her. "I'll hold on to these."

The diversion the beer promised would help get Leslie through the evening. It was bad enough being at the river again, but the strange feelings Luke aroused amped up her craving for alcohol.

Luke popped the top on his beer, surveying the hangout. "So, this is the river."

Leslie fumbled with the can, her cheeks burning.

"Let me get that for you." Luke took her beer and opened it.

She grabbed her drink back. "I can do it. My fingers get numb when I'm cold."

Luke motioned to her coat. "Is that why you're wrapped up like an Eskimo?"

Kelly grumbled, "Might be hard for someone from Boston to understand, but people feel the cold down here more."

He grinned at Kelly. "Where's your coat, then?"

"Ah, I like the cold." Kelly lowered her gaze and bit her lower lip.

Leslie suppressed the urge to groan. *Is everyone hot for the new guy?*

A scream rose above the loud music and conversation.

Sara danced on a picnic table, kicking up her high-heeled black boots and swinging her black shirt around. Then she reached behind to the clasp of the lacy bra that barely kept her large boobs covered.

"Oh shit," Luke mumbled.

Leslie needed to curb Sara's outlandish behavior before it got back to Gage. He'd tasked her with keeping her friends under control.

"Go get her." She pushed Kelly toward the benches. "Before she does something else stupid."

Kelly ran, slogging through the sand to get to the picnic benches.

Sara stumbled when she spotted Kelly closing in. She tipped over the side of the table, flapping her arms like a bird trying to stay upright, but it was hopeless. She landed face first on the beach.

Applause, along with a few congratulatory whistles, broke out.

"Is it always like this?" Luke asked.

Leslie watched as Kelly helped Sara to her feet. "No. It used to be a lot wilder when Beau ran the river."

"Beau Devereaux? I've heard a lot about him around town. Did you know him?" He sipped his drink, keeping his attention on her.

Leslie studied his high cheekbones, regal forehead, and straight nose, debating what to say.

"Yeah, I knew him," she admitted. "He went to St. Benedict High." Her tone was flat, sounding as emotionless as Gage.

"Doesn't sound like you cared much for him."

She gazed into his green eyes, fighting the urge to reveal more than she should. "Beau dated my sister before she died. I wouldn't say I got to know him well, but what I did know, I didn't like."

His eyebrows shot up. "Really? Everybody in town makes him out to be some kinda saint. Quarterback of the football team, great student, model citizen. You're the first to tell me the truth."

A stab of panic took Leslie's breath away. "The truth? How would you know—"

"In my experience, when someone seems perfect, chances are they're far from it. Perfect is an act meant to deceive. The losers, failures, lost souls—those are people I believe in because they're real." He glanced over his shoulder at a path leading to the parking lot. "The people of St. Benedict believed the illusion of Beau Devereaux. But if he was all that, I doubt he would've ended up as dog food."

She sipped her beer, trying to chase away the memory of Beau surrounded by The Abbey's charred beams. "He had a place in the cells behind The Abbey where he used to take my sister. She was crazy about him almost 'til the end."

"Almost?" Luke tilted his head, appearing intrigued. "She changed her mind?"

Leslie fiddled with the pop-top on her can. "Beau did."

"Where's this abbey?" Luke peered around the beach. "I've heard it was quite a place before the fire."

The fire. The memory of that night at the hospital repeated in an agonizing rush. She'd cried, screamed, and begged to see her sister, but her father had kept her out of the hospital room.

"Would you like to see it?" she asked without thinking.

Luke's brow wrinkled. "Are you sure? Didn't your sister die there? Going back might be—"

"Dawn didn't die there," Leslie interrupted. "She died at the hospital after the fire. I've avoided The Abbey ruins for long enough."

Luke tapped his can against hers. "Then here's to putting those demons to rest."

Leslie took a sip of beer and summoned her courage. The last thing she wanted was to lose it in front of Luke.

I hope you know what you're doing.

She gestured to the path that led to the iron gate. "Follow me."

Chapter Nine

Black clouds blotted out the stars, but Leslie's discomfort with the darkness eased when she glanced at Luke walking beside her. Her feet sank into the sand as she made her way along the shoreline. They approached the gap in the bushes, revealing the path to the rusted gate, and Leslie reconsidered being alone with him.

But despite her apprehension, Luke gave her something Derek hadn't—a sense of peace. Maybe it was the idea of unloading her burdens on a stranger, sort of like a makeshift confession.

They arrived at the gate with the *No Trespassing* sign. Decorated with crosses and swirls, it marked the entrance to The Abbey grounds. She kept her head down as they stepped through, afraid to peer up at the once-imposing structure.

Luke stopped abruptly at the edge of the overgrown field. "Holy shit."

A charred clump of broken beams, tumbled red bricks, and blackened limestone walls rose from a twisted mass of debris that had partially collapsed into the structure. The masonry steps to the entrance were intact, and the grounds no longer reeked of smoke—the only scent was the sweet essence of grass. One spire rose upward toward the sky. The black ribbons climbed the smooth surface and faded at the top, leaving the white block pristine.

"Must have been impressive in its heyday. A shame it ended up like this." Luke set out across the high grass, heading toward the cells.

Leslie's apprehension skyrocketed. What awaited her in the ruins? She didn't know what she'd do if she ran into a ghost, let alone her sister.

Dead leaves crunched beneath her feet as she hurried to catch up with Luke. The grass got thicker and higher as she neared him. He was bent over, examining something. When she reached his side, Leslie saw the remains of the triple-tiered fountain. The angel that had sat on top, along with most of the masonry below it, had crumbled into the stagnant water.

Leslie hated that the forgotten angel didn't survive. It would've been like having a memorial to her sister there.

She turned to the charred remains of the cells, squinting into the darkness. A tickle rose along her spine, and then a shadowy form wavered next to the rubble. She held her breath, willing her gaze to remain on the structure, not wanting to turn tail and run.

The shadow loomed by what was left of the craggy entrance to the cells as if beckoning her closer.

"*I killed the wrong Moore twin.*"

Luke stepped away from the fountain, heading back toward The Abbey.

When Luke moved, the hold Beau had on her broke, and Leslie hurried after him, pushing away thoughts of the past.

He stopped to eye the lone spire. "What was it like before the fire?"

"There used to be two of those," Leslie said, stopping next to him. "Most of the structure was intact. The roof had a few holes in it, but the inside still held much of the original decoration. Birds nested there. Sometimes the wild dogs would get in."

His brow creased. "Wild dogs?"

"They roam the grounds. The legend has it they once belonged to the lady in white who haunts the place. Some believe she was a gamekeeper in love with a monk at the seminary. She hanged herself from a tree in the woods, and the monks left her dogs behind when they vacated the property."

Luke pointed at the mound of charred debris behind The Abbey. "What was that?"

Leslie pulled her coat closer. "Beau's favorite spot—the cells."

A mournful howl ripped through the silence around them.

"That was dramatic." Luke chuckled.

"It's the dogs. We should go."

She was about to turn away when he held her arm. "Don't worry. Wild animals aren't going to attack us."

"You don't understand. When the dogs appear, death is near." She tugged to get free.

Luke kept a tight hold on her. "Wild animals don't attack unless provoked. They must be starving or really tempted to go after prey larger than themselves. With all the game in these woods, I'm sure they're well fed. If we encounter one, remain calm, don't run, speak softly, and don't make any sudden moves."

She remembered the bulky man who had shoved her out of The Abbey the night Beau died. After rounding up the trained attack dogs, the man Gage had hired to kill his son ordered her to go home.

"How do you know so much about animals?"

"Animal behavioral science." Luke let go of her. "I took a few classes. I wanted to be a vet, but then I changed my mind."

She took a moment, attempting to figure him out. He was confident, friendly, and interesting, and nothing like Derek. "I don't see you as a vet."

"I love animals more than people." He raised his head to the dark sky. "What was that you said about the dogs and death?"

"When the dogs appear, death is near."

His eyes flashed in the low light. "Is it true?"

The sway of the trees yielding to the breeze hypnotized Leslie. "The last time I heard them, my sister died."

His gregarious smile disappeared as the moon dipped behind a cloud. Leslie shuddered.

He leaned into her, and his warm breath touched her cheek. "What happened to your sister?"

She didn't know where her courage came from, but suddenly, she wanted to share Dawn's story.

"We were getting ready for the Halloween party at the river, and Derek was coming with us. We were going as the Three Musketeers." She paused and grinned as she remembered the day they'd gone shopping for the outfits. "We were home, preparing for the party. I remember Derek called, and then she started rushing me, telling me to get ready. She was already dressed and wanted to leave, which was funny because Dawn was never early for anything." Leslie took a deep breath, finding the strength to continue. "When I got out of the bathroom, she was gone. She'd taken my car and my phone. I had to go to the neighbor's to call Derek, but he didn't answer. I found out what happened when my parents got home, and we went to the hospital. The son of a bitch who did it beat her, and I suspect raped her, then set her on fire. My father still refuses to tell me what really happened."

Luke moved in front of her. "Did they find who killed your sister?"

Black hate rose to the surface, sweeping away her other emotions. "They never caught him." Bitterness permeated her voice. "We were twins, and I hoped that bond would somehow connect us even in death. But she has never come to me. Does that sound silly?"

"No, not at all. I was the same way after my mom died. I was little and wanted to hear from her, but never did."

His grief resonated with her. She raised her head, taking in the twinkling stars. How could such a beautiful heaven bear witness to such ungodly acts?

"I heard Beau Devereaux died here, too," he whispered.

She tore her gaze away from the sky.

Luke glanced around the remains, crinkling his eyes. "Do you know where?"

She wiped her cheek, suddenly ashamed of her tears. She seemed to cry without provocation lately. "Yeah. I'll show you."

The high grass tickled her fingers during their trek to the gate. No matter the season, green remained on the trees. Leaves never fell, and grass never died in Southeastern Louisiana.

They strolled through the gate, and she directed him back toward the party. When they made it to the beach, shouting and laughter greeted them. The music was louder, and there were a few people dancing in the sand.

She kept along the beach, heading past the picnic benches and fire pits until they found a quieter spot a few yards away.

"Around here." She gestured to the yellow sand. "This is the place they kept showing on the news."

She stood, sinking into the sand, relieved she'd not witnessed this part—the last moment where Beau's bleeding and battered body had ended up on the beach surrounded by the attack dogs. Gage had never shared how he intended for Beau to meet his end, but she assumed the dogs had been part of his plan.

She stared at Luke, admiring his striking good looks. Her sister had drooled over every cute guy she saw, while Leslie was never fazed. Until now.

"I've been asking around about the Devereaux family," he told her. "I've heard a lot of good and bad."

She folded her arms. "I'd suggest you not do that. If you ask too many questions, it'll get back to Gage Devereaux. He's a man you don't piss off."

He tilted his head to the side. "How do you know?"

Leslie analyzed his features, wondering why he was so interested. Then she scolded herself for being so suspicious. Gage Devereaux was the patriarch of St. Benedict. Anyone would want to know more about him. "My dad works with him. He knows Mr. Devereaux very well. They went to high school together."

A menacing shadow crossed Luke's face as he stepped beneath a tree branch. For a split second, she swore Luke had the same cruel grin as Beau.

"I bet you know a lot more about the Devereaux family than most in town."

She twisted her hands. "Yes, I do."

Luke closed the distance between them. "What do you know?"

She hesitated. Lying to her parents, and even Derek, had come easily. Maybe too easily. But Luke seemed to suck every secret out of her like a vampire.

"Hey, I was looking all over for you."

Leslie stumbled back when she saw Derek. He wore a tense smile as he crossed the beach, his black loafers sinking into the sand.

She glared at him. "What are you doing here?"

"I heard everyone was coming to the river tonight. Thought I might stop by and see how you were." Derek glanced at Luke and slipped his hands into his trouser pockets. "Are you all right?"

An uncomfortable feeling gnawed at her stomach. "What do you mean, am I all right? What are you doing out here, Derek? You hate parties at the river."

He nodded at her. "So do you."

Luke stepped forward, extending his hand. "We met at The Bogue. I'm Luke Cross."

Derek kept his hands in his pockets. "I'm Derek. The ex-boyfriend."

Leslie's cheeks burned, and she wished she could be swallowed whole by the sand.

"Ah," Luke lowered his hand. "I asked Leslie to show me The Abbey and where they found Beau Devereaux."

"You didn't bother to let anyone know you were out here?" Derek scowled. "I asked several people at the party where you were. No one had a clue."

There it was—that condescending inflection, mixed with his perpetual concern and topped off by hints of mistrust. She'd become a master of the many intonations in Derek's voice. His uncertainty was her specialty.

"You need to quit checking up on me. My mother told me you showed up at my house. Did you follow me here?" The question rushed out with more sarcasm than she'd intended.

"Someone has to keep an eye on you." Derek stepped in front of her, blocking her view of Luke. "Or have you forgotten there's still a killer on the loose?"

"Hey, man, relax." Luke put a friendly hand on his shoulder. "I'm not a creeper. Leslie was showing me The Abbey. That's all."

Derek wheeled around to him. "She's mine, dude. You got that."

Leslie slapped his back. "You asshole. I don't belong to anyone. When are you going to get that through your thick head?"

She'd never seen this side of Derek before. He'd always been the mellow, respectful boyfriend she'd counted on. This person was a stranger.

"You haven't known this guy more than ten minutes, and you're wandering off with him at night, alone." Derek pointed at her. "You're smarter than this."

Luke's posture became rigid, showcasing the tension in his shoulders and neck. "Derek, you should leave."

Derek kept his gaze on Leslie. "Is that what you want?"

"I told you before. We're through." She raised her voice. "Leave me alone."

"I'm not going to do that. You're in danger, and until you wise up, I'm going to make sure you're safe." A reddish hue tinged Derek's face. "Do you want to end up like Dawn?"

Leslie balled her fists. "I can take care of myself, Derek. I'm a lot better at it than you can possibly imagine." She stormed off the beach and found the path leading back to the party. She slapped away a few low-hanging branches, giving her exasperation an outlet.

Derek had gone too far. Now that he'd seen her with Luke, Leslie feared he'd never let her go.

Chapter Ten

Gage sat at his desk, watching the blanket of early morning sunlight creep across the parking lot of the brewery's administration building. He'd been there since before dawn, debating what to do. The note crumpled in his hand had created a problem—one he would need to eliminate before the person behind it carried out their threats.

He checked the small mahogany clock that Elizabeth had given him on their tenth wedding anniversary.

He tossed the ball of paper on his desk. He'd seen signs of Beau's instability about a year before he attacked Elizabeth. Even as a child, the boy had been fascinated by pain. When he killed the family pet, Elizabeth became unhinged. By that time, Gage had realized it was too late.

He wasn't sure when his love for his son dissolved into doubt. There wasn't a time in their relationship he could pinpoint. But when the moment arrived to have Beau killed, he had not hesitated.

The office door opened without warning, taking his attention from the balled-up note.

"Good morning, Gage," Joe said, standing in his doorway.

He'd expected the visit. It was the reason for his early arrival at the office. It wasn't a meeting he looked forward to every month. "Joe, glad to see you're as punctual as ever."

Joe Cannizzaro strolled up to his desk, his bald head gleaming beneath the overhead lights. Short and stocky, he walked with a limp, something he accredited to a run-in with a nasty customer. With a jovial smile and cherubic cheeks, he was far from intimidating, but then again, he wasn't the one who did the dirty work for his organization. Gage had dealt with enough of his employees to know what Joe was capable of.

"I always look forward to driving up here to visit you." Joe took a seat in front of Gage's desk. "I need to get out of the city every now and then."

"How's everything in New Orleans?" Gage asked, making polite conversation.

"We have a new police chief. Eager man, but I've got the mayor straightening him out on the finer points of looking the other way."

Gage grinned. He'd educated his sheriff on such *finer points*, especially when it came to his son.

Joe sat back in his chair, the leather groaning in protest. "How's the national campaign going? Are you putting my investment to good use?"

Gage tapped his finger on his desk. "The ads should be hitting in another few days. I'm waiting on Mark Haskins to get the commercial contracts in order before we begin."

"Haskins?" Joe raised his black eyebrows. "He's the father of one of the girls you're taking care of, right?"

Gage nodded. "Taylor. She's one of Beau's fuckups."

Joe dusted a piece of lint from his coat sleeve. "Yeah, they did add up. I hope you can keep them quiet. The last thing my associates and I want is loose lips sinking this money ship."

Gage bristled at the comment. "I have them under control."

"And the girl found buried at the river?" Joe tilted closer to the desk. "Whose fuckup was she?"

Gage's stomach tightened. "Sheriff Davis is looking into it. So far, no one has claimed her. No one around here knows anything."

"The press made a stink out of it. They linked her with the other girl found at the river and your son. Not the kind of publicity we need right now."

"I agree." Gage leaned back, letting his detached business persona take over. "People in town will get restless, and you understand what that means."

Joe eyed the partially wadded ball of paper. "Keeping everyone in check is important to the success of the brewery. I know some residents are resentful of the Devereaux hold, but others are loyal to your family. Just make sure you keep a lid on things here. Any hint of scandal would hurt business."

"You know I do everything I can for this business."

Joe glanced up. "Like killing your son. You would do the same to anyone else causing trouble. Right?"

Gage hesitated before picking up the note from his desk. He uncrumpled the message and handed it to Joe. "This was left on my doorstep the other morning."

Joe took the wrinkled sheet and carefully read it. "Who's Eva?"

Gage folded his hands, choosing his words carefully. "My sister. She died when I was six. I barely remember her."

Joe's volume rose along with the redness on his cheeks. "Were there any mysterious circumstances around her death? Anything we should be concerned about?"

Gage shook his head. "But whoever uncovered her existence means to make her a problem, especially now with the new campaign about to launch."

Joe weighed the paper in his hand. "I see your point."

Gage hated to dig a deeper grave for himself, but he had no choice. He needed to put Joe's connections to use before word leaked out. "Can you find out who did this?"

Joe slid the note back across the desk. "What about the girls you're supporting? Could any of them be behind the note?"

Gage chuckled. "I seriously doubt it. They're more enamored with the new cars and clothes I provided. They have too much to lose by causing trouble."

"Teenage girls are the definition of trouble." Joe tossed up his meaty hands. "I know, I have two of them. I'm going to have them followed, just to be sure."

Gage believed the girls were a waste of time, but he didn't express his objections. His father had taught him that when dealing with men like Joe Cannizzaro, the less you said, the better.

"Let me know when you find the culprit." Gage placed the note in a desk drawer. "I'd like to ask them some questions."

"Leave the questioning to me." Joe grinned. "I'll take care of everything."

Gage had never considered him a friend. Joe had a propensity for violence and murder that disturbed him. But they were necessary evils if Gage wanted his business to thrive and his secrets to remain buried. The hefty price he paid for Joe's expertise was worth it in the end, because whenever a problem got in Gage's way, Joe got rid of it—permanently.

Leslie strolled into The Bogue, and a welcome blast of heat relieved her constant chill. Guilt over putting off college applications nagged at her. She needed to figure out if she wanted to go or take a gap year to get her head straight.

The chatter of familiar voices drew her attention to an orange vinyl booth in the back of the dining room. Taylor, Kelly, Sara, and Luke were in a lively conversation. She headed in their direction.

"There she is, finally," Sara announced in her overly dramatic style.

Leslie set her book bag on the bench. "What's so important that I had to rush here?"

Kelly motioned for her to sit. "We've been talking with Luke about The Abbey."

Leslie's breath hitched. *That doesn't sound good.*

Luke leaned across the table to her. "It's my fault. I was asking about the ghost at The Abbey, and Sara concocted a plan."

Sara gave her a cocky grin. "How about doin' a séance at The Abbey?"

A nauseating wave swept through Leslie. She wasn't ready to deal with whatever ghostly horrors rose from those ruins. "Are you crazy?"

Sara held up her hand, urging calm. "Luke mentioned your little adventure at The Abbey and how Derek showed up out of nowhere." She feigned a grimace. "Super creepy."

Kelly took her hand. "We're worried for you. Luke especially."

Luke raised one side of his mouth in a sexy half-smile. "I saw how upset you were when Derek arrived. The situation was pretty uncomfortable."

Leslie's stomach fluttered. She had to stop letting Luke get to her. Every time she stared into his green eyes, she turned to butter. *Damn it!*

"No, it's all good." She hoped to sound genuine. "Derek was just being Derek."

Taylor pointed at Leslie. "You've got a stalker."

The accusation ruffled Leslie. "No, it's nothing like—"

"Tell her about the ghost," Kelly insisted, cutting her off.

Sara's eyes widened. "Luke said he saw somethin' back at The Abbey."

Leslie's stoic façade cracked. "What did you see?"

Luke ran his hand through his thick hair. "After you took off, I went back to The Abbey. I didn't see anything specific, just a white blur running across the grass. But I heard a woman scream."

Goose pimples rose on Leslie's arms, and for several seconds, she forgot to breathe. She sat frozen on the bench, her worst nightmares playing in her head. Was Dawn trapped at The Abbey because of the hell Beau had inflicted?

"We think he saw the lady in white." Taylor's excited pitch was at odds with her flat, emotionless features.

Leslie dug her nails into the tabletop. "How do you know it wasn't someone else?"

Luke and her friends stared at her, frowning.

"Do you think Dawn could be there?" Kelly finally asked.

Leslie shoved her hands under the table and clenched her fists. "Ghosts are said to haunt places where they suffered great pain, and people around town have reported seeing her. So yeah, she could be there."

"There's only one way to find out for sure." Sara slapped the table, rattling their cutlery. "We have to summon the spirits at The Abbey."

Leslie's heart sank. Séances were what people did when they were drunk, or in a scary movie where everyone dies in the end—but in the middle of the woods by the river?

"I don't think that's a good idea." Skepticism laced Taylor's words. "I've read about that shit, and if it goes bad, or you summon a demon or evil entity, we could all—"

"She isn't going to summon a demon," Kelly argued. "Where's your sense of adventure?"

Sara sneered at Taylor. "What's wrong with you? We have to know if Dawn is there. Leslie needs to know."

Leslie clasped her clammy hands together. What if Beau appeared at their séance?

"How do you feel about this, Leslie?" Luke asked. "Are you up to it?"

His smoky voice chased away her dark thoughts and she raised her head, attempting to appear confident. "Performing a séance at The Abbey is a good idea. When nothing happens, maybe the rest of the town will stop whispering about Dawn haunting the place."

"It's settled." Sara clapped her hands. "We'll head to The Abbey Friday night around seven and see who will answer our call."

Taylor shook her head. "This is stupid. We're asking for trouble."

Luke spotted more customers heading in the door. "Helping someone is never stupid. It's the right thing to do."

Kelly looked him over as he stood. "Are you someone who likes to help people?"

He flashed a breathtaking smile. "I like to think so." Luke rushed toward his new customers.

Leslie fixated on him as he walked away.

"Careful, there," Kelly whispered in her ear. "If you play with fire, you're gonna get burned."

Chapter Eleven

Bright beams from the noonday sun reflected off the sidewalk outside Dottie's Boutique on Main Street. Sheriff Kent Davis lowered his sunglasses as he stood next to his cruiser and eyed the picturesque window displaying a mannequin in a low-cut blue dress and fancy blue ostrich feather hat. He couldn't see any woman he knew wearing such a getup, but what did he know. He did his shopping online, and then only bought jeans.

The rest of the shops along the central roadway in and out of St. Benedict had a smattering of customers, but not a lot of the locals would be out so early. Most of the businesses in town didn't get busy until after five, when people got off work at the brewery and students roamed the streets looking for something to amuse themselves.

He walked toward the boutique entrance, reviewing the questions he had in his head for the owner, Dottie Norway. The older woman had an eye for people and a memory better than anyone he knew.

He pushed the glass door open, and the gardenia-scented aroma of his wife's favorite perfume hit him. Dottie was the only merchant who sold it.

Bright yellow, pink, and turquoise hues cluttered the racks and adorned the mannequins. He'd never understood why women needed so many clothes. But he'd learned never to question his Emma about her shopping charges on their credit card. He wanted to live a long life, and fighting with a woman was a sure way of dying young.

"Kent, how can I help you?" Dottie walked around a rack of silky dresses. "Are you shopping for Emma's birthday next month?"

Dottie's perfume was hypnotic at first, but then Kent had to fight an urge to sneeze.

Her eyebrows went up, and she gave him a coy smile. "Or have you got another woman?"

He sighed. It was one of Dottie's most annoying habits—gossip. If St. Benedict had an annual gossip festival, Dottie would be its queen.

A model in her youth, she'd left St. Benedict to seek fame and adventure in New York City, only to return a few years later, pregnant and abandoned.

Despite her age, Dottie's legs could still turn a man's head. She reminded him of a modern-day Scarlett O'Hara—the woman Scarlett might have become if her tale had taken her into middle age.

"I'm here on official business, not shopping for Emma. I need to know if you remember any girls coming through town about twenty-five years ago. Late teens, early twenties. May have been with a man."

Dottie frowned at the red St. Benedict clay on his boots. "You're talking about that girl you found at the river."

He nodded, knowing whatever he said would be all over town by sunset. "You always keep track of everyone coming and going. Wondered if you might help me."

She straightened a yellow dress with white flowers on the rack next to her. "Not a lot of strangers come to my boutique. But when I read the story, I recalled a girl who shopped here a few times one summer long ago. Had lots of money to spend, but claimed she knew no one in town. I remember thinking there was something off about her."

Kent's fingertips tingled. "Off how?"

Dottie crinkled her pale brow. "I couldn't put my finger on it. She just felt different. Sort of like a melody you've heard a thousand times before but played differently."

He bit his tongue to keep from commenting. Dottie always was melodramatic. "You got anything a bit more substantial?"

She crooked her finger at him. "Come with me. I have something that might help."

Dottie led the way to the back of the store. The colorful dresses, an array of sheer lingerie on a wall, and display cases filled with flashy jewelry and perfume confounded every one of his male senses. He wanted to run for the hills, but he had a job to do.

They walked through an open door with *No Admittance* across the top. A storage room waited on the other side. Dottie eased across the white-tiled floor, her heels tapping as she went. She stopped at the far wall and eyed a bulletin board with dozens of photographs tacked to it.

He drew closer and scanned the pictures. They were all of women, smiling for the camera. None of the faces he recognized, but a slow burn awakened in his stomach. It was the same sensation he'd gotten back in New Orleans when working a homicide. It usually meant he was on to something.

Dottie selected a faded Polaroid of a beautiful young woman with long strawberry blonde hair. "I often take pictures of customers who're not from around here. Her name was Lila, Lila Price. She told me there was a price to being her. I always wondered what she meant by that." She handed him the photo.

Kent studied the girl's high cheekbones, perfectly curved jaw, full lips, porcelain skin, and playful eyes. It was her. He knew it in his gut. And he felt confident he had a name. That might not seem like much, but for him, it was huge. He had a person to focus on, not a pile of bones. People needed justice. Bones only needed a grave.

"Any idea where she was from?"

Dottie shook her head. "She never said. And I did ask. You know me, Kent. I can't pass up a juicy piece of gossip." She rested her arm on top of the water cooler next to the bulletin board. "She was in here during the summer of 1990."

"How do you know?"

She pointed at the photo. "The date's on the back."

He turned the Polaroid over and saw the name Lila Price, June 1990, scribbled in black. "You should've been a cop, Dottie."

She chuckled. "My son says the same thing."

"How is Jacob?"

Dottie pursed her lips, adding to the lines around her mouth. "The last postcard I got was from Germany a few months back."

"He still with his band?"

The glint in her eyes dulled. "He dreams of being a rock star. I tried to tell him I had big dreams, too, and ended up coming back to St. Benedict when they fell apart. But kids don't listen."

Kent thought of his two boys and all the battles he'd waged to guide them. "No, they sure don't." He held up the picture. "Can I keep this?"

"Go ahead. I hope it helps." She moved away from the cooler. "You hear anything on that new boy in town? The one Carl has working for him at The Bogue."

Kent tucked the picture into the top pocket of his shirt. "No, why?"

Dottie led him back through the storage room. "I just hear all the girls talking about him when they come into the shop. Apparently, he's become the hottest thing in town."

"Which girls are these?" he asked, slightly concerned.

Dottie headed through the door leading to the showroom. "Sara Bissell comes in pretty frequently with the new girl—Kelly something. Her mother moved here from Covington to work for Mr. Devereaux."

"Norton, Kelly Norton." Kent eyed the dresses in the store. He had seen a few receipts from his wife's forays into Dottie's place and knew it wasn't cheap. "Those girls usually shop here?"

Dottie tossed her head. "No. They just started coming by. I figured they're spending the big raises Mr. Devereaux gave their parents because of the national campaign."

Kent pressed his lips together as he considered the possibility. He knew about the raises and had seen Sara Bissell, Taylor Haskins, and Leslie Moore driving new cars around town. Something didn't fit.

"Thanks for the picture and the information, Dottie." He turned toward the entrance.

"Do you want to get Emma's perfume for her birthday while you're here?" Dottie asked.

Kent tipped his hat. "I'll be back for it. Not to worry."

He walked out of the shop, the burn in his stomach getting stronger by the second. Other people had gotten raises, but their children hadn't flaunted it like those four girls. What was the connection?

Kent always prided himself on staying on top of the happenings in his town, but for the first time since becoming sheriff, he felt like his grip on St. Benedict had slipped. He needed answers, and there was only one person he trusted to tell him the truth.

Kent gazed up at the two-story building covered with pale gray, weathered cypress boards. The windows had green shutters, and red brick steps led to french doors. There was a short faux balcony with a scrolled iron railing along the second floor. It reminded him of the Creole cottages in the French Quarter, but unlike those historic homes, this one was constructed ten years ago when Gage wanted an office building in town. He'd hand-picked the businessmen who would set up shop there—the primary one being his attorney and friend, John Moore.

Kent got out of his car and placed the manila folder he'd brought from the station under his arm. John had grown up in St. Benedict and would have been around Lila Price's age when she'd died. Kent needed more than Dottie's picture to piece together what had happened to her. He had to find out why she'd ended up buried at the river and who had put her there.

A brass plate beside the double glass doors listed the building occupants with John Moore's name at the top.

Kent stepped through the entrance, rankling at the high temperature inside the lobby. He preferred a frosty nip to the stuffy heat—it helped him think.

He veered into a narrow hall with doors on either side stained to resemble bleached cypress. Black suite numbers marked each office.

When Kent arrived at suite three, he saw John Moore's name and *Attorney at Law* engraved on a brass plaque next to the door.

Kent cringed—his conditioned response after years of dealing with so many corrupt attorneys in New Orleans. The cases he'd lost because of favors paid to judges or backroom deals had been too many to count. Kent hated to think of the dangerous criminals who had walked away without serving a day of jail time because of a broken legal system.

He turned the brass handle, putting the past behind him, or trying to. It was always there, the guilt over letting the victims down. Maybe it was why he felt so determined to find Lila Price's killer. He wanted the satisfaction of making the bastard pay.

The reception area, furnished with only two wingback royal blue chairs, had a wilted potted fern that looked close to death. A few posters of local festivals decorated the walls. Kent's gaze went to the Ponchatoula

Strawberry Festival poster. Last year, he'd attended with Emma and they loved the strawberry wine.

There was no receptionist, no desk, and no way for him to let John know he was there.

A door on his right, painted to match the ones in the hall, opened and John Moore barged into the room. Kent inspected his baggy khakis and a slightly wrinkled long-sleeved blue shirt. He suspected John's association with Benedict Brewery had him working long hours lately, but the man hid any hint of fatigue behind his welcoming grin.

John sauntered up to Kent, exuding his usual amiability.

"I thought I heard someone come in." John extended his hand. "Good to see you, Kent."

Kent shook his hand while keeping the manila folder tucked under his arm. "You got a minute?"

John gave him a pensive going-over through the thick lenses of his glasses. "Sure. Come inside."

Kent followed him into a bigger room. With dark paneling, brown leather furniture, and a mahogany desk that reminded Kent of the one Gage sat behind at the brewery, the office reeked of authority.

An array of framed diplomas and commendations crowded the wall. John Moore might have been the only attorney in St. Benedict, but his clients hailed from all over St. Tammany Parish. However, most of John's endeavors went toward his biggest client, Gage Devereaux.

John motioned for Kent to take a seat in one of the brass-studded chairs in front of his desk. "What can I do for you?"

Kent placed the folder in front of him and opened it to the autopsy picture of the bones. "I need your help identifying this girl. She was pregnant when she died, and her neck was broken, indicating it was a homicide."

The moment John sat at his desk, the color drained from his cheeks. His reaction brought back memories of when Dawn had died. Kent had questioned an ashen John and almost catatonic Shelley while trying to hold it together. He'd known the girl and watched her grow up. That night still haunted him. It was every parent's worst nightmare.

John pulled the folder closer, attempting to read the coroner's report. "You have any idea who she is?"

Kent removed the Polaroid of Lila Price from his shirt pocket and dropped it on top of the report. He noted John's reaction, the way he stiffened with a fleeting look of horror.

"I think her name's Lila Price. Dottie took a picture of her in 1990 when she shopped at her store that summer." Kent watched as John sat back in his chair. "That's when you and Gage graduated high school, right?"

"Yeah, sure, but I don't remember anyone by that name. It was a long time ago."

"Do you recognize her?"

John picked up the photo. His brow wrinkled as he scrutinized the picture.

Kent noted the way he bit his lower lip. The nervous gesture told him a lot about what was going on inside John's head.

"Beautiful girl, but she doesn't look familiar." John handed the Polaroid to Kent. "I wish I could tell you more, but we graduated in 1990. Everything is kind of a blur from back then."

Kent dropped the photo into his top pocket. "I understand. High school was a crazy time for all of us." Kent decided to change tactics to see if he could help jog his memory. "What about a strange girl hanging out around town?"

John shook his head. "I never met anyone who looked like that. I'd remember her, Kent. Hell, the whole town would. Strangers stick out around here."

Kent suddenly felt like an ass. Here he was asking questions about a girl no one knew from twenty-five years ago when the man's daughter had been murdered only a few months ago by someone they had yet to find. "I'm sorry, John. I didn't think."

John ran his hand through his brown hair. "Please tell me the person who killed my daughter wasn't responsible for this girl, too."

"It's highly unlikely, but this crime has less chance of being solved than Dawn's."

John's lips formed a firm line, adding an emptiness to his bloodshot eyes. "When are you going to find out who killed my baby? Dammit, Kent, I saw the autopsy. My daughter was beaten, raped, and left to die in the fire."

Part of Kent wanted to reassure him they would find the son of a bitch who had brutalized Dawn, but his law enforcement side kicked in. You never gave assurances to a victim's family. You presented facts, timelines, and procedures. Hope didn't lead to a conviction in a court of law. "You know how this goes, John. It takes time."

He could sense the frustration in John because he felt it, too. The scene of the attack at the cells behind The Abbey had been destroyed by the fire, eradicating precious evidence. There had been little left on Dawn's burned body to get the hair and skin samples needed to ID a suspect.

John nodded and dropped his gaze to his desk. "I understand."

Kent closed the manila folder and tucked it back under his arm, his churning stomach urging him to leave the office.

"Thanks for your time." He stood and waited for John to rise. "Give Shelley my best."

John slipped his hands in his pockets. "I will. She's still struggling with things, but I hope in time she'll get back to her old self."

Guilt plagued Kent. "How's Leslie?"

John's features lifted slightly. "She's been having a tough time. She broke up with her boyfriend, Derek, out of the blue, which worries me. He was a lot of help to her after Dawn died."

"That's a shame. Carol Foster's boy is a good kid." Kent knew he should go, but the conversation with Dottie still nagged at him. "How does your daughter like her new car? I've seen it around town. Nice wheels."

John's color returned. "She was glad to get rid of her old car. Too many memories of her sister."

That sounded logical to Kent, but something felt off. "Seems a lot of kids in town got new cars for Christmas."

"Well, several employees got great Christmas bonuses from the brewery. Maybe that's why so many kids benefited."

John's deadpan reaction didn't surprise Kent. He was skeptical, but didn't bother to probe deeper. "You're probably right. I'll be on my way. Will let you know what I find out." He shook John's hand and left the office, convinced there was more to Lila Price than John was willing to admit.

He'd known the dead girl. Kent would stake his badge on it.

Chapter Twelve

John deliberated his next step and then grabbed his cell phone. Beads of sweat broke out on his forehead as he waited for the call to connect.

"Hello, John." Gage's voice vibrated through the speaker. "What's up?"

John shut his office door. "I need to talk to you. Where are you?"

An edgy silence followed. Knowing Gage as he did, John suspected he was with one of his mistresses.

"Is something wrong?" Gage asked.

"Kent Davis just came to see me." John wiped his brow. "He was asking questions about Lila Price."

More silence.

"Give me a couple hours and meet me at the brewery," Gage instructed. "Bring your briefcase and tell anyone who might ask it's a business call."

A cold dread spread through John. "Who might ask?"

"Just do as I say. We'll talk when you get here."

John hung up, wishing he'd taken the job in New Orleans with a big law firm several years ago. He'd covered Gage's ass more times than he cared to remember, and he worried the patriarch of St. Benedict would go down in a ball of flames one day, taking John with him.

John opened one of the many files piled on his desk and checked his watch. He had two hours to kill. Two hours to worry about what Kent Davis knew. How long could he keep Gage's unsettling past a secret?

After leaving his office, John had gone straight to the brewery. To see Gage's devoted assistant, Connie, already gone for the day surprised him. She was a friend from high school, though they weren't close. A quiet girl who loved horses and always stayed at home, Connie never partied with Gage or John—and thankfully had never seen Gage's dark side.

Pins and needles shot through John's fingers as he sat, keeping a death grip on his briefcase. Gage paced the floor, the red evening light pouring in through his office windows. Lately, things seemed to intensify whenever he dealt with Gage. There was something disconcerting about his biggest client lately, but John couldn't decipher what it was.

"In other words, he knows nothing." Gage stopped and looked at him.

John fidgeted. "He has a name and a picture."

Gage returned to his chair and dissected John with his gaze.

John had always hated the man's steely stare.

"What did you say?" Gage asked.

John fought the dryness in his mouth. "I didn't tell him anything. Did you know she was pregnant?"

He waited for his friend's reaction, but the always-in-control Gage Devereaux never let his emotions slip.

"No." Gage laced his fingers together. "Did he say anything else?"

John relaxed his grip on the briefcase and set it down. "He just asked if I remembered her or saw any unfamiliar girls hanging out around town."

Gage put his hands down. "We'll need to get our stories in order. I'll repeat what you said when he comes to me."

"You think he'll question you?"

Gage nodded. "Kent is a thorough little rat. That's why I hired him."

"Not thorough enough to find my daughter's killer. If I didn't know any better, I'd swear he's dragging his feet on purpose."

Gage's scowl slipped a little, and for a moment, John spotted something akin to regret in his eyes.

"I'm sorry," Gage said, his voice uncharacteristically soft. "I know how hard it is to lose a child. Elizabeth hasn't been the same since Beau."

John silently chastised his disregard for another's suffering. He wasn't the only parent in the room to be gut-punched by grief.

"When they first told me what happened to Dawn, I wanted to kill someone." John remembered that night in the hospital, holding his little girl for the last time, and his throat tightened. "I'm still angry, but it seems pointless. It won't bring my baby back, won't heal her mother's broken heart, won't replace the sister my daughter lost."

John wondered if it was worse for Gage, having lost his only child. He still had Leslie.

"You'll never know how sorry I am about Dawn," Gage muttered. "She deserved to be happy, safe, and achieve her dreams."

The comment wasn't something he'd expected from the reserved man. Gage never became sentimental, at least not around John. "What about Beau? He deserved the same."

Gage turned to the window. The last rays of the sun showed the stubble on his jaw. "We both know Beau had his faults."

"He was a kid, Gage." John observed his clenched hand. "Boys always try to act like badasses. Remember how we were?"

Gage spun his chair around and faced him. "But you were never the badass. That was my job, and I did it well."

John chuckled. "Yes, you did."

"I spend a lot of nights wide awake, going over everything I did with Beau. All the talks, the lectures, the fights." He stood. "Was I too strict, or not strict enough? Did I turn too much of a blind eye? Should I have kept him from the river?"

John watched as Gage leaned on the edge of his desk, his mind somewhere else. "I do the same thing," he said. "But with girls, it's different. I often question if I left her mother to deal with the tough subjects too much. Was I a good example of the type of man she should look for? I don't sleep much, either."

Gage folded his arms and stared at John. "If anyone asks about Lila, you don't know anything. I can't have the town finding out about her, especially now. The national campaign will hit in a few days, and that kind of press would kill everything we've worked for."

John sighed and rose from his chair. "As your attorney and oldest friend, I'm warning you to be careful. Kent sounds pretty damn determined to find out what happened to the girl."

Gage gripped the edge of his desk. "Then we have to make sure he never gets more than that picture." His knuckles shone white against the dark wood. "Let's keep this between us. No one can find out about my family's past."

John picked up his briefcase. "There's one more thing you have to consider. Carol."

Gage's expression became as hard as stone.

John realized he was about to reopen an old wound. "Remember, Carol came to me that summer after graduation and asked if there was someone else. She said she saw you once with another girl she didn't recognize. I told her no, but if Kent goes to her, she could bring that up."

Gage squeezed the back of his neck. "Shit. I didn't think of that. I haven't spoken to Carol Foster since ..."

John patted his shoulder. "Maybe it's time." He walked out of the office and headed to the back stairs, anxious to be on his way. John wondered if he'd done the right thing by encouraging Gage to talk to Carol. But if Gage wanted to protect his name and his company, he would have to go to the one person who knew him better than anyone.

Outside, John took in the dying red embers of the sun. The nip in the air briefly invigorated him, but as the drive home loomed, he pictured his wife numbing herself with bourbon and his daughter's hollow eyes. His family was falling apart, and there wasn't a damn thing he could do about it.

His house wasn't a home anymore. It had become a space where the dead lived—a place occupied by the lost and brokenhearted.

Chapter Thirteen

The treetops in the parking lot swayed when the night wind brushed across their branches. Leslie eyed the play of shadows while listening to Kelly's breathing. Her insistence on coming along had not been unexpected. She had stuck close since Leslie's breakup with Derek.

"You're sure you can do this?" Kelly asked.

Leslie turned off the engine and put her keys in her pocket, striving to remain calm. "This is something I have to do."

She shoved open the car door, hiding her apprehension from Kelly. If her sister could communicate, it would solidify her resolve to stay in St. Benedict. How could she go on with her life if Dawn remained trapped in such a desolate place?

Leslie headed to the dirt path leading to the river. When she landed on the sandy beach, the breeze welcomed her with a bone-chilling embrace. She shivered, praying this evening didn't turn into the disaster Taylor had predicted.

She made her way along the shoreline, but when Leslie arrived at the rusted iron gate, Kelly put her arm across the threshold, blocking the way.

"What are you going to do if you see her? How will it make anything easier?"

She pushed past Kelly, not wanting to admit she'd been asking herself the same thing. "Nothing will make her death easier, but if I see her, then I'll know she didn't leave me." Leslie bit her bottom lip to keep it from trembling and marched through the gate.

Ahead, hidden among the high grass stalks, the bobbing rays of flashlights scoured The Abbey grounds. They were not the first to arrive.

"Thank God," Taylor said, running up to her. "Sara's driving me nuts."

Leslie rubbed her arms. "Why?"

Taylor directed her flashlight at the gate. "She's been Miss Bossy Pants since we arrived. I've been unloading shit out of her car for an hour."

A figure in a black robe approached from the last-standing archway over The Abbey entrance. It floated down the steps, a platinum-blonde ponytail peeking out from under the hood.

Leslie would give Sara credit for her dramatic outfit, but guessed she'd gotten the idea from the lady in white.

"'Bout time your asses showed up." Sara sauntered toward her. A heavy coat of black lipstick contrasted against the paleness of her skin.

Kelly took in Sara's robe with an amused grin. "You're gonna run the ghosts off in that getup."

"Just goes to show how little you know about speaking to the dead. Black is a soothing color to them. It invites them to communicate with us."

Kelly chuckled. "I bet you just made that up."

Leslie surveyed their small group. "I'm surprised you showed, Taylor. I thought you said this was stupid."

"It is," Taylor told her. "I just hope she doesn't raise Beau instead of your sister."

Sara laughed as she tried to roll up the sleeves of her robe. "We ain't here to raise that asshole. If Beau shows up, I'll be the first to send him back to Hell."

Leslie scanned the charred beams of The Abbey's remains. "What about Luke?"

Sara glanced at the gate. "Here he comes now."

Leslie quickly spun around.

Luke came through the gate, carrying an ice chest in one hand and a flashlight in the other. The moonlight highlighted how his T-shirt clung to his chest as he crossed the grassy field.

Kelly pointed at the ice chest. "Please tell me that's beer."

Luke covered the last few feet and dumped the chest at Leslie's feet.

"Not beer. Soft drinks and leftover pizza. I didn't think mixing alcohol and summoning the dead was a good idea."

"Damn," Kelly mumbled. "You don't have anything else besides pizza? I'll be sick as a dog if I eat that crap."

Sara stepped forward and twirled around. "Whatcha think? Spooky enough?"

Luke stroked his chin. "I'd say so."

The gesture made her wary. Leslie had seen Beau do the same thing many times before, usually when he sized up a woman.

Then Luke's interest shifted to her. "Are you sure you want to do this?"

Leslie tossed up her hands. "Yes, for the twentieth time. Why does everybody keep asking me that?"

Taylor nervously scoured the darkened terrain. "Can we get on with this? I don't wanna be here all night."

Sara pouted her black lips. "Fine. Come on." She turned back to The Abbey entrance. "I set up under the remains of the doorway."

Kelly rushed to catch up with Sara. "But Dawn was in the cells, not The Abbey. Shouldn't you set up by them?"

An icy foreboding raced through Leslie. Now that she was here, confronted by the possibility of seeing her sister—no matter how remote—she feared what they might uncover. She stood in the grass, unable to move.

Luke touched her elbow. "Hey, you okay?"

His comforting presence displaced some of her anxiety, but not all of it. "I just want to get this séance underway."

"You might want to." Luke peered ahead to The Abbey. "But I'm not too keen on meetin' any ghosts."

At the steps, Sara and Kelly went around a ring of candles, setting flame to the wicks with their lighters. The flickering sent a halo of glowing light to the arch above, creating ominous shadows.

Leslie trekked through the tall grass while Luke kept up with her. "Do you think Sara can summon the dead?"

Luke's deep chuckle charged the air. "Hell no. All she'll do is make a fool out of herself and us for going along with this."

"You didn't have to come," she whispered to him.

"I know, but I wanted to be here for you. Friends support each other, no matter how crazy the adventure."

"Hey," Sara shouted from the steps. "I need you two to concentrate on the spirits, not each other."

Leslie sheepishly hid her grin. "Sara's going to be impossible if she pulls this off."

"Don't worry," Luke told her. "I have a feeling all Madame Sara's gonna summon is a few loud yawns."

Leslie giggled as she climbed the steps. Then she stopped, appalled by the sound of her flirty laughter.

What the hell am I doing? I don't giggle.

She arrived at the makeshift altar Sara and Taylor had created.

Seven black candles had been arranged in a circle around several objects Leslie recognized. A cheerleading uniform from St. Benedict High lay on a white towel. On top of it was a red ribbon and a framed picture of Dawn doing cheers with her squad.

Seeing the objects forced Leslie to take a startled step back. She didn't recognize the picture, but her sister's smiling face stirred a slew of memories. She regretted not attending more football games to see Dawn cheer. Her reasons for staying away struck her as childish. She should have supported her more and been there when she needed a shoulder to cry on. All the arguments, the differences, the spats seemed so stupid. If she could only go back and change how she'd behaved, maybe her sister would still be alive.

"This is," Luke scratched the stubble on his cheek, "uncomfortable."

Sara passed her hand over the items in the circle. "We need power objects, things the spirit of the dead person will recognize and will help summon them."

"Oh, brother," Kelly mumbled.

Luckily, Sara didn't hear her. She was too busy getting into her role as master of ceremonies.

"Taylor and Leslie, stand by me. Luke and Kelly, you go to the other side. Everyone must concentrate on the objects in the circle and think of Dawn."

"What do I think of?" Luke asked. "I didn't know her."

Sara pointed at the picture atop the uniform. "Focus on that. Think about how much you would like to see her. How she was connected to Leslie." She waved her hand in the air, seeming frustrated. "You can come up with something."

Luke lowered his voice and said, "I'm glad we've settled that."

Kelly giggled next to him.

Leslie stiffened. It was the same flirty giggle she'd just shared with Luke. The sound Dawn made whenever Beau was around. She chastised herself for making such an idiotic noise and swore never to do it again.

"Now, call your sister," Sara ordered.

Leslie gaped at her. "What?"

"Call her. Ask Dawn to join us. She'll come to you, not me." Sara pushed her toward the ring of candles.

Leslie stumbled forward, not sure of what to say.

"Go on," Sara insisted, raising her voice. "We ain't got all night. The portal between worlds only opens for a short time."

Leslie attempted to concentrate on her sister's photo and ignore the stares of the others. Luke's heated gaze felt particularly discomforting.

She closed her eyes and thought of Dawn. Her laugh, smile, penchant for leaving behind a mess, and her love of clothes. A rush of happy memories from their childhood came and went. She could hear Dawn's high-pitched voice, see her hair caught in the wind of an open car window, and smell her favorite food—boiled crawfish. A thousand images from her sister's brief life flashed through her mind, and Leslie found comfort in every one of them.

A low howl resonated across the church steps. It was a long, drawn-out, mournful cry that silenced the crickets and saturated the air with unease.

Leslie's eyes flew open, and a shiver ran up her spine.

Sara glanced back at the woods. "They're here."

"Who's here?" Kelly asked in a shaky voice.

"When the dogs appear, death is near," Luke whispered.

Leslie looked across the dancing candlelight at Luke as he stared into the woods.

He glanced back. "Anybody got a gun?"

Taylor kept her gaze focused on a clump of trees close to the steps. "Yes, but I left it at home."

Everyone turned to her.

Leslie's shock briefly chased away the worry of being attacked by wild beasts. When had the girl gotten a gun?

Taylor acknowledged the curious stares with a half-shrug. "My dad gave it to me. He wanted me to be able to protect myself."

Kelly gripped Leslie's wrist, squeezing hard. "We need to get out of here."

Sara scowled and then yanked Kelly's hand away from Leslie. "Are you serious? The howlin' means we're close. You can't leave."

Kelly shoved Sara away. "I'm not going to end up as supper for some rabid dog."

Leslie stepped in to stop them from coming to blows. "Wild animals don't attack unless provoked," she pointed out, remembering what Luke had told her.

Luke flashed a smile, seeming pleased. "She's right. We're safe as long as we don't confront them."

Leslie's anxiety receded. She no longer cared about the hungry hounds or the creepy woods surrounding them. They would survive no matter what crept out of the shadows. He gave her that kind of confidence.

"What do we do?" Taylor demanded, darting her gaze from Luke to the woods.

"We go on." Sara raised her head to the sky. "We're on the brink of makin' contact."

Leslie wanted to disagree. Then again, she wasn't the expert. She'd never seen a ghost, but could always sense her twin when she was close. There was nothing like that around her now—no sense of Dawn's energy, exuberance, innocence, and determination.

"Dawn Moore," Sara called out, disturbing the stillness of the night. "Your sister's here. She wants to talk to you. Can you give us a sign you're with us?"

The hair on Leslie's arms rose, and her skin danced with a strange energy. A loud *crack* came from inside the ruins.

Kelly gasped, Luke tensed, and Sara slyly smiled.

Another mournful howl tore through the grounds, but this time it sounded closer. A lot closer.

The air grew colder—or was it her imagination? She looked at the others in the circle. They were all perfectly still, listening intently. Leslie's heart thudded in her ears.

Then a flash of white in the darkness of the derelict church coiled her stomach into a knot. She held her breath, anxious for any sign, any hint that someone unearthly had joined their group.

Dawn?

A streak of bright light to the left of the steps distracted her. Leslie watched the specter fly through the woods, darting along the edge of the grounds and weave in and out of the trees.

She thought it was a trick of the moon reflecting off a bird's wing, but then the streak elongated. It morphed in size, growing taller until it took on the shape of a long white billowing cloak. It hovered and then floated up as if caught in the breeze.

Mesmerized, Leslie observed the strange phenomenon. *This can't be happening.*

Curiosity tempted her to chase the apparition and see if it were real. Then the light shifted. The ghostly figure appeared to turn and suddenly faced The Abbey.

Leslie moved closer to the steps, straining to see what remained hidden beneath the hood. Then the moonlight filtered through a few tree branches and illuminated the shadows under the folds. A small nose, full lips, and eerily glowing white skin appeared. The features seemed human, but then they flickered as if fighting to stay in the world of the living.

An eviscerating terror urged Leslie to turn away, but something kept her glued to the spot. The otherworldly being stopped and stared, looking right at her before the woman tilted her head and studied their group.

Then a voice in her head shouted, "*Run!*"

Chapter Fourteen

A rush of adrenaline sent a searing burst through Leslie. Her legs carried her away before her mind registered the movement. She took off, ran down the steps, and leaped into the high grass. Bile rose in her throat, brought on by panic. She dashed in the opposite direction of the specter—anything to get as far away as she could.

The high stalks slapped against her, and Leslie's chest burned, but she kept running as if her life depended on it. She headed toward the river, thinking somehow the water would keep her safe.

"Leslie!"

A man called to her. Was it Luke? All she could comprehend was the thing she'd seen wasn't her sister.

It didn't take long before she hit the brush. The twigs snapped against her arms like whips, flaying her jacket. A sharp branch hit her face, but she needed to keep going.

Leslie broke through a thick line of trees and came to a sudden halt when a slender stretch of beach blocked her way. The rumble of the river rose as she wheeled around, looking for another route of escape.

Numbing hysteria crawled along her skin, pleading with her to keep moving. But the brief respite allowed a thread of sense to break through the screaming in her head.

What are you doing?

She took several deep breaths and was thankful when her mind began to clear.

No way that was real.

She wanted to laugh, and then began second-guessing what she saw. But no matter how many rational explanations she put forward, Leslie could not explain away the woman's face beneath the hood.

She'd seen her, and she was real.

A figure emerged from the brush. Leslie tensed, waiting for the spirit. When she saw Luke, she released a long sigh of relief.

"Why did you run away like that?" He rushed toward her. "What happened?"

She felt foolish. "I'm sorry." She turned to the water, hiding her embarrassment. "I got spooked by the howling and ..."

"And what?"

Luke was right behind her, but sounded far away. She could feel the heat of his skin through her jacket. It was like she was a ghost, and he the one she haunted. Leslie swallowed hard, nervous about being alone with him. It wasn't that she didn't trust him—she didn't trust herself.

She twisted her hands together as she faced him. "I think I saw something back there. In the woods. A woman in a white cloak." She waited, expecting him to laugh, but he didn't.

Luke put his hands on his hips and peered out over the water. "I saw her, too, by the trees. She appeared as a beam of silver light and then formed into a person. She had a white cloak that partially hid her face. I thought I was the only one who saw her."

Thank God. She wasn't crazy.

"When I first spotted her, I thought maybe she was your sister." Luke batted away a leaf clinging to her arm. "I wondered if that was why you ran."

Sweat trickled down Leslie's brow. "I wouldn't have run away from Dawn. I would've run after her shouting her name, asking why she did what she did."

Luke pressed his hands into her shoulders and stared directly into her eyes. "Then what? If you'd learned the answer, what would it change? Dawn would still be dead. Knowing why she did anything before she died won't make her death any easier."

She liked his practical, straightforward manner.

"You sound like me—or the old me. My sense of self has taken a beating since my sister ..."

"You're still you in there." He pointed at her chest. "You'll find your way back."

"Will I?" She shook her head. "I feel like I'm losing my mind. Seeing ghosts, attending séances in the middle of the woods. What's next?"

He took her hand and led her back to the trees along the shore. "I saw the ghost of the lady in white, too. I've never been a big believer in psychic phenomenon, but she was real."

They journeyed up the embankment in silence while Luke pushed a few branches aside. Her fright eased, and that funny calm he instilled returned.

She noticed his broad back and the way his biceps flexed as he cleared the path. "Have you ever done anything like this before?"

He snapped a yellowed leaf from an oak. "Not like that." He chuckled. "But when I was a kid, my best friend talked me into using a Ouija board to contact my mother. I was always trying to find a way to speak to her back then."

"How old were you when she died?" she asked, trying to picture him as a small boy.

"Around four, almost five, I guess."

They walked along the path to the rusted gate as they chatted. Leslie concentrated on his voice instead of searching the trees. Luke's deep melodic tone hypnotized her.

"She painted and sketched all the time. I can still see her face. She was happiest when she created her art."

The affection with which he spoke moved Leslie, and she touched his sleeve. "You miss her, don't you?"

He held the gate open for her. "Every day, but you learn to go on."

"Do you?" She shook her head. "I can't imagine that."

He walked alongside her, the burble of the river accompanying them.

"Tell me about Dawn. What was she like?"

Leslie tried her best to keep it together while straining to find the right words. "She loved being a cheerleader and was captain of her squad. She thought about giving it up for a time, but I talked her out of it."

"Why did she want to give it up?"

"Beau," she said with a hint of disgust. "She found out he wasn't who he pretended to be. She'd called it off, but he wormed his way back in. Then she left him for good before she died." Flashlights on the trail ahead sifted through the trees. "That must be the others."

Luke urged her on with a hand on her elbow. "Probably still looking for you."

They rounded the end of the trail and stepped onto the white sands of the beach. They hurried past the green picnic benches, firepits filled with black ash, and garbage cans to the path that led to the parking lot.

The glaring beams of car headlights forced her hand to her eyes.

"Where the hell did you go?" Sara sounded angry.

Leslie went to a spot where the light wasn't as bright, and when she lowered her hand, Sara stood in front of her, glowering.

"You broke the circle. We were almost in contact with your sister."

Kelly and Taylor were right behind Sara, waiting next to a black truck. Leslie wasn't about to let them know what she saw. She'd never hear the end of it. "The howling freaked me out, so I ran."

Sara wiggled out of her dark robe, revealing her jeans and black top underneath. "What did you see? Tell me."

Leslie cringed. How would she talk her way out of this one?

Luke stepped around to Leslie's side. "I got a glimpse of the lady in white. I even saw her face."

"Yes!" Sara pumped her fist in the air. "I knew it worked."

Kelly frowned at her. "I thought we were supposed to summon Dawn?"

"We got a ghost, and that's what matters." Sara hooked Luke's arm. "Now, tell me everything. We've gotta keep a record of what you saw."

Sara ushered him to the Mustang at the corner of the lot. Taylor dutifully followed, her long brunette ponytail swishing across her back.

The normal sounds of crickets in the woods, and the distant rumble of a car passing on the road, did little to offset Leslie's discomfort.

Kelly eased in next to her. "Do you want to tell me what really happened?"

Her accusatory inflection infuriated Leslie. "What? You think I ran off with Luke for a quickie on the beach?"

Kelly paused and then folded her hands. "Did you?"

She reminded Leslie of an impatient parent putting up with a screaming toddler.

Sara's hearty laugh drifted over to them. Leslie suspected her flirty mood was in overdrive.

Leslie glanced across the parking lot and removed her keys from her pocket. "Let's go. We've wasted enough time chasing spirits."

"You okay to drive?" Kelly asked. "You look pretty shaken up."

Leslie might have felt frazzled, but she wasn't about to let Kelly drive her home. The last thing she wanted was to appear weak in front of the others. If she fell apart, Sara, Kelly, and Taylor would soon follow. "Don't worry about me." She watched Luke with Taylor and Sara, discussing what he'd seen at The Abbey. "I'm not the one in danger here."

Kelly followed her gaze to the others sitting on the Mustang. "He's not interested in them. Only you."

The comment created a fluttering sensation in Leslie's stomach. He was too handsome not to have a boatload of women in his past, but she suspected the voraciously chatty Sara and tight-lipped Taylor were not what he craved. Luke had a calculating side—she could sense it when he talked to her. It gave Leslie the impression he would want more from a woman than just sex. Luke was after something else, but she couldn't get a handle on what that was.

Leslie walked with Kelly to her car as Luke chatted a few feet away, not appearing to care if they left. She opened the driver's side door and, with a weary sigh, slipped into the comfy seat.

"We're heading home," Kelly shouted through her open window. "You guys gonna be all right?"

Sara waved. "Go on. See you Monday at school."

Kelly sat back and reached for her seat belt while Leslie turned the key in the ignition.

The engine didn't make a sound.

"Oh no." Leslie tried again, but the engine sputtered briefly and died. She scowled at the console. "It shouldn't do that. It's new." Leslie pictured her father's reaction when she called to say her car had stalled at the river. He wouldn't be happy.

She pushed open her door and got out, cursing under her breath.

Kelly followed her to the front bumper and stood by as she lifted the hood.

Engines were a complete mystery. The maze of wires, cables, and plastic coverings left her utterly confused.

Luke approached the car, his gaze focused on the raised hood. "What's wrong?"

"Won't start," Kelly told him.

Sara and Taylor weren't far behind—their interest more on Luke than her engine troubles.

Luke removed a small flashlight from his back pocket and shined the light under the hood. He inspected the engine, a frown creasing his brow. Leslie found the way Kelly and Sara stared at Luke's butt entertaining.

"Here's your problem." Luke pointed at the front of the engine. "Loose connector cable on your battery."

Leslie moved closer to the bumper. "How did that happen?"

Luke held the flashlight in his mouth as he reattached the cable.

Leslie admired his hands as he worked. She wasn't sure if it was his confidence in dealing with a subject foreign to her or how he'd taken command of the situation, but it reinforced her feelings for him. He didn't coddle her or try and protect her, as Derek had.

Luke backed away and wiped his hands on his jeans, leaving a black stain along his thigh. He removed the flashlight from his mouth. "That should do it. Give it a try."

Leslie ducked into the car and put her key back in the ignition. The engine purred to life.

Luke slammed the hood. "The cable probably got knocked loose on the local roads. Happens sometimes when they aren't secured properly."

She turned off the engine and walked toward Luke. "It's a new car."

Luke chuckled. "New doesn't mean it can't break."

"Unless someone messed with it," Taylor suggested.

Leslie couldn't believe Taylor had made such a bold accusation. That wasn't the timid Taylor she knew.

Luke turned, flexing his shoulders slightly. "What are you insinuating? That I did it?"

Taylor folded her arms. "A lot of strange things have happened since you arrived in St. Benedict. Why is that? Did you come here to get rid of us?"

"Taylor!" Sara shouted. "Would you shut up?" She faced Luke, putting on a fake smile. "Ignore her. She rambles. Complete idiot."

Luke shifted his gaze to Leslie. "What's Taylor talking about?"

Sara glared at Leslie and then went up to Luke, slipping her arm around his waist and de-escalating the situation. "Damn, you're good with cars."

Luke ogled Sara's ample bosom spilling over the V-neck of her shirt. "Yeah, I'm good with my hands."

Sara traced her finger along his thick forearm. "I bet you are."

Luke grinned as he allowed her to lead him away.

The interlude puzzled Leslie. She'd thought him more discerning. All it took was big boobs and a pretty face, and Luke turned to putty.

Derek never did that.

Without warning, her love for *that boy* pressed down on Leslie like an anvil. There were moments when she wanted to run to him and beg for forgiveness, but then her secret would slink its way into her thoughts and stifle the desire. She'd made her decision. There was no going back.

Kelly went to Taylor's side. "You need to ride home with Leslie and me." Kelly shot Leslie a pleading *we've-got-to-get-her-out-of-here* look.

"Yeah, come with us," Leslie called to Taylor.

Leslie returned to her car door and glanced back at Luke and Sara crossing the lot to Luke's GT. Sara might aggravate her sometimes, but Leslie was grateful she'd kept Luke from interrogating Taylor.

One slip, and Gage would hear about it. She didn't want to consider what he'd do to her and the others if that happened.

"That was close," Kelly said over the roof after getting Taylor in the back seat.

Taylor tugged the seat belt over her shoulder. "Thanks for the ride. I'm glad to get away from Sara."

Leslie shut her door and started the engine. "Why did you accuse Luke of tampering with my car?"

Taylor sat back, staring blankly out the window. "He shows up out of nowhere, gets cozy with the four of us, and then wants to come to The Abbey. Don't you see what he's doing? He's trying to worm his way into our lives because he wants something."

"Would you get real?" Kelly spun around to face Taylor. "He's new in town and making friends. He's not out to kill us."

"We can't trust him," Taylor insisted, putting a hint of displeasure in her mousy voice. "He's manipulative, too quick to help, and way too friendly with everybody he meets. He's Beau all over again. He even has the same smile."

Leslie shuddered and gripped the steering wheel while maneuvering the dark street toward town. "He's not Beau. You know what an asshole he was."

Taylor slapped the back of Leslie's seat. "If we aren't careful, Luke will hurt us just like Beau did."

To Leslie, the ominous threat was ridiculous. Beau Devereaux was dead, and his evil with him. She hoped whatever had prompted Taylor's outburst would evaporate once she got to know Luke. She brushed her thumbs against the leather steering wheel and searched for the best way to assure Taylor. "Give it time," she said while glancing at her friend in the rearview mirror. "You'll soon discover not every man you meet is like Beau."

Kelly put on a warm smile for Taylor. "Yeah, Leslie found Derek, and he's a real good guy."

Taylor sank into her seat. "If he's such a good guy, why did she dump him?"

Kelly arched her eyebrows at Leslie. "She does have a point."

Leslie wanted to strangle Kelly, but stifled her frustration. "You both know why I called it off. Derek has no idea what we've done. If he ever did, he'd hate me, and it would put him in danger. I can't live with that."

"I get it," Taylor added. "You've done things you regret. Kept secrets from friends and family. Still, it seems sad to give up on someone you love because of someone you hate."

A trickle of suspicion worked its way through Leslie. She eyed Taylor in the rearview mirror as she pressed the gas pedal. "You're wrong. I don't give up on those I love."

Leslie had sacrificed her relationship with Derek to keep him safe. What kind of life could they have together if all she did was lie?

Gage had warned her, when they embarked on their plan to get rid of Beau, that one day she could pay a price for her involvement. That day had arrived.

Chapter Fifteen

The morning sun spread welcoming rays across the parking lot of Mo's Diner. When Gage got out of his car, he took in the glowing white neon letters above the entrance. The blue booths, where he'd spent a great deal of time with Carol during high school, could be seen through the front windows. Her laughter, as light as a summer shower, filled his mind. Those were the happiest days of his life.

John had told him she still frequented the establishment before heading to her job in Covington. Gage hoped to catch her and somehow tell her about Kent's investigation. Just the thought of speaking to her again after so many years rattled him. How could he tell the only woman he'd ever loved to keep quiet when he'd ruthlessly cast her aside?

His hand trembled before yanking open the door. He needed to forget about the past and concentrate on the future of his business and his family.

The pungent aroma of coffee and chicory teased his nose. The overhead fluorescent lights still flickered just as they had the last time he'd walked in the door. Even the patrons looked the same, slouched over the glass-covered counter, drawing strength for another day from their caffeinated beverages.

A few customers were in the booths set along the windows facing Main Street, but Carol wasn't among them. Gage worked his way along the aisle, a few wide-eyed glances following him. When he made it to the booth farthest from the entrance, he eased onto the blue bench and waited.

An older woman with silver hair approached him, carrying a pad and pencil. "What can I get you, Mr. Devereaux?"

"Good morning, Sylvia." He nodded to the waitress who had once worked at his brewery. "Coffee, black."

"Sure thing." She jotted down the order. "You still looking for help at the brewery?" she demurely asked. "My boy's back in town and needs a job."

Her tired eyes resembled so many he'd seen around St. Benedict—longtime residents down on their luck. His father had warned him everyone would turn to him for help. "Sure. Tell him to stop by the brewery office. We'll get him started."

Her smile burst at the seams with hope. "Thank you, Mr. Devereaux. Thank you."

Sylvia hurried away as though afraid to overstay her welcome.

He flexed his shoulders, still tense from his morning workout. The added weights had done little to offset his edginess. He'd be sore soon, but pain kept him sharp.

Gage drummed his fingers along the dinged Formica table. The small bell above the door tinkled, and his throat tightened.

A slender woman with a glowing smile and lovely brown hair entered. Her movements still intoxicated him. During their years together, he'd often watched her when she wasn't looking. Her grace had given him sustenance on his darkest days.

His hand twitched as she stopped at the counter and greeted a few of the diners. She was the same, still as bewitching as he remembered.

He waited, holding his breath as Carol turned. When their eyes met, he'd hoped for a glimmer of fondness, but what he got was utter disbelief.

Gage stood, too antsy to sit still any longer. The walk toward her was the longest in his life. His stomach twisted.

The sunlight filtered through the glass doors and settled on her face. Lines of worry marred her lovely, light brown Creole skin, but she was still beautiful.

"Gage?" She twirled a lock of hair around her finger.

He noted the gesture and grinned. She'd done the same in high school when anxious.

"Hello, Carol." He adjusted the sleeve of his shirt. "I was hoping I'd run into you."

He surveyed the diners who were taking in their every word. No doubt news of their reunion would spread across St. Benedict before sunset, but he didn't care. He'd lived under the scrutiny of the town all his life. Let them stew on this development.

"You're here for me?" she asked timidly.

He motioned to his booth. "Can we talk?"

Gage waited for her to step in front of him. He liked the fitted pantsuit she wore and the way it hugged her slim figure. He remembered her always wearing sundresses and flowing outfits in high school.

He waited until she took a seat at his booth before sitting across from her. The nervous energy between them could have lit up St. Benedict for a month.

"Why now?" she said, cutting to the chase. "All these years, and now you want to talk?"

He folded his hands and placed them on the table.

Sylvia returned at that moment, two piping hot mugs of coffee in hand.

"I put cream and sugar in yours, Carol." She nodded to her former colleague. "I have your cheesecake bagged whenever you're ready."

Sylvia scurried away. Gage was grateful she hadn't lingered.

He studied Carol's face, overjoyed to be with her again but sick about the reason. "You still like their cheesecake, huh?"

"You remember." She blushed and giggled.

The sound clawed at him. Just one of many things about her he'd desperately missed. "I spent a small fortune in this place feeding you strawberry cheesecake." He ran his fingertips across the table's surface. "I heard you got a job here after you left college."

She closed her hands around the warm cup of coffee. "Had to make a living."

"How's your boy, Derek?"

"He's good. Hoping to go to LSU." She ran her thumb along the rim of her mug. "I'm sorry about Beau. I wanted to call or send a card, but I figured you probably had enough to deal with."

"Thank you. I appreciate the thought."

She patted the table. "I can't believe you're here. I used to hope you would stop by. I always wanted to share a cup of coffee with you and find out what happened." She lowered her gaze to her mug. "That summer you returned from Boston, I tried to talk to you, but you ignored me. Why?"

He pushed his coffee away. "You know why. My father never approved of our relationship. He let us alone in high school, but after that, he insisted I toe the Devereaux line."

"But you always said what he wanted didn't matter."

Gage rubbed his face, wishing he hadn't come. The past still pained him more than he'd realized. "I've often wondered what would've happened had my father not interfered. He hurt so many people keeping us apart."

Carol nodded. "You, me, Elizabeth, my son, your son, the entire town. The list of people damaged by Edward's aspirations is pretty long."

His hatred for his father seared through him. "I should have ignored him and married you. You could have saved me from myself."

She set her coffee aside and clasped his hand. "What are you talking about?"

Her touch aroused feelings he thought he'd buried. Gage wanted to berate himself for being so stupid, for thinking that letting her go was for the best.

"Forget it." He straightened up, pulling his hand away. "I need to talk to you about something."

Carol picked up her coffee. "Kent Davis already asked me about a woman named Lila Price. The whole town is buzzing about the investigation."

His mouth went dry. "What did you tell him?"

"The truth. I've never heard of her."

He sagged in his seat. "I was hoping to warn you before he got to you."

"Warn me? Why?" She looked alarmed.

"Kent's being particularly relentless on this case. I didn't want him bothering you and bringing up a bunch of bad memories."

"My memories of you and high school were never bad. Far from it."

The smile he offered her was slight, but genuine. "I'm glad to hear that."

"What have you got to do with this Lila Price?" She took a sip of coffee. "I know you, and you would never have come to see me after so long if you didn't have something to lose. What's going on?"

He gazed into her eyes, wanting to share the hell he'd endured since leaving her, but knowing such a revelation would only end badly. His transgressions were hard enough for Elizabeth to live with, but unloading those burdens on Carol was unimaginable. He wasn't the Gage Devereaux she'd loved in high school. The man he'd become would disappoint her.

"I don't know anything. I just wanted to make sure Kent didn't grill you like he did me."

"I appreciate your concern." Her smile dwindled.

Her voice was no longer soft and inviting. The magic between them had died.

Gage rose from the booth. "Thank you for taking the time to talk. John Moore tells me you have a new job in Covington working for some attorneys."

"Yes, I'm doing well."

"I'm happy for you." He took out his wallet and put a fifty-dollar bill on the table. "Take care, Carol. I wish you and your son only the best."

He walked briskly away and left the diner.

Once in the comfort of his BMW, he sucked in a deep breath. He hunted for Carol in the diner windows and found her still at their booth, wiping her eyes with a napkin.

Shit!

She got up and headed for the door, but Sylvia stopped her and handed her a small white bag.

Gage longed to start his car and drive away, but something compelled him to wait. He wanted to watch Carol a little longer. Seeing her again had been painful, but also wonderful.

When she stepped outside, she almost ran into a young man. Tall and fit with a head of thick, sun-kissed hair, he seemed familiar, but Gage couldn't place him.

The newcomer spoke to Carol. She smiled as they chatted. The distress of their encounter no longer darkened her features.

She shook his hand, intriguing Gage. He wasn't sure how he knew the stranger, but had the feeling he'd met him before.

A car pulled into the parking lot and stopped outside the entrance, blocking Gage's view.

He recognized the person behind the wheel—Derek.

Carol climbed into the vehicle, and her son drove away.

The young man she spoke to at the diner entrance eagerly watched their car. His interest seemed too intense to be casual, heightening Gage's dismay.

Who is this kid?

Growing more suspicious, Gage opened his door.

When the young man spotted him, Gage never averted his eyes. But instead of turning away, the stranger smiled and set out across the blacktop toward him. His gait was casual, but he carried tension in his shoulders.

"I was hoping to run into you, Mr. Devereaux."

With a square jaw, chiseled cheekbones, and green eyes, Gage thought he was a good-looking kid.

"My name is Luke Cross." He held out his hand.

The air siphoned out of Gage's chest like a sliced tire. "The sheriff mentioned you. From Massachusetts, right? You don't sound like it."

His gaze held no animosity as he nodded. "I went to a private school outside the area."

"What brings you to St. Benedict, Mr. Cross?"

Luke appeared unruffled. "To find my family. My mother was Pamela Cross. An old friend of yours from college, I believe."

Gage's wrath would boil over unless he got it under control. He took a breath, held it as he counted off ten seconds, and then let it go. He kept his tone friendly and asked, "What did Pamela tell you about our time at school?"

Luke's grin alluded to a calculating mind behind the mellow exterior. "That you two were close."

The subtle hint wasn't lost on Gage. Had Pamela told him the truth? "Where's your mother now?"

"She died when I was four." Luke's voice sounded cold and empty. "My grandparents raised me."

Gage remembered the beautiful strawberry blonde with a captivating smile. When they met, he'd been drunk at a party, lamenting over a girl who broke his heart. Pamela had a similar laugh and reckless disregard for rules. He looked at her, and Gage couldn't stop seeing the other young woman. When he finally kissed her, his infatuation with the girl who nearly destroyed him took over. His guilt from their one-night stand remained. Pamela's letters, voicemails, and pleading at his door all came roaring back.

"I'm sorry she's gone," Gage finally said. "I remember she was a promising artist."

"My grandparents said my mother had many demons. They drove her from art to a life of drugs. She tried to explain her actions in a letter I received when I turned twenty-one."

Gage leaned against his car, wary. "What did the letter say?"

"She told me who you were, where you were, and how to find you."

Dread tensed every muscle in his back. Gage had spent his life paying for what he'd done in Boston. Now, his sins had come back to haunt him in the guise of Luke Cross.

"What did you hope to accomplish by coming here?" he asked in a bitter tone.

Luke inspected the car behind Gage. "You got a 4.4 V8 in that 750?"

Gage moved away and glanced at his car. "You know cars?"

"Engines," Luke corrected. "I rebuild them." He motioned across the lot. "Let me show you my baby."

Gage had loved rebuilding engines, but his father forced him to give it up. He still admired expensive machinery—his garage could attest to that. But Edward Devereaux had never wanted him to dirty his hands with what he called menial labor. "Where are you staying?"

Luke stopped before a dark green 1966 GT Mustang. "I've got an apartment at the end of Main Street."

Gage didn't hear him—he was too preoccupied with the car. He walked alongside the sleek machine and ran his fingers over the hood. Then Gage noticed the dent in the front bumper. He yanked his hand away, his stomach churning.

"I had a car like this in high school. Even had the same dent on the front bumper. I was angry and hit a tree by the river."

Luke nodded, coming closer. "The car belonged to my mother. She left it to me, along with the letter. I kept it exactly as it was, dent and all."

Gage examined him. "Is blackmail your motive for being here?"

Luke squared his shoulders. "I didn't come here to blackmail you. I wanted to meet my father and my half-brother, but it seems I arrived too late. I'm sorry for your loss."

Gage could see Beau saying the same thing, lacing his poisonous words with just enough charm to trick a person into believing he cared.

"Claiming you're a Devereaux will make you more enemies in this town than friends. I suggest you watch your back."

"Why? Are you going to put a knife in it?" Luke studied Gage. "Tell me, is that girl they found at the river your doing, or did another Devereaux take care of her?"

Gage disliked it when rivals baited him. It was a tactic often used by those bluffing in poker when they had a shitty hand—better men than this boy had tested him. "Careful, Mr. Cross, or you might end up in the river, too."

Luke took a set of keys out of his pocket. "And just when I thought we were getting along so well."

He climbed into the Mustang, and the *vroom* of the engine vibrated through Gage. He'd loved that throaty sound.

Once in his car, Gage watched with interest as Luke pulled out of the lot. He touched the steering wheel and stared at the veins in his wrist that disappeared beneath the sleeve of his white shirt.

Blood. It was what his father had raised him to respect. Luke's arrival had been ill-timed, but could be fortunate.

He carefully deliberated how to proceed. The eyes of the world would soon be on him, and he couldn't have anything overshadowing the brewery's success—even his newfound heir.

CHAPTER SIXTEEN

Derek squinted at the foggy windshield distorting his view of Gage and Luke in the parking lot across Main Street. He'd decided to wait in the car while his mother ran into the local drugstore. She claimed to have a headache, but he knew the real reason for her red eyes and runny nose—Gage Devereaux.

That his truck had broken down and he needed his mother's car was opportune. Derek had planned to investigate Luke Cross, but seeing him with Gage caused even more concern.

He watched as Luke showed Gage his Mustang. Derek was too far away to read their faces, but by the way Gage lovingly stroked the hood, he could tell he had a thing for classic cars. He thought Gage Devereaux, like Beau, was only interested in himself. He couldn't imagine the man hunched beneath a hood with grease under his fingernails.

"Whatcha looking at?" Carol asked when she slid into the seat next to him.

Derek pointed across the street. "Never figured those two for friends."

Carol stared out the window. "I bet Gage is captivated by that car." She sat back, a small white bag in her hand. "He used to have a similar one in high school. We took it to the river every weekend."

"I don't get what you saw in him."

She retrieved a bottle of aspirin from the bag. "He was different then, honey."

"What were you talking about with Luke?"

She worked the cap off the bottle. "Is that his name? I don't recall. We only spoke for a moment. He asked me about the cheesecake at Mo's."

"He's the guy from Boston I told you about," Derek said with a hint of distaste.

She wistfully tilted her head. "Ah, yes. The one Leslie's friends were all over. I can't say I blame them. He's handsome."

"He's trouble."

Carol dropped two white tablets into her hand and then set the bottle in the cup rest. She took a moment and studied the men across the street. "He reminds me of Gage at that age. Looks a little like him. All the girls were crazy about him, too."

Derek tapped his fist on the steering wheel, fighting to hold in his anger. "Yeah, well, Leslie is acting just like her friends. I think she may have something going on with Luke."

Carol sagged into her seat. "Leslie? I know you said you two called it off, but I think you're both being foolish. You've been crazy about her since the day you met."

Derek jutted out his chin. "Feelings change, Ma."

"Do they?" She closed her fist around the aspirin. "I might have believed that once, but not anymore. You love Leslie, and she loves you—no matter what you think you see. She's not the kind to go flitting from one guy to the next."

"She's been spending a lot of time with him. Something's up."

Carol tossed back the pills and made a face as she gulped them down. "Maybe this Luke is giving her something she needs right now."

Derek rocked his head back. "That's not helping me, Ma."

She slapped his thigh. "I'm talking about being a friend. Maybe he's listening to her in a way you couldn't because you were too close. Sometimes, when you've been through a great loss, you need someone far removed from the situation to help give you perspective."

The explanation did nothing to quell the churning in his stomach. "Then why did she push me away? After all we went through together, why'd she tell me to stay out of her life?" He closed his eyes, inundated with the memory. "I'd never heard her sound so hateful. It was like the girl I loved had died."

Carol put a hand on his shoulder. "She's confused. Give her time. Everyone must come to grips with grief in their own way. You can't force it. She's been through a lot."

"But how long do I wait?"

Carol peered out the window, observing Mo's parking lot. "Who can say? Eventually, she'll come around. When you love someone, a part of them never leaves you."

The longing in his mother's voice urged him to follow her gaze. Across the street, the roar of Luke's Mustang drowned out the small-town noise. Then the rigid figure of Gage Devereaux walking back to his car sent a shiver through him.

Why, after all her suffering, did his mother still love such a man?

Elizabeth Devereaux strolled out of Dottie's Boutique, excited and laden with shopping bags. The sexy, low-cut dresses and sheer lingerie were meant to keep her husband enthused about their baby-making activities. The past few weeks with Gage had conjured up images of their honeymoon, with a few added twists. New things Gage introduced in bed. His not-so-gentle take on sex didn't turn her off like it had when she'd been a naïve bride.

She remembered the feel of Gage's hands on her body and the woodsy fragrance of his cologne. The first time he was rough, she'd been frightened. The next night, she'd asked him to do it again.

Elizabeth set her bags in the trunk and, with a sly smile, headed to her driver's side door. Something flapped on her windshield—a piece of folded paper secured beneath a wiper. Annoyed, she retrieved the flyer and saw it wasn't an ad, but a copy of a picture. In the photo, her husband sat at a booth in Mo's Diner—a place he'd refused to take her.

Across from him was Carol Foster.

The loving way her husband gazed at the woman obliterated Elizabeth's cheerful mood. He'd never looked at her that way. She'd never felt even an iota of emotion that he conveyed in the image. Tears blurred her vision, but the words printed below the photo dried them instantly.

Are you worried? I would be.

A sick feeling laced through every fiber of Elizabeth's being.

She spun around, searching the street. Everyone knew about Gage and Carol. She'd lived with the whispers for years after moving to the provincial hovel. What had changed?

With paranoia ripping through her, she got in her car, debating if she should call Gage. Then another, more disturbing thought occurred to her—why was Gage with Carol?

His affairs had been with various professional and not-so-professional women, but none of them had been Carol. Elizabeth had spent a small fortune on private investigators to make sure. But if he had found his way back to the one woman he'd really loved, Elizabeth felt certain her marriage would end.

But he won't leave you and a baby.

Her inner turmoil cooled. Gage would never walk away from an heir. His damn name and legacy meant too much to him.

She started the engine, a slight grin on her lips.

"Time to step up my efforts." Elizabeth crumpled the paper. "I'll give Gage a baby, even if I have to dig up someone else to be the father."

Chapter Seventeen

A gentle breeze shook the leafy branches of the oaks lining Huntsman Road. The early evening light filtering through the branches created peculiar patterns on the sidewalks as Leslie drove along, looking for the familiar single-story ranch home where Taylor lived.

A stack of books sat on the seat next to her, stuffed with assignments Taylor had missed. She'd been out sick for almost two weeks, supposedly with the flu. Leslie didn't buy it. She'd spoken to Taylor a few times on the phone and not once had she sounded ill. Leslie volunteered to drop off her missed schoolwork, hoping for an opportunity to find out what was up.

She arrived at a red brick house boasting a bed of purple and yellow pansies in the garden. The yard appeared freshly mowed, the porch swept of leaves, but the porch light was lit, which struck her as odd considering it wasn't dark yet.

Leslie lugged books up the inclined walkway to the back gate. Taylor had asked her to come to the rear entrance when she called to say she was on her way.

At the gate, an unsettling breeze swept over her. She turned and glanced back at the street, expecting to see someone, but there were no cars or people, only the wind stirring the trees. The black gates to the Devereaux Estate were right across the street. How Taylor spent her days looking out on that entrance perplexed Leslie. The constant reminder of Beau would have driven her mad.

She slipped through the side gate and peeked into the garage. Taylor's Jeep was there, but the other two stalls were empty.

Leslie climbed the rock steps to the back door. A creepy feeling came over her. There it was again—the sensation of someone watching her.

The country-style door flew open, and Taylor stood before her. Her sweatpants were wrinkled, her sweatshirt had several colorful stains, her brown hair was a nest of knots, and dark circles rimmed her eyes. Not only was she unkempt, but the hollows of her cheekbones had her looking like the walking dead.

"What's wrong with you?" Leslie plowed through the door, worry replacing her doubts about Taylor's illness. "Have you seen a doctor?"

Taylor stuck her head outside, scanning the backyard. "Were you followed?"

Leslie went to a table by the back door and set down the books. "Followed? By Derek?"

Taylor shut the door and set the latch. "Not Derek. Someone else."

Leslie observed Taylor's jerky movements, and her distress intensified. "Who do you think would be following me?"

Taylor inspected the book bag. "People who don't want to be seen."

A sickening feeling twisted Leslie's stomach. "Taylor, what's going on? Why haven't you been in school?"

Taylor took her arm, and Leslie got a whiff of her.

"When was the last time you showered?" She looked around. "Where are your parents?"

Taylor pulled her deeper into the home, past a room with assorted green plants and a pool table. "Dad went out of town to do PR work for the brewery, and Mom went with him. They'll be back later tonight."

"They left you alone like this?" Leslie didn't hide the astonishment in her voice. "Do they know you haven't been in school?"

Taylor's flat expression never changed. Her eyes remained lifeless and empty. "I told them I was fine when they left. I had more important things to do than go to school."

Leslie stayed close as they entered a narrow hallway. "Taylor, you're not making any sense. What could be more important than graduating?"

Taylor walked into an oak-paneled living room, flourishing her hands. "This."

Diagrams, papers, sticky notes with words scribbled on them, and open books were strewn across the dark wood coffee table, taped to the red brick hearth, spread out on the hardwood floor, and scattered across the green sofa. The entire room looked like a cyclone had hit it.

Leslie crept across the hardwood floor, staring in fascinated horror. "What's all this?"

Taylor stood in the center, wildly waving her hands. "My research. I've spent every hour since my parents left digging into everything I could find." She went to an open laptop on the coffee table, several sticky notes attached to the screen. "I'm putting it all together."

Leslie gingerly stepped over open books on the floor—a few had *St. Benedict Public Library* stamped inside their covers. She knelt to get a better look at a stack of maps of the Mississippi River. "What are you researching?"

"The Devereaux family, of course. You won't believe what I've found." Taylor darted across the room, a blur of movement. Then she returned to Leslie's side, a piece of paper in her shaking hands.

"This is a bit extreme." Leslie slowly got to her feet.

Taylor tipped her head awkwardly. "No, it's not. To conquer an enemy, you have to learn everything you can about them." She pointed at a set of windows with their shades drawn. "I've spent months watching those gates—watching that family. There's something wrong with them."

Terror raked through Leslie's insides. She didn't know what to do, and the only person she could think to call was her father. She held up her hands as if calming a skittish horse. "We need to get someone who can help you."

Taylor let out a high-pitched laugh that sounded nothing like the girl she'd once been.

"Help?" Taylor went to the fireplace and lovingly caressed the maze of papers taped to the bricks. "The Devereaux family are the ones who need help. Their history is filled with violence, corruption, and madness." She paced in front of the hearth. "Their name had to be changed from Frellson to Devereaux to cover up their crimes. The Frellsons had a reputation for murder and mayhem from here to the brothels of New Orleans."

She picked up a book from the floor. "Do you remember when I told you about Gerard Frellson? He built what is now known as the Devereaux Plantation. Gerard was the bastard son of a wealthy plantation owner who lived outside of New Orleans. He was also a gambler who hustled travelers on riverboats. He shot a man and married his widow. Then he strangled her and married her daughter. Gage's grandfather, Jacques, was accused of rape. A girl in New Orleans got pregnant by him. He forced her to have an abortion, unheard of at the time, and she died because of it. Her family was paid off when they spoke out. Edward Devereaux had a great-aunt who committed suicide in the plantation home. Another cousin hanged herself. Gage Devereaux had a sister who died under mysterious circumstances in that house."

Leslie hesitated and then moved closer, her curiosity sweeping aside her concern. "Wait, what sister?"

"I found her obituary in the old newspapers. Funny, no one in town ever mentioned her existence." Taylor looked through notes attached to the mantle. "There were duels on the grounds, and several of the losers were buried where they got shot. Some say their ghosts walk around the property at night." She snagged one of the yellow slips of paper and shoved it at Leslie. "The Frellson family was related to Madame Delphine LaLaurie—the woman who tortured slaves in the French Quarter. That is where some speculate the Devereaux curse came from, but they don't know the history of the land their property is built on."

Her unease returning, Leslie pushed the piece of paper back at her. "Curse?" She paused and debated what course of action to take. "Taylor, why don't you come home with me. You might feel better if you get away from this stuff."

Taylor gaped at her with bulging eyes. "I can't leave. Not when I'm so close."

Leslie tried to smooth her matted tresses. "So close to what?"

Taylor recoiled from her touch. "To finding out why he did it. Why Beau did those horrible things to me, Kelly, and Dawn. Don't you want me to expose the truth about the madness in their family? Don't you want to see them stopped?"

Luke's advice about dealing with wild animals came back to her. Leslie hoped it proved to be as effective with humans. "You can't do that." She softened her tone, wanting to come across as non-threatening. "We promised, remember? We agreed we wouldn't speak to the police or go after the Devereaux family. Our revenge ended the night we left Beau at The Abbey."

Taylor tilted her head and backed away. "Did it?"

Leslie almost tripped on a book as she stepped toward Taylor. "What are you saying?"

Taylor remained quiet for a moment and then narrowed her gaze.

Leslie regrouped. Taylor was in no shape to answer a barrage of questions. "Maybe you should consider therapy. I'm sure Mr. Devereaux would pay for it. He wants to make amends for what his son did to us."

"We made a deal with the devil. We should have told the world what Beau did."

"Mr. Devereaux is not the devil. He wanted to get you help before. We all did." Leslie gestured to the papers spread throughout the room. "This will make everyone think you're losing it. If your parents come home and see this, they will want to—"

"They won't see it. I'll have everything put away by then." Taylor snapped up the papers attached to the mantle and hugged them to her chest. "I just needed time to sort it all out, to finish my research before ..." She stared at the blackened grate in the fireplace. "Thank you for bringing my homework. You should go see Derek. Get back with him before it's too late."

Leslie wasn't about to leave her, not in this state. "You know I can't do that."

Taylor wrinkled her brow, intensifying the emptiness in her eyes. "He needs you, and you need him. Tell him the truth. The lies we protect aren't worth the burden of guilt they create."

Leslie didn't know how to deal with Taylor's ramblings, but her friend couldn't be left alone. She had to find some way to help her. "Why don't I hang out with you?" She removed a few papers from the pile in Taylor's arms. "Until your parents come home."

Taylor's lower lip trembled. "It's not safe."

Tingling erupted along the back of Leslie's neck. "Why isn't it safe?"

Taylor snatched the papers out of Leslie's hands. "Go. I'm okay. Promise."

Leslie touched Taylor's cheek. "I have a better idea. Let's get you into a hot bath and find a change of clothes." Relief washed over her when the girl didn't pull away. "When was the last time you ate?"

Taylor took the papers to the coffee table and set them down. "I can't remember."

Leslie forced a weak smile. "Why don't I fix something while you get cleaned up? How does that sound?"

"Okay." Taylor nodded. "I'd like some scrambled eggs." Without looking back, she headed out of the room.

Leslie wanted to make sure Taylor didn't do anything foolish, but she wasn't suicidal. She was too intent on revenge for that. The post-traumatic stress of Beau's rape had shattered her resilience. All of them had taken different measures to deal with life after Beau. She couldn't fault Taylor for searching for a reason why the twisted shit had inflicted such horror.

Leslie spent most nights lying in bed, waiting for Beau's shadow to haunt her. The rest of the time, she blamed herself for Dawn's death. She'd often replay Beau's dangerous behavior leading up to that Halloween night, stumped by why no one believed her warnings. If they had, Dawn would be alive.

With hands on her hips, Leslie considered which mountain to tackle first. Cooking, or cleaning the mess in front of her.

The quacking duck ring from her cell made Leslie jump. She retrieved her phone from her pocket and saw Sara's name on the screen.

"Hey, I'm glad you called," Leslie whispered.

"How's Taylor?" Sara asked, sounding unusually compassionate. "I'm worried about her."

Leslie picked up a book from the floor. "Not well. The entire living room is covered with paper. She has pages of notes, newspaper articles, and books all over the place. She's been studying the Devereaux family and is convinced insanity—or better yet, a curse—is why Beau did what he did."

"Where is Taylor?" Sara sounded frantic.

Leslie rubbed her forehead. She didn't have the stamina to deal with Sara's crap right now. "She's taking a bath. She looks like she's been living in the same clothes for days. Her parents went out of town, and she's been holed up here ever since. I don't think she's eaten much, either."

"What're you gonna do?" Sara demanded. "You can't leave her. She's dangerous to us right now."

There she was. The selfish Sara had returned.

"Would you stop? I'm not leaving her." Leslie paused and thought of her parents, guessing what they would do. "I'll get some food in her first and straighten up. Then I'll talk to her parents when they get home."

"I'll come over and help. We can collect all her research and make sure no one finds it."

Leslie hesitated as she looked around. "Stay away, Sara. I mean it. I'll take care of this. One person is about all Taylor can handle right now."

"I'll have my phone if you need backup. Remember, get rid of the evidence. We can't trust her to do that on her own. She proved that with the video."

Leslie stared at the paper and books strewn across the living room. "What am I supposed to do with all this shit? There's a ton of it."

"Stuff it in a garbage bag and take it with you," Sara snapped. "Don't leave a scrap for that little idiot to do something stupid with."

Sara hung up, and Leslie sighed.

That girl can be a heartless bitch.

Leslie went in search of a garbage bag. She wished she knew how to handle a friend's breakdown, but high school hadn't prepared her for such an event. She knew Gage would pay for her therapy. He wouldn't refuse—he was anxious to make sure no one ever found out about Beau.

But what would happen if Gage stopped taking care of her friends? What would happen then? Leslie hoped that day never came. She didn't have the strength to weather such a storm.

Chapter Eighteen

Moonlight filtered through Leslie's bedroom window as she tossed and turned, agonizing over the information Taylor had collected. She couldn't afford for anyone to discover the meticulous research still locked in her trunk. But, of all Taylor's ramblings, the one thing that stood out was the mention of Gage's sister.

Why has no one ever mentioned her before?

The questions tumbling through her head wouldn't stop. Giving up on sleep, Leslie tossed her covers aside and climbed from her bed.

It's going to be a great Monday. She winced.

Once on the stairs, she noticed the silence in the house. Rarely was she up before her father. He was the early riser—and the one who made the coffee.

Leslie trudged toward the kitchen, frustrated that she would have to wait for her caffeine jolt to percolate. Then something in the living room brought her to a grinding halt.

A shadow moved aimlessly in front of the fireplace, blocking the family pictures cluttering the mantle. Leslie assumed her mother had come downstairs to wander the house, something she usually did when she couldn't sleep. But as Leslie drew closer, the figure swayed and billowed as if caught in a gust of wind, and then colors appeared inside the black mass.

Brunette hair pulled back in a messy bun appeared, and then red sweatpants materialized, accentuating a young woman's body. But it was the white T-shirt with the roaring red St. Benedict High dragon that stunned Leslie. The clothes were the same she'd helped Taylor into earlier.

"Taylor? What are you doing here?"

The ashen color of Taylor's cheeks and deathly pale lips startled Leslie. The girl's dull eyes didn't register a speck of light as she floated across the living room, her bare feet never touching the floor.

A hole opened in Taylor's right temple. Red drops trickled from a pulsing wound. The ribbons slid down her cheek and along the nape of her neck. Crimson streaks mixed in her hair and dripped to her chest until blending with the dragon on her T-shirt.

Leslie became consumed with the color and texture of the falling liquid. "Taylor, what happened? Who did this to you?"

Taylor opened her mouth and her head bent back, widening the gap between her lips. The painful contortion wiped away her recognizable features until all that was left were the raised voices coming from the black hole that had been Taylor. A loud cry spilled from the darkness and wrapped Leslie in an unearthly chill.

She wanted to scream, but then the black mist morphed into a devilish hand with tapering fingers. The thing stretched, coming at her. Leslie remained frozen, unable to break free. The icy hand touched her wrist, and fingers slowly wrapped around her flesh.

"I have something to show you."

Beau Devereaux leaped from the stone steps of The Abbey, his heart pounding, and took off the moment his feet touched the grass. Beau ran as fast as he could from the derelict structure still stinking of smoke. His wrists burned where the zip ties had cut into his flesh, and his head felt cloudy from the drugs Leslie, Taylor, Sara, and Kelly had doped him with.

Ahead, the trees blocked all light from the night sky. He needed to reach the woods and hide. His legs were heavy, but he ran as if heading for the endzone to score a touchdown. It wasn't an ache for victory that spurred him on—it was revenge.

I'll get those four cunts if it's the last thing I do.

Beau was almost to the trees when he glanced over his shoulder at The Abbey. No one waited for him on the steps. Whoever had cut him free from the chair wasn't following.

He sucked in the fresh night air, fighting to clear his head. His thighs burned as he reached the tree line at the edge of the clearing.

Disoriented, Beau attempted to figure out which way led to the parking lot. He could then make his way back to town. Gage would be furious over what the four had done and use every ounce of Devereaux power to destroy them and their families.

A tree branch cut across his cheek, stinging like hell as he stumbled over something on the ground. A log? It was so damn dark that Beau didn't know how he would find his way back.

He stopped and rested his hand on a tree trunk, taking a moment to wipe the sweat out of his eyes. He needed to get it together.

A crunch to his right made him spin around. He wasn't alone.

Beau peered into the blackness. A white-cloaked apparition moved between the low-hanging branches. The last thing he remembered was Leslie taunting him at The Abbey in such a getup.

"I'm gonna kill you, bitch!" He tensed, waiting for any hint of movement.

Her laugh, a high, airy trill, carried on the night wind.

A foul odor like an old coat left in a moldy closet and rolled in dirt wrinkled his nose. Then the low rumble of a deep growl pierced the air.

Beau's heartbeat quickened, and a bitter taste rose in his mouth. He scoured the woods for any sign of the creature that made the unholy sound. The dogs inside The Abbey had terrified Beau. Had they followed him? He crept forward, hopefully heading toward the river. He would be safe if he could find the shoreline.

Beau clung to the cover of the trees, his eyes darting back and forth, searching for whatever was stalking him.

Another glimpse of white dashing from one tree to the next jarred him. Beau broke into a run.

This isn't funny anymore.

He barreled through the brush, smashing dried leaves and twigs. The noise would let the dogs know his whereabouts, but what choice did he have?

A howl erupted close by.

Beau ran faster, no longer caring about the loud crashing sounds as he charged through the brush. Terror tightened around his chest. It got harder to breathe, and panic turned his thoughts of revenge to those of survival.

The thrashing behind him grew louder. This wasn't an act of vengeance meant to terrorize him. Someone wanted him dead.

Beau saw the faces of those he'd had fun with, but one stood out from the blur of others. The girl who'd gotten away. Leslie.

A wet trickle ran down Beau's cheek. In a ray of dim starlight, peeking through the trees, he caught a swath of red on his fingertips. Blood. Then cuts along his arms and hands appeared. Dodging trees, he forgot his wounds and concentrated on staying ahead of his pursuer.

There was another howl, and then something broke through the trees next to him. It wasn't the figure in white. This creature ran on all fours, and the pungent stink of its matted brown coat surrounded Beau.

When the dogs appear, death is near.

Beau darted to the left, hoping to lose the beast. The air cleared of the revolting smell, and then something else hit him—water.

The river. He was almost there. The realization gave him renewed energy. Beau pumped his weary arms and legs harder. The thicket of trees thinned, and the night sky glistened on the water's surface.

The ground dipped when he hit the embankment, but Beau couldn't slow his momentum. He lost his footing and tripped over a dense bush of white camellias. When he emerged on the other side, he tumbled onto sand.

When he landed face down next to the Bogue Falaya River, he relaxed. Then a chill ran up his spine.

Panting and putrid warm air filled his ears. A prickly sensation raised the hair on the back of his neck.

Beau slowly turned over. His eyes widened when he spotted three large dogs standing over him. Bared white fangs gave away their deadly intent. The beasts remained still, as if waiting for something to make the first move. Their massive, drooling muzzles hovered inches from his face and left him paralyzed with fear.

Something behind the dogs caught his eye. A figure, the face undetectable behind a dark hooded cloak, stood watching.

"Help me," he stammered.

The specter raised a milky hand. The sound of snapping fingers bounced off the water and Beau shuddered, knowing what would happen next.

He didn't see the dogs attack. All he registered was a haze of black and brown fur, the atrocious smell, and then the pain.

The animals gave no warning before they sank their teeth into him. The orchestra of flesh tearing and his high-pitched screams proved this was no nightmare. This was his end.

The metallic taste came after one of the deadly hounds went for his throat. Beau couldn't scream anymore, no matter how hard he tried. The warmth of his blood spilling out on his chest comforted him. At least he wasn't cold anymore.

By the time the dogs tore open his abdomen and removed his bowels, the pain had turned into one giant wave of unrelenting agony.

Black spots crowded his vision as the figure moved closer.

Leslie?

He raised his hand to her, no longer caring about the dogs lapping at the blood pooling on the sand around him.

You were the one I always wanted.

Beau's head lolled back as he took a last look at the stars above. Then his hand fell into the waters of his river, the edges of the shoreline now a dreadful shade of crimson.

Chapter Nineteen

Leslie bolted upright, gasping for air, and clutching her covers. Sweat trickled down her temples, and then she saw the rays of morning light streaming through her bedroom window.

A dream. It was a dream.

She took a steadying breath, grateful to be awake.

Leslie remembered Taylor and how she'd moved through her home as if she were a ghost. And then there was Beau's horrific end. She could still hear his screams.

The nightmare quickly faded when the uproar of voices filtered through her bedroom door.

Frightened, Leslie jumped up and grabbed her robe. No one had shouted in her home since the death of her sister. She hurried toward the stairs, tying her robe as she went. Rounding the bottom of the steps, Leslie turned to the family room, unsure of what she would find.

Sheriff Davis and a deputy stood talking to her parents. The warmth drained from her cheeks.

"Leslie?" Shelley walked toward her, fully dressed.

It had been months since she'd seen her mother wearing anything other than a robe. The shock added to her burgeoning alarm. "Mom, what's going on?"

Shelley's brows drew together. "Sheriff Davis needs to ask you a few questions."

Leslie swallowed hard. Her first thought was Beau. They had found something at The Abbey—something that led them back to her. She glanced at the hearth, seeing her favorite picture with Dawn on a fishing trip. She'd survived losing her other half, and nothing these two men did or said would ever be as devastating.

Kent held his Stetson. "Leslie, I need your help."

Leslie planted her feet in front of him and waited for her world to crumble.

"Where were you Saturday night?" Kent shot a glance at her father.

"I was at Taylor's house. Taylor Haskins. Why?"

The sheriff nodded. "Her parents said you found her in a rather bad way and stayed with her until they returned from their trip."

Leslie's insides turned to mush. "This is about Taylor?"

John Moore put a gentle arm around her shoulders. "Leelee, Sheriff Davis needs to know more about what state of mind Taylor was in. Her parents said when they went to check on her Sunday morning, she wasn't in her room."

Shit! The little idiot was doing what she, Sara, and Kelly had feared—drawing unwanted attention. "Did she run away? She never said anything to me about leaving."

The adults gave each other apprehensive glances.

Her stomach dropped. This was about more than Taylor flying the coop. "What is it?" Leslie turned to her father. "What's wrong?"

John guided her to the sofa to sit down. "Leelee, something has happened." He took her hand. "Taylor was found at the river yesterday. Her Jeep was in the parking lot." He lowered his gaze. "She's dead."

"What?" Leslie whispered, feeling like someone had punched her in the gut. "That can't be." She blinked back tears.

Since first noticing Taylor's bizarre behavior, Leslie had imagined several outcomes for the traumatized girl, but this hadn't been one of them. Then her hideous dream repeated in her head, and suddenly Taylor's death didn't seem so farfetched. Sorrow enveloped her, but she pushed it away. She wasn't about to lose it in front of the officers.

She wrapped her arms around herself and squeezed, fighting to hold in her emotions as she spoke. "What happened?"

Sheriff Davis appraised her reaction. "It appears she took her own life."

Leslie's façade cracked. Air—she suddenly couldn't get enough of it. The room shrank as darkness blotted out the walls and furniture.

"Honey, calm down." Her mother cradled Leslie's face. "Breathe deep, slow breaths."

Shelley, talking her through each gasp, helped, but in her mind, all Leslie could see was Taylor's hollow cheeks and frightened eyes.

Soon, the room returned, and Taylor's image faded. "When I left, she was in bed," Leslie said between raspy breaths. "I checked on her right before her parents got there. After I spoke to them, I came home."

"When was that?" Sheriff Davis had his phone in his hand.

"Ten, ten-thirty." She wiped her eyes, annoyed with her tears.

"You're sure she was actually in the bed?" Kent leaned closer. "She could have fooled you."

The comment irked the crap out of Leslie. She knew the difference between a bunch of pillows versus a person under the bed covers. She'd lived with Dawn's sneaking around for far too long. "Yeah, I'm sure."

He typed something into his phone. "Taylor's parents said when you stopped by, she wasn't doing well. Can you tell me about that?"

Leslie laced her fingers together, carefully weighing her words. "Taylor had been out of school with the flu. She asked me to drop off her assignments."

Kent never looked up from his phone. "What did you find at her house?"

"She was a mess. She looked like she hadn't had a shower or eaten for days. She was nervous and talking loudly. I could hardly get her to sit still."

Her father's lips were set in a firm line. "What was she nervous about? Did she give you a reason?"

Leslie hesitated, searching for a lie to appease the adults. She found it amusing how easy it was for her now. Dawn had been the twin who hid everything from their parents—the daughter who broke the rules. When had she turned into her sister?

"School," she said in a restrained voice. "She'd been having problems in a few of her classes. There was a guy she liked who hurt her, ignored her. She also felt guilty about Dawn. She always said she should've done more to save her."

"Oh, God." Her mother put her hand to her mouth and closed her eyes.

John Moore hugged his wife. The gesture took Leslie back to those horrible hours in the hospital when Derek had held her and never let go.

Derek. She wished he were there. He'd kept her focused and given her strength. She missed him more than ever.

"*The lies we protect aren't worth the burden of guilt they create.*"

Taylor's words returned, and then she pictured the blood from her dream and the ugly wound on the side of Taylor's head as she floated above the living room floor.

Leslie shuddered and then asked, "How did she die?"

Sheriff Davis put his phone in his pocket. "Gunshot to the head."

A thick blanket of denial settled over Leslie, insulating her from the blow of the sheriff's words. "No, that can't be. Taylor would never have killed herself. That's not her. She wasn't suicidal. She even admitted—"

"The evidence says otherwise. She used the .357 her father purchased back in December. Mark Haskins bought it because Taylor kept saying someone was following her. After everything that's happened lately, he wanted protection for his family."

"Someone was following her?" Shelley put a protective arm around Leslie. "Could it be the same person who hurt Dawn?"

Images of Taylor's erratic behavior, paranoia, and resolve that someone had been following her, sent a prickling unease over Leslie's arms. She remembered the feeling of being watched when she went to Taylor's.

Kent raised his hands to Shelley. "We've been combing St. Benedict for new faces, strangers, any reports of people passing through. We're keeping a sharp eye out, don't you worry."

Leslie's eyes widened. "Someone did this to her. Can't you see that? You have to find her killer."

Kent Davis widened his stance, exuding authority. "For now, we're working the case as a suicide, even though Taylor didn't leave a note. But I assure you I'll investigate all possibilities, Leslie. I promise. We'll find the truth."

After Kent thanked them for their time, her father showed the sheriff and his deputy to the front door.

Shelley gave her a half-hearted embrace. "Stay home from school today. I'm sure it will be traumatic enough when the school is informed of Taylor's death."

There was too much at stake to stay home and hide. She wiggled out of her mother's arms. "I want to go to school."

Shelley's stern frown highlighted the lines between her brows as she brushed a wisp of hair from Leslie's eyes. "Are you sure?"

Leslie instinctively shied away. Her mother wasn't tender, not with her. Theirs had been a relationship steeped in friction. "I'm sure."

John returned to the room, his head bowed.

Shelley motioned to Leslie. "She wants to go to school. That's a bad idea. Tell her, John."

Her father, the paragon of reason in a house filled with temperamental women, straightened his stooped shoulders. "If she wants to go, let her."

Shelley's face flushed. "After everything she's been through? Do you know what the stress of that could do to her? The godawful memories it could rekindle?"

"For you, or for her?" John exhaled in frustration. "Your daughter's living her life, Shell. We're all trying our best to live day by day." He paused, his face a network of deep lines. "We can only get through this together, and for so long, you haven't been here. You need to be part of this family again."

"Enough!" Leslie shouted. "We're not a family anymore. We stopped being one the moment Dawn died."

Shelley clasped her hand over her mouth, the color draining from her face.

John stepped closer. "Leelee, you don't mean that."

The fire inside Leslie charged to the surface. "What kind of family stands by and does nothing after what happened. Aren't you angry? Don't you want revenge?"

John lowered his glasses and pinched the bridge of his nose. "I believe the police will find the killer, and we will have our day in court. Justice will prevail."

Leslie's scornful laugh carried across the room. "Revenge is sweeter than justice can ever be."

John grabbed her shoulders, his fingers digging into her flesh. "You don't think I want that? To tear apart whoever killed my daughter?" He let her go. "But I also believe in the law, as do you."

Leslie crossed her arms. "I'm not so sure I believe in anything anymore. That same law you admire has let rapists and murderers out onto the streets without a second thought about the victims and their families. That's not law. It's politics, and I want nothing to do with it. Playing by the rules gets you nowhere."

Shelley stifled a sob. "Where is this coming from? This isn't my daughter."

"It's all right, Shell." John went to his wife's side. "Leelee isn't thinking clearly. She's upset about her friend. That's all."

Leslie marched to the base of the stairs and then faced her parents, no longer afraid to speak her mind. "Oh, I'm thinking clearly. For the first time in my life, I see how things really are. How the world works and people who follow the rules only get screwed. That's why I don't want to be a lawyer anymore. And don't ask me what I'll do instead or how I'll make my way. I haven't figured that out yet. You just need to understand, I don't have the same goals as before. I've changed."

John stormed toward her. "When did you decide this? Why didn't you come to me?"

Leslie planted her hands on her hips. "When was I supposed to do that? When you were at the office or hiding away here?"

"How could you?" The obstinate Shelley Moore revived. "Do you want to destroy your future? You never stop to consider the ramifications of what you do."

Her mother's words deepened Leslie's wounds. Her courage disintegrated, and sharing her plans with her parents became too painful. Instead of standing up to Shelley, Leslie ran up the stairs.

She'd once heard a cop on TV say, "*The ultimate price of revenge is regret.*" The line had stuck with her, but its true meaning hadn't clicked before now.

Leslie slapped away a tear as she stomped into her bedroom. Her hate had driven her to take part in Beau's death, but remorse had ignited a bonfire in Leslie's gut. It burned day and night. Now she was sure it would explode since Taylor had shown her how Beau died.

One day she'd confess her sins, but not for many years, and by then, the Devereaux family would hopefully be long gone. Only whispers about the deaths along the banks of the river would remain.

Chapter Twenty

Leslie sat in her car, staring at the gloomy clouds over St. Benedict High. They mirrored her dismal mood. The incident with her parents would make her home life intolerable, but Leslie vowed never to take back anything she'd said to them. Her fingers tingled, and she loosened her grip on the steering wheel. She needed to get it together. Otherwise, she'd turn into a zombie like her mother.

Leslie shut off the engine and took a moment before heading to class. She thought of calling Derek—if only to tell him of Taylor's death. The news would be as jarring to him as it had been to her.

A knock on the window made her flinch. Kelly and Sara stood next to her car with worried scowls.

When Leslie got out, a brisk breeze hit her. She'd left the house without a jacket. How had she not felt the cold after living in an icy hell for months?

"Did you hear about Taylor?" Sara asked as she stroked the collar of her black faux fur coat.

It would seem CNN had nothing on the St. Benedict rumor mill. "Sheriff Davis was at my house this morning, questioning me."

"You? Why you?" Kelly bit her lower lip. "Did he ask about Beau?"

Sara elbowed her. "Would you shut the hell up?"

Thankfully, Sara blocked the wind. Leslie reached into the car for her book bag, hoping to find a sweater.

"She was with Taylor last night," Sara said, eyeing Leslie. "I called after she'd dropped off her homework. Apparently, Taylor lost it."

Kelly frowned. "Lost it? I don't understand."

Leslie lugged her bag out onto the blacktop and knelt to rummage through it. "She was erratic and had papers plastered all over the living room. She kept going on about the Devereaux family and some curse."

"What about all her research?" Sara's voice crept higher. "What did you do with it?"

Her preoccupation with the papers bugged the shit out of Leslie. She pointed at her trunk. "It's in there."

Kelly chewed on her fingernail and then lowered her hand. "This is going to come back on us. I know it. Everyone is saying Taylor shot herself."

Leslie found a sweater in the bottom of her bag and struggled to remove it from under everything else. "No, she didn't. That's not Taylor." She glanced up at Sara. "You knew her. Did she ever seem suicidal?"

"She was a little nuts," Sara said. "She never confided in anyone. She hung out with us, but I never talked much to her. Did you?"

Leslie yanked out a red sweater. "Yes. After Beau did what he did to her, we talked. She told me what happened. Maybe I should have listened more."

Kelly touched her arm. "Even if we all did, I doubt it would've stopped her from ..."

Leslie lowered her gaze, guilt eating her alive. "The sheriff said there was no note. People who commit suicide leave a note."

Sara winced. "Well, not everyone. Lots of people kill themselves, and the police never figure out why."

"You know damn well that wasn't her," Leslie snapped.

"Whoa." Kelly gasped. "Wait a minute. Are you saying someone killed her?"

Leslie shrugged on her sweater. "Did either of you know Gage Devereaux had a sister?"

Sara's eyebrows squished together. "What does that have to do with anything?"

"Taylor showed me an article about the little girl who died when Gage was six. Don't you think it's weird no one in this town ever mentions her?"

"They never mentioned her to us, but we're not from here." Kelly motioned to Sara. "Maybe outsiders don't get included in stuff like that."

Leslie hugged the sweater closer. "My father grew up with Gage, and I was never told about her. I want to know why she's been such a secret."

Sara grimaced and then blew out a long breath. "Do you think Taylor was murdered because of what she dug up on the Devereaux family?"

The idea sounded preposterous, but Leslie would believe that before she could fathom Taylor putting a gun to her head.

Kelly's eyes widened. "Or she talked about what Beau did, and Mr. Devereaux found out. What if he thinks none of us can keep our mouths shut? We could be next." She pointed at Leslie. "You promised he would take care of us."

Leslie let out a disgusted sigh as she picked up her book bag. "He *is* taking care of us. Gage Devereaux doesn't want to hurt us, he wants to help us."

"How do you know what that man wants?" Sara challenged. "My dad says he has mob connections fundin' his national campaign. He could have offed Taylor because she ran her mouth. We all know what Beau was like. Who's to say his old man ain't the same?"

"We're all gonna die." Kelly slapped her hand over her mouth.

"Stop it, both of you." Leslie slung the book bag over her shoulder. "First off, the whole town knows about Gage's underworld connections, and no one else has ever died when they spoke out against him or spread rumors about his family. Why would he start now?"

"Because he's about to launch a big national campaign for the brewery." Kelly sounded almost frantic. "The last thing Mr. Devereaux needs is four girls talking to the press about his sadistic son."

Leslie's certainty about Gage Devereaux wavered. She knew protecting his family name meant everything to him and that was why he'd struck a deal with her. But as she weighed the possibilities, Leslie began to question if Gage Devereaux would stick to his end of the bargain.

Maybe he is just like Beau.

After a brief, tense silence, Kelly asked, "Should we go to the police?"

"Are you for real?" Sara spun around, checking the quad behind them. She turned back to Kelly, lowering her voice. "We can't chance anyone findin' out about that night. Then we'd be accused of killin' that piece of shit. No, we keep our mouths shut and lay low. Let's see if the sheriff digs up anything."

Kelly put her hands on her hips, not seeming happy with the suggestion. "You want us to wait around until we're picked off like Taylor?"

Their petty bickering ignited Leslie's fury. "For goodness' sake, pipe down. We're not going to get *picked off.* I know Gage Devereaux. He has no interest in harming us."

The first warning bell screeched across the quad. Students sitting on benches and huddled in small groups on the grass gathered up book bags and headed for the main doors.

"I wish I had your faith, but I don't trust anyone." Sara's platinum blonde mane whipped in the breeze as she eyed the students. "Taylor's suicide is gonna make it a lot harder to fly under the radar. Everybody will be watchin' us, thinkin' we're next. We'll probably have teachers and counselors up our asses for weeks."

Leslie glowered at Sara. "Taylor didn't kill herself."

"Whether she did or didn't won't matter." Kelly moved away from the car. "We were her only friends, and until we're no longer living in a fishbowl, we can't be stupid."

Leslie fell in step behind them as they strolled across the blacktop to the sidewalk. Stares and whispers rose around them. Leslie longed for the day when she could walk into a room and be like any other student. She thought of Dawn and how much she would have loved the attention. A crippling pang stung her chest—the wrong Moore girl had survived.

Before she climbed the steps, Leslie scanned the parking lot. There was no sign of Derek's blue pickup truck. He'd either caught another ride or decided to stay away.

The thought of not having him in her life saddened her. It seemed their destiny was the same as the star-crossed lovers she'd studied in English lit, doomed because of the intolerable burden of tragedy.

CHAPTER TWENTY-ONE

Fatigue wracked Leslie's body. Her bones ached, and her head pounded after the emotionally arduous day. She yearned to go home and crawl back in bed, but having another confrontation with her parents was the last thing she needed. Instead, she turned her car into the parking lot of The Bogue Falaya Café.

Students sat in booths by the windows, chatting. She envied them. Between the mass assembly to discuss the pain of suicide and the constant questions about her dead friend, Leslie's tolerance for people had hit a new low.

She knew that many of those who had stared and whispered as she passed by in the halls of St. Benedict High were there. She was about to leave when Sara's black truck pulled in close to her driver's side door.

Kelly hung out the window and waved as Sara laughed behind the wheel. Their chipper attitude shocked Leslie.

Taylor is dead, and these two idiots look like they're ready to celebrate.

"I wasn't sure if you'd come," Kelly shouted.

Leslie opened her door. "We have to talk." Glancing around, she was skeptical of how much privacy they would have to discuss Taylor. She dug through her book bag, hunting for her wallet, when a nagging sensation gripped her.

"*Were you followed?*" Taylor's words echoed through her head. Had she known something?

"Hey!" Kelly got out of the truck. "Ready to eat?"

Leslie clasped her wallet, her hands shaking. "I thought we came here to talk."

"And to eat." Sara sauntered toward Leslie, her black outfit matching the blacktop. "I skipped lunch. Who can eat that crap in the school cafeteria?"

Kelly grinned. "I love their food. I can't get enough of it."

Sara hooked Kelly's arm. "You scarf that cafeteria garbage but can't stomach pizza at The Bogue. What's wrong with you?"

The two girls walked ahead. When they stepped inside the restaurant door, Leslie held her breath. Fortunately, heads didn't turn in their direction. No one seemed interested.

Kelly led the way down the narrow aisle, waving at a few people she knew. She selected an empty orange booth in the back of the dining area and sighed as she eased onto the bench. "It's not the same without Taylor."

Leslie sat across from her, sensing the change in the air. "Yeah. It doesn't feel right."

Sara eased in next to Kelly. "Taylor was messed up. And her fascination with the Devereaux family history? You can't tell me you weren't sick of that shit."

Kelly sniffled, holding back tears. "How can you say such things? It's cruel."

Sara glared at her. "It's the truth. Jeez, pull it together."

After Sara rolled her eyes at Kelly's outburst, she eagerly scanned the crowd. Suspicions about her loyalty hounded Leslie. Sara was a hothead and unpredictable. If she decided to turn on them, Leslie would have no means of stopping her.

Leslie patted the table, getting Sara's attention. "What are you looking for?"

"Who," Sara corrected with a smirk. "Who do you think?"

Leslie's cheeks burned. Luke wasn't the reason they had come to the diner—Taylor was.

"Oh, there he is." Sara sounded way too exuberant.

With a dab of flour streaked across his brow, Luke stepped from behind the counter, carrying a large pie on a flat metal pan. A white T-shirt clung to his broad chest, and faded jeans showed off long, athletic legs.

Luke spotted Leslie after he set down the pizza and then accidentally smeared flour along his jaw. His smile was slow but magical. The way he didn't seem to care what others thought of him added to his charm.

"Mmm." Sara made a lustful groan. "Damn, that man's got it."

"For God's sake, Sara, how can you act like that when our friend is dead?" Leslie chided. "We're here to talk about Taylor, not for you to drool over Luke."

When Leslie glanced up the aisle again, an unexpected customer moved from behind Luke. Derek. Her heart plummeted.

Shorter and less muscular, Derek looked like Robin standing behind Batman. He also lacked Luke's upbeat attitude.

He settled next to the counter, and his gaze connected with hers. Derek didn't make a move to approach their booth. He'd drawn a line in the sand and dared her to be the first to cross it.

An uncomfortable knot formed in her stomach. Should she stay in the booth and deepen the divide between them?

You can't let this go on.

"I'll be back." She scooted to the edge of the bench.

Sara grabbed Leslie's arm. "Do you want to end up like Taylor?"

Her question sent a tremor through Leslie. "What makes you think that'll happen?"

Sara's grip tightened on Leslie's arm. "What if someone is watchin' us? Watchin' you? You could risk our lives if you take him back."

Kelly gazed at a few tables close to their booth. Several diners had turned to take in the disagreement. "Stop it," she said in a hushed tone. "People are starting to stare. She's only going to speak to him."

Sara released her grip. "I'm just remindin' her what's at stake."

Leslie nursed her sore arm and stormed away, cursing. Sara appeared to be getting paranoid, and she didn't like the change in her.

She took the last few steps toward the counter and eased alongside Derek, focusing on the task at hand. "We need to talk," she said softly to avoid being overheard.

He scowled. "You made it pretty clear you wanted me to stay away from you."

She rested her elbow on the counter. "I'm sorry for how I acted. I was confused and angry about Dawn, and it was wrong to say what I did. I never meant to—"

"Break my heart?" His huffy voice teemed with sarcasm. "Well, you did. You dumped me for your new friends and haven't acknowledged me for weeks. So why are you here? To make yourself feel better about hooking up with Pizza Boy?" He turned away.

She edged closer, wanting him to look at her. "Luke is a friend, nothing more. And I didn't break up with you because I wanted to spend more time with friends. There's so much more going on than you can understand."

"Oh, I understand, Leslie. You made everything perfectly clear that day at your house."

"Hey, Derek," Luke said, approaching them at the counter. "Your order is ready."

Derek nodded, avoiding her. "Make it to go."

Luke hesitated as his attention darted between Derek and Leslie. "For two?"

"Just one." Derek took out his wallet. "I've got to get back to work."

His iciness rattled Leslie.

Luke took in their interaction with interest, then patted the countertop. "Okay, be right back."

Derek grabbed a napkin from a dispenser and wiped his hands. It meant he was nervous. His palms always got sweaty when he was nervous. "I heard about Taylor. I'm sorry. I know how troubled she was, but I never imagined she'd kill herself."

"She didn't kill herself." Bitterness seeped into Leslie's voice. "She was on edge, but she wasn't suicidal."

Derek faced her, and his scowl softened. "They found her shot, and the gun was there. How can you believe she didn't kill herself?"

Leslie gazed into his wonderful eyes, itching to tell him everything about all the players in the game of lies she'd become entangled in. But she remained silent, reminding herself he'd be safer that way.

Leslie choked back emotion. "She didn't leave a note."

"That doesn't mean anything," he argued. "We all saw how she dressed and acted. Taylor was disturbed. Everyone at school knew it."

His indifference added to her sorrow. "Well, you didn't know her."

Luke returned from the kitchen with a white pizza box. "Here you go. Sausage, jalapeños, and mushrooms."

Leslie lowered her head and hid a smile as she left Derek at the counter. A splinter of hope penetrated her broken heart. He had not given up on her completely—he'd ordered her favorite pizza. It was the first ray of sunshine in her dark day.

"Wow, that looked intense." Kelly inspected her with a concerned frown. "Are you okay?"

"I'm fine." Leslie slipped back into the booth, keeping her stoic mask in place.

"What did you say to him?" Sara questioned.

"We talked about Taylor." Leslie shifted in her seat. "I wanted to make sure he knew."

Sara's expression darkened. "That's it?"

Kelly elbowed Sara. "You sure you want to call it quits with Derek? I thought you two had plans for the future."

"Plans change." Leslie streaked the condensation on the side of her water glass. "People change."

Sara folded her arms and reclined against the bench. "Bullshit. You're still crazy about him, but you need to be careful. We have to be on our guard, especially after the stunt Taylor pulled."

Luke strutted toward their table, his gaze settling on Leslie. "I heard about Taylor. You guys okay?"

Sara leaned in, showing off her substantial cleavage. "It's so horrible. But she had issues."

Kelly's mouth dropped open, as did Leslie's.

"Taylor's *issues* were no different than ours." Leslie tempered her irritated voice.

Luke raised his eyebrows and removed a pad from his white apron pocket. "Well, I'm sorry to hear about her death. She seemed—"

Flashing lights at the windows made Luke pause.

Two patrol cars parked by the side entrance, almost blocking the doors. The dining area stilled as patrons peered outside.

Leslie's hands shook as she pictured an officer cuffing her and taking her to jail. Sheriff Davis must have discovered something that connected her to Beau's death.

Luke returned his pad to his apron pocket. "I'll be back in a minute to take your order."

He went to the side entrance as two deputies pushed open the door.

Once inside, they squared their shoulders and tugged at their gun belts.

Sweat beaded Leslie's upper lip as the men in dark blue uniforms spoke with Luke. She rose from her bench, straining to get a better look.

Luke smiled and gestured into the dining room, appearing as if he were offering them a table.

Then the two officers closed in, obstructing most of Leslie's view.

Oh shit.

One of the officers spoke softly, and Luke's smile faded.

A hush rolled through the restaurant. Diners ignored their food, craning to get a better view of the encounter. Cooks came out of the kitchen, wiping their flour-dusted hands, appearing eager to discover the reason for the sudden quiet. Even the jukebox stilled—its last song played out.

Luke gave the officers a brief but nervous nod and turned to the counter. He removed his white apron and then said something to one of the cooks. The heavyset man took a few apprehensive steps forward, but Luke held up his hand, stopping him.

To Leslie's astonishment, Luke calmly walked out of the restaurant escorted by the deputies. She, and the rest of the customers, gravitated toward the windows. Leslie pressed against the glass, studying the patrol cars.

The officers stopped at the first car and put Luke in the back seat.

Leslie wanted to rush outside and remind them of his rights—as her father had taught her—but thought better of it.

Leslie watched as the flashing red and blue lights danced across the restaurant walls. She got a quick glimpse of Luke in the departing patrol car, his head bowed.

"What the fuck?" Sara said a little too loud.

Several other diners gave her disparaging glares.

"Why are they arresting Luke?" Kelly spun around in her seat. "He hasn't done anything."

Leslie rushed to collect her wallet. "They didn't arrest him, but they obviously want him for something." She climbed out of the booth.

Sara stood, frowning. "What could they want him for?"

Leslie pulled her keys from her sweater pocket. "I don't know, but I'm going to help him."

"How?" Kelly followed them out of the booth. "Because it sure looked like he got arrested to me."

Leslie stopped and faced her. "When they arrest you, they cuff you. Luckily, he didn't resist." She turned away. "I have to go."

Sara yanked her arm. "Go? You can't. We've gotta stick together."

"I have to talk to my dad," she said, shaking off her grip. "Luke's gonna need a good attorney."

CHAPTER TWENTY-TWO

Gage slammed his gearshift into park as soon as he arrived at the St. Benedict Sheriff's Department in a converted brick warehouse. He got out and stared at the arched stone portico over the entrance that read *The Edward Devereaux Building*. He'd just refurbished the place with bulletproof windows, and this was how they repaid him? With his keys digging into his closed fist, Gage marched up the red brick walkway, ready for battle. "These assholes better remember how much they owe me."

Gage entered the building wanting to bash heads together. Kent Davis had given Luke his phone number, creating a whole new set of problems. He didn't need disparaging stories about his mistake with Luke's mother jeopardizing his business.

He arrived at the enclosed reception desk, fuming. He should have forced the boy to leave town as soon as he knew who he was, but like most situations in his life, Gage hoped to come to an amicable financial agreement to make his problem go away.

"How can I help you, Mr. Devereaux?" The woman behind the front desk asked, a silver shield on her dark blue uniform glistening in the fluorescent light.

"Amy, I'm here to see Luke Cross."

She quickly tapped a button on the side of her desk. A buzzer sounded, and a glass door to the right popped open.

"Through there, Mr. Devereaux." She pointed at the door. "I'll let Sheriff Davis know you're here."

"Thank you." Gage reminded himself to be cordial, just like his father had pounded into him. "How's your mom?"

"She's good." Amy seemed to relax a little. "Enjoying retirement from the brewery."

He didn't bother coming up with any more small talk. Gage could barely remember who her mother was, but he owed Amy the courtesy—she'd let Beau off for speeding on several occasions.

He headed down a hall lined with oak doors to the interrogation area. Gage had personally overseen the refurbishment of the building. It had been right around the time Beau started getting into trouble, and he'd wanted to ensure he was familiar with the place in case his son ever ended up in jail.

He went to the last door off the hall and nodded to the lanky officer stationed outside. "Is Kent in there, Owen?"

Owen bobbed his head. "Ah, yes, Mr. Devereaux. He's with Mr. Cross and Mr. Moore."

Gage stopped suddenly. "John Moore?"

Owen met Gage's blistering stare. "Yes, sir. He arrived soon after Mr. Cross was brought in for questioning."

Gage hid his displeasure behind a well-practiced smile. "Thank you, Owen."

Without asking permission, he stepped past the officer and reached for the door handle—time to find out how far this crap had spread.

The room was windowless, with white-painted cinderblock walls, and reeked of day-old coffee and recirculated stale air. In the center was a rectangular wood table marred with dents and scratches. When he found Luke hunched over with red stains on his white T-shirt and flour dust in his hair, everything changed. Gage no longer saw a stranger he wanted to run out of town, but someone he felt compelled to help.

He'd fought for years to keep Beau out of any situation resembling this. He shut the door, determined to intercede.

"Gage." John Moore stepped forward. "Luke said he asked to call you. I'm glad, but confused."

Kent Davis waited behind John, his grim frown, wide stance, and folded arms adding to the grave atmosphere. "Thank you for coming."

Gage ignored the sheriff and turned to the young man.

Luke raised his head. He didn't smile, didn't react, and his empty gaze added to his miserable expression.

Gage scrutinized Kent's authoritative pose. "Why is he here?"

John faced the sheriff. "Well, Kent? This is your circus."

Gage was glad John had said what he was thinking.

Kent relaxed his arms and stepped forward. "I brought him in for questioning about Taylor Haskins and to get a voluntary DNA sample."

Gage approached the table. "I was told it was suicide. Why bring Luke in?"

"It wasn't a suicide, but made to look like one," John said, and motioned to Kent. "He showed me the coroner's report. There was no gunshot residue on her hands. She didn't fire the gun that killed her."

"There was a skull fracture at the back of the head." Kent cast one of those patronizing stares Gage hated. "Whoever killed her knocked her out first."

Fuck. This was all he needed—another murder in St. Benedict.

Gage looked at Kent while pointing at Luke. "And you think he did it?"

"No." John sat on the corner of the table. "But since Luke is new in town, he wanted to question him."

"Then you showed up," Kent added with a touch of sarcasm. "Why did he call you? What's your connection to him?"

Gage shifted his attention to Luke, debating a course of action. The truth would start a shitstorm, but if he spun it a different way, it would also allow him to keep Luke under a watchful eye. He didn't trust him—Gage didn't trust anyone—but having the boy under his thumb was a better way to control him.

Gage went to Luke's side and placed a hand on his shoulder. "I met Luke's mother, Pamela Cross, when I was in school in Boston." Gage glanced at John. "You remember how much I fought with my father about Carol. I was going to marry her, but he wouldn't allow it. He sent me away to college to separate us. In my freshman year, I met Luke's mother."

John moved forward and cleared his throat. "Gage, as your attorney, I must advise you to carefully consider what you say in front of witnesses."

Gage ran a hand across his mouth, attempting to hide a grin. "I'm well aware. Thank you, John."

Kent twisted his lips. "Are you saying what I think you're saying?"

Gage admired Luke's strong good looks and thick head of hair. It was just like his. "He's my son."

"Whoa." John's eyes bulged behind his glasses. "Hold on, Gage. You don't know for sure he's your son."

"I know." Gage adjusted the sleeve on his jacket. "Luke's Mustang was mine. When Luke's mother said she was pregnant, I didn't believe her. But, to cover my ass, my father said to pay her off. So, I had to give her my car and told her to get an abortion. I thought that was the end of it. Then I saw Luke's car—my car." He stepped toward Kent. "The day you told me about him, mentioned his last name and where he was from, I suspected who he was. I didn't know he was mine until we met."

Kent went to Luke's side. "Is that why you came to St. Benedict? Because you knew Gage Devereaux was your father?"

Luke folded his hands on the table, his face a blank canvas. "My mother told me about him in a letter. She said their affair was brief, but I was the result."

Gage bristled at the use of the word *affair*.

"When I left college, I wanted to find my father, so I took the car my mother left me and came here."

"I'll vouch for him, Kent." Gage stood to the right of Luke's chair. "How are you connecting him to Taylor?"

Kent stroked his chin, studying Luke.

"You already know he has an alibi, Kent," John added. "He was working late at The Bogue and left the restaurant after one in the morning. You can check the security footage to verify."

Gage was pleased John had taken over Luke's counsel. He didn't understand how he'd gotten there ahead of him, but was relieved he had.

Kent looked at Gage. "According to the coroner, the Haskins girl died between midnight and one in the morning. So, as long as his story checks out, it would seem your boy is in the clear. For now."

"You could have figured that out without hauling him in." Gage scowled. "You just wanted to question him about why he's in St. Benedict."

"I'm doing what you hired me to do. He's free to go." Kent pointed at Luke and left the room.

Gage considered his next move. He'd claimed the young man in front of his attorney and the sheriff. He would have to act quickly to keep the situation from blowing up in his face.

John moved closer, with his hands in his pockets. "Was that wise?"

Gage peered over his shoulder at Luke. He was still plagued with concerns about trusting the boy, but what choice did he have? No one with Devereaux blood would serve time in jail on his watch. "He's mine, John. But a DNA test should appease your concerns. It won't take Kent long to get the results."

"Are you going to claim he's yours legally?" John lowered his head. "You do understand what's at stake if you do?"

All Gage could think about was he would have an heir. His family name and legacy would live on. He would've preferred a legitimate son, but the situation would resolve once Elizabeth got pregnant. "Of course, I understand."

John leaned in and whispered, "But you don't know anything about him."

"I'm not a raving psycho." Luke raised his eyes to Gage. "Or a rapist."

Gage's heartbeat quickened. Did he know about Beau?

"I'm sure you're not," John said to him. "But to be a son of Gage Devereaux, there's a lot you'll need to learn."

Beads of sweat dotted Luke's upper lip. "All I've ever wanted was a family, Mr. Moore. I'll do whatever it takes to have one."

Luke's politeness and reserved manner pleased Gage. Maybe fate had spared this boy from having Beau's appetites. A second chance sat before him.

"Thank you for coming, John." Gage patted his shoulder. "Now, tell me how you got wind of this."

John nodded. "Leslie and Luke are friends. She was at The Bogue when they took him in for questioning. She called me immediately."

Gage had always known Leslie was a clever girl. He was grateful she'd reacted quickly. "Thank her for me."

"What do you want me to tell her when she asks what happened here?"

Gage squared his broad shoulders. "The truth. Everyone in town will know soon enough."

"We should proceed slowly," John suggested. "Maybe take care of this legally before we go making announcements."

Gage noted how John's eyes disappeared behind his glasses as he squinted. He seemed worried.

"Luke, how would you like to come and live with me?" Gage asked. "We'll collect your belongings from your apartment, and you can stay in one of my guest rooms."

Luke stood, his eyes wide with astonishment. "You're serious?"

John held up his hand, urging restraint. "Gage, shouldn't we check out a few things first?"

Gage waved off his reservations. "No. I know a Devereaux when I see one."

Mumbling, John collected his briefcase. "Then I'll leave you to it. Call me later. We have a lot to work through."

Gage waited for John to exit the small interrogation room. Once the door closed, he went to the table.

"He's right, you know. As a Devereaux, there'll be expectations. Are you sure you want this? Maybe you should take some time to consider."

Luke ran his fingers over the top of the table. His hands reminded Gage of Beau's. They were the same length, with tapering fingers and wide palms. But the man Beau had turned into became his worst nightmare. This boy was different. He had to be.

"I don't need to think about it." Luke eased away from the table. "For years, I've wondered who you were. Now that I'm here, I realize this is what I've been missing all my life—a father."

Gage grinned. He could even bullshit like Beau. A true Devereaux.

"Then let's go grab your things." Gage removed his keys from his pocket. "It's time you get to know where you came from."

Chapter Twenty-Three

Streetlamps nestled between tall oaks illuminated the way to Gage's black wrought iron gates. The heater in his car kept the chill at bay, but did little to offset the icy hush between him and Luke. His newly found son sat in the passenger seat, staring at the gated property. Luke's stoic countenance betrayed nothing. He was Gage's son, all right—he never let anyone see what he was thinking.

"How much land do you have?" Luke asked.

Gage typed his code into the keypad. "Devereaux Plantation is a hundred and fifty acres, including the brewery. When our ancestors settled the area, they owned everything to the Bogue Falaya River. The Abbey is built on the ruins of the original Frellson family chapel. Gaston Devereaux gave the chapel and some land to the Benedictine monks so they could put a seminary there."

"Why did he give it away?"

"My guess would be guilt over something. Our family has made a lot of mistakes through the years." Gage chuckled as the gates slowly swung open. "My grandfather, Jacques Devereaux, tried to drown his sins in beer. He's who built the brewery. It became his passion."

Luke turned to him, his gaze cold. "Is it your passion?"

Gage never considered beer anything but a business. He didn't even like the taste, but he knew more about making, bottling, selling, and marketing it than anyone who worked for him.

"Not particularly." He viewed the lights of the brewery in the distance. "But I do like the thrill of business."

Gage steered the car along the concrete drive. Darkened oaks draped with Spanish moss cast sinister shadows. The eerie night bothered Gage. His discomfort stemmed from the ghost stories his grandmother told. When he'd taken over the house after his father's passing, he installed extra lights inside and out. Gage had enough specters in his past without having to confront more around his home.

Yellow beams broke through the branches, and the unsettling darkness retreated. Four white Corinthian columns shone first. Then the ornate balconies trimmed in wrought iron appeared. Finally, the car cleared the last clump of trees, and the porch decorated with white rocking chairs materialized.

Gage kept an eye on Luke, anxious to see his reaction to the three-story Greek Revival plantation.

Luke sat forward, the wisp of a grin across his lips.

Light glowed from large windows, and the Spanish moss-covered oaks framing the pre-Civil War home swayed in the breeze.

"You'll get a better appreciation during the day." Gage nodded at the gardens of gardenias lining the front porch. "It always looks a little creepy at night. Some say spirits dwell among these trees. Wouldn't surprise me if they're demons. Our family history is littered with violence."

"Taylor found stories about your family," Luke told him. "She was particularly obsessed with the rumor of mental illness in the Devereaux family. Any truth to that?"

Gage eyed the lights in the round cupola atop the red-slated roof. "Every family has its skeletons."

Luke glanced up at the balconies trimmed in the same swirling design as the gates. "Why did the Frellson name change to Devereaux?"

"My grandmother told me my great-great-grandfather, Gaston Frellson, was—and I quote—a ne'er-do-well who owed a lot of money. His father didn't want to sully the family name and planned to cut him out of the will. It was rumored that Gaston killed his father to inherit the estate. To hide from his past crimes, and as a parting shot, he took his mother's maiden name. We've been the Devereaux family ever since."

Luke tugged at the hem of his T-shirt. "Do you think it's true? That he killed his father?"

Gage glanced at Luke as he drove up to the five-car garage. "I wouldn't put it past him. Gaston Devereaux was a powerful man."

"Just like your father." Luke shifted in his seat. "I heard he was a state senator. People in town still talk about him."

"He was well-connected, and I still have influence in Baton Rouge because of him. When I need political favors, his name moves mountains." Gage pulled into the garage.

Luke emitted a low whistle. "Is that a McLaren 570GT?"

"A present I bought myself." Gage admired the sleek lines of the luxury vehicle. "My wife called it a waste of money. Beau agreed with her because I wouldn't let him drive it."

Luke stared, starry-eyed, at the red car. "Money spent on a piece of automotive excellence is never a waste. It's a treasure."

Gage had become accustomed to having so little in common with Beau that Luke sharing his interests surprised him. He shut off the engine and stepped out of the car.

Luke grabbed his bag from the back and joined him.

Gage showed Luke through the mudroom and past the etched glass doors decorated with peacocks. Luke stopped and inspected the six framed magazine covers featuring the home.

"The house is a registered historic landmark. We get a lot of magazines wanting to photograph it. These were some of the better ones."

Luke examined one of the pictures. "I've always really liked old houses. Their history and grandeur."

Gage suppressed a grin. He'd always loved his home, but Beau hated it. Yet another thing he had in common with Luke.

They walked into the kitchen. The aroma of freshly brewed coffee lingered in the air. It meant Elizabeth had waited up for him. She usually put on a new pot when he arrived home from the brewery—her subtle hint that he would need the caffeine for the long night ahead.

Gage had not warned her about their new guest. He could imagine how she'd react—frigid on the outside, but a raging hurricane within. That about summed up his wife since their son's death. Everything she said or did roused his suspicion. She wasn't the quiet, doting woman he'd married.

The digital lights from the numerous appliances reflected off the copper-topped breakfast bar.

Gage tapped the built-in onyx refrigerator. "We have a cook. Her name is Leah. She comes in every morning, so let her know what you like to eat."

Luke set his duffel bag on the breakfast bar. "I can cook for myself."

The hint of rebellion sounded oddly familiar—another Devereaux trait. "She shops for us, too. You can let her know what you want."

Luke caressed a slight dent left in the copper, a relic from one of Beau's tantrums.

"I appreciate you taking me in," Luke said. "But I don't want to be a bother."

Gage rested his hands on the cool surface of the breakfast bar, hoping to sound genuine. "I don't know what your mother told you about me, about us, but I can assure you, I never knew you existed until the day I saw you outside of Mo's. Had I known you were in Massachusetts, I would have come for you after your mother died."

Luke slouched, appearing a little lost. "I asked my grandparents about you. They told me they had no information about my father. It wasn't until I read her letter that I knew your name."

"I'm sorry. I wish—"

Elizabeth walked into the kitchen. Her silky black dress and red lipstick hinted at what she'd planned for her husband. She halted and stared at Luke.

"Elizabeth." Gage went to her side, hoping to fend off any of her questions. "I'd like you to meet Luke Cross." His arm slipped around her waist.

Her gaze shifted from the young man to him. The color of her lips disappeared as she pressed them tightly together.

"Luke is the son of Pamela Cross. A friend I knew in Boston long ago." He dropped his voice, letting her know he would not tolerate any outburst—not yet anyway. "He will be staying with us."

She stiffened under his arm. He knew her well enough to sense the swell of outrage roaring through her veins.

"This is a surprise." She stepped away from him. "I haven't had time to prepare any of our guest rooms. You should have told me sooner."

Luke shook his head. "No, please. I don't want to be a bother. I can go back to my apartment."

Elizabeth's tense posture eased.

"Your apartment is a hovel and no place for you." Gage turned to his wife. "All the bedrooms in this house, and we don't have a single one ready?"

Elizabeth's cheeks pinked. "I believe the yellow bedroom is adequate for tonight. I can have our maid prepare one of the bigger rooms in the morning."

Gage nodded, pleased with her response. "I'll take him upstairs and show him where to go."

Elizabeth relaxed her hands. "Welcome to our home, Mr. Cross. We're happy to have you."

Luke collected his duffel bag. "Thank you, Mrs. Devereaux. You're very kind to put up with my intrusion so late in the evening."

Elizabeth mustered a sweet smile. "Not at all. Let me know if you need anything."

Gage showed him out of the kitchen and glanced back at his wife. "I'll come down after I see him to his room."

Gage left her, knowing a heated discussion was sure to follow.

He escorted Luke to the main hall, avoiding the shortcut to the staircase through the cypress-paneled dining room. The portraits of former Devereaux men might be too much, just yet. Slow and steady was Gage's plan to introduce Luke to his new life. He wanted to avoid the hell he'd suffered with Beau. The new Devereaux needed to be tested and observed before taking on any real responsibility. Gage hoped he proved up to the task.

They passed the door to his office and the peach-painted parlor Elizabeth treasured. Luke's astonished stare entertained Gage as he took in a massive, gold-framed painting of New Orleans and life-sized portraits of deceased Devereaux family members.

What if he turns into Beau?

Gage raised his head to the elegantly curved mahogany staircase as he considered the years he'd spent dealing with his psychotic son. Beau had made Gage a master at eliminating the most troublesome problems. If Luke followed in Beau's footsteps, Gage would have his associates do away with him, too.

I'll protect the Devereaux name at all costs.

Elizabeth paced the red rug covering the hardwood floor in Gage's office. The picture of Gage and Carol together at Mo's still haunted her. She wanted to scream and claw out his eyes, but her position relied on providing her husband with an heir. Until she had another child, she had to keep quiet.

The room smelled of his expensive cologne, and the masculine, dark décor matched his personality to a tee. The wide walnut desk, burgundy leather furniture, and engraved map above the hearth of the original Frellson Plantation oozed the family's lineage and privilege—all the attributes Gage exuded.

Elizabeth was from an old, blue-blood New Orleans family who had been on friendly terms with Gage's mother, Amelia Devereaux. The daughter of an English Earl, Amelia was also known in the city for her powerful husband, Edward, and handsome son. It wasn't long before Amelia and Edward deemed the former debutante a suitable candidate to marry Gage.

Her father had pressed for the match and Elizabeth readily agreed, believing she'd find happiness. How she wished she could go back and start over.

The click of the door brought a halt to her pacing.

Gage strolled in wearing his usual scowl. "I got him settled in."

Elizabeth folded her arms. "Who is he?"

Gage went to his desk and put down his phone.

Something was up. He only avoided wielding his intimidating stare when bad things happened. He'd done that on the morning he told her about Beau. He'd sat calmly at the breakfast bar and revealed how her son had been found dead by the river. She recalled every detail—the dispassionate way he'd described Beau's injuries and cause of death.

Gage sat behind his desk and opened a drawer. He pulled out a bottle of scotch and two glasses.

Elizabeth sashayed toward him, staring at the liquor. "A few months ago, you would've hidden that from me."

Gage poured two glasses. "You've changed. And you're going to need it. I have something to tell you."

Shit. He's leaving me.

"Which is?" Her heart raced.

He pushed the glass toward her. "Luke Cross is my son."

Elizabeth almost laughed out loud with relief. She'd expected something much worse. She ran through what he'd told her in the kitchen, and one thing stood out—Boston.

She peered into the dark liquid. "He's her son? The woman Edward used as leverage to make you marry me?"

He examined the design etched into his old-fashioned glass. "He didn't make me marry you, but yes, she was the main reason we were thrown together."

"Did you know she was pregnant?"

He responded with a curt nod. "She said she was. I gave her my car to pay for an abortion. The same car the boy drove to St. Benedict. Poetic justice, I guess."

Elizabeth ran her finger along the rim of her glass. "Is a car the only evidence he's your son?"

Gage glanced at her untouched scotch. "I'm having Kent Davis run a DNA test. He took Luke in for questioning about the Taylor Haskins murder."

Elizabeth put her hand to her chest. "I thought she committed suicide."

"No." Gage stood, carrying his drink. "They've ruled it a homicide. And since Luke is new in town, our ambitious little sheriff decided to question him. Luke called me for help."

"And you waltzed in to the rescue, telling everybody he was your long-lost son." A bitter taste filled her mouth. "Why bring him here? Does he even know what you did to his mother?"

Gage cocked an eyebrow. "What I did? You don't even know what I did."

She pushed the drink away, not wanting to fall into that trap again. Elizabeth needed to think about her future baby's health.

"Your son left behind a lot of evidence about his sexual proclivities. I can guess where he got that from."

"My son's inclinations are not mine." Gage took a sip of his drink.

"At least Beau wasn't sloppy. What else would you call that young man upstairs in our guest room?"

Gage tipped his glass to her. "Touché. But that boy might be the answer to my prayer. An heir to keep the Devereaux line going."

The comment stiffened her back. "A bastard? You're joking."

He set the drink on his desk. "Why not? My family has had several bastards. Luke will be no different. Blood matters more than legitimacy."

Her insides twisted. "You know nothing about this boy."

"I have someone checking him out. I'll know more than he does about himself soon enough."

Ah, there it was—that unflappable Gage Devereaux confidence. He'd always been so hell-bent on controlling everyone that he never considered the emotional impact of all his plotting. Beau had paid heavily for it, and she expected Luke would, too.

"What about our baby? What do we do with him when I get pregnant?"

Gage looked her over. "You're not pregnant yet."

Elizabeth's knotted stomach registered the slight, but she didn't give Gage the satisfaction of seeing her distress. She needed to drive a wedge between the two men. "You can't trust him."

Gage chuckled and picked up her untouched glass. "I can't trust anyone, so what difference does it make? Starting tomorrow, I'll be introducing our newest Devereaux to our way of life, and you will help me."

The idea of catering to Gage's bastard disgusted her. Was she to become the forgotten wife and humiliated stepmother to Gage's illegitimate heir?

"What if he turns out to be like Beau?" she asked, hoping to play the only card left.

Gage shot back the scotch in Elizabeth's glass. "I've thought of that, but Beau showed signs when he was young. You have the scar to prove it. Luke has a different temperament."

"He could change. Just like you do when you're pushed into a corner."

Gage set the glass down with a thud. "Make sure you don't push him, or me, and everything should be fine. Take him shopping tomorrow. He has nothing appropriate to wear." He opened his office door. "After that, bring him to the brewery. I'll show him around. We'll need to guide him to conform to the expectations of our name. Can you do that?"

She walked toward the door, aware of the way he appraised the swing of her hips. "I've followed your orders for this long." She stopped and turned to him. "But when I give you a son, promise me he will come before Luke."

Gage gave her a sinewy smile. "I promise. And he will share in what's mine and what I'm building."

She stood on her toes and kissed his lips. "I'll be in my room waiting for you."

He wrapped his hand around her neck and gave it a light squeeze. "I have a few calls to make, and then we can play."

She removed his hand. "No more bruises for a while. At least until he leaves."

Gage's eyes burned into her. "Who said he's leaving? This is his home now."

He closed the door, and when the lock clicked, Elizabeth's temper erupted.

His home? She charged toward the stairs. *We'll see about that.*

Reassured by Elizabeth's compliance, Gage returned to his desk and retrieved his phone. He sat, studying the dark screen, carefully thinking through everything he would say. The call was one he'd dreaded, but he needed to know if his friends had created more complications.

After three rings, a grizzled voice answered. "Is there a problem?"

Gage clenched his jaw. "A situation. Did you do anything about the Taylor Haskins girl?"

Joe's long sigh rattled him.

"I don't remember her being a problem. And no. We've had eyes on her and the others, but that's it."

"She's dead." Gage waited for Joe's reaction, but there was none. "She was murdered, according to my sheriff."

"Not by our hands. Sounds like you have another player in town."

The blistering turmoil spreading through Gage wasn't familiar. The situation was beyond his ability to contain, and he hated it. "Thank you. I'll be in touch."

The line went dead, and Gage tossed his phone down. This was unacceptable on the eve of the brewery's national debut.

He curled his hand into a fist and slammed it into his desk. A momentary pain ran up his arm. He concentrated on his throbbing hand, finding power in the sensation.

Self-control in all things. Never let them see who you really are.

Chapter Twenty-Four

Leslie reclined on the grass in the quad, her face to the sun but shivering in the frigid breeze. She'd missed her second period class and opted to remain outside. The crowded school building and buzz of conversation in the halls were too much for her.

She'd sought refuge in nature, wanting to feel something real against her skin, but what she needed most was peace to think.

Her father's revelation about the murder when he'd come home from the sheriff's station left her numb. She'd been right about someone killing Taylor. Leslie would bet that someone had followed the frightened girl around before her death, exacerbating Taylor's fragile state of mind.

The reveal about Luke's paternity hadn't shocked her as much as it should have. Luke had never behaved like Beau, which only added to her conflict. There were moments he seemed so much like him. Luke was a Devereaux, but had also become a friend.

Taylor hadn't trusted Luke—and now she was dead. Coincidence? Her head hurt considering the possibilities.

"Hey." Sara had a seat next to her and zipped her black leather jacket. "What's up? You never skip class, but here you are."

Leslie rubbed her hands together, trying to get the feeling back in her fingertips. "Shouldn't you be in chemistry?"

Sara shook her head. "Not when my friend is out here all alone. You look like you could use a drink."

Leslie raised her head to the passing clouds, wishing she could float away on one. "You ever been so wrong about someone, you begin to question what you're right about?"

Sara eased back on the grass, resting on her elbows. "Please tell me this isn't about Derek."

"No. Luke Cross."

Sara bobbed her eyebrows. "Now, that's a subject I can grab with both hands."

Leslie plucked a few blades of grass. "Not if you knew the truth about him."

Sara sat up. "What are you talkin' about?"

If Leslie said anything, the whole town would know by lunch. But if she didn't, the entire town would probably still know by lunch because the sheriff's wife was the queen of St. Benedict gossip.

"Luke is a Devereaux. He's Gage's son."

She expected shouts of joy or a moderate bit of celebratory dancing, but Sara remained unusually still.

"Fuck me."

Leslie chuckled. "Seems he already did that to both of us. Figuratively speaking."

Sara scooted around in front of Leslie, her long black skirt trailing on the grass. "He knew. That's why he showed up in St. Benedict. To find Gage."

Leslie hugged her legs, pulling her knees close. "He picked our brains about Beau and his family, knowing full well who he was. He used us."

"That little shit." Sara swatted at the grass. "I wanted him. Still do. But knowin' who he is makes it kinda weird."

"Yeah, being Beau's half-brother puts him in a whole new light."

Sara flopped back on the ground. "We should tell Kelly. She's got the hots for him, too. It's a shame. He seemed so normal."

Leslie tipped her head closer. "Yeah, but for how much longer? You know the saying; absolute power corrupts absolutely. Beau proved that."

Sara struggled to stand, her boots getting caught in her flowing skirt. "Come on. We're headin' to Kelly's. She's home with some stomach bug, again."

Leslie studied the red brick school building across the quad. "I should get back. I have French in ten minutes."

Sara tugged at her jacket sleeve. "So? Skip it. With your GPA, you could fail every test from now until graduation and still pass." Sara put her face closer to Leslie's and grinned. "You don't want to be little miss perfect your whole life, do you?"

Leslie had strived to be a stellar student—never skipped class, never in trouble, and took on extra credit assignments for fun. Suddenly, she itched to break free and do something reckless. Maybe this was the guilt or grief getting to her, but there was another part of her that wanted to live life the way Dawn would have.

"I'll drive," she said as she got to her feet. "I'm not riding in your truck."

Sara stuck out her chin. "What's wrong with my truck?"

"Nothing, but if we're gonna skip class and leave, I suggest we go low-key."

Sara dusted snippets of grass off her skirt. "Fine. Let's stop by Mo's and get coffee and strawberry cheesecake to go. I'll text Kelly and tell her we're on our way."

Leslie stared at her. "I don't think we should be bringing her coffee and cheesecake if she's sick."

Sara pulled out her phone and started typing. "She's fakin' it. You know what a drama queen she's been lately."

Leslie grabbed her book bag and dug out her keys. "There's something else you should know about Taylor."

Sara sent her text, never glancing up at her. "Like what?"

Leslie drew in a fortifying breath. "Taylor didn't kill herself. She was murdered."

The phone wobbled in Sara's hand. "No way."

Leslie checked to see if any other students were around. "My dad said the sheriff found forensic evidence confirming Taylor didn't pull the trigger." She expected Sara to shake or cry out, but her blank stare remained. Leslie touched her shoulder. "You okay?"

"Taylor was right. Someone was after her. After us." The words tumbled from her black-painted lips. "We have to do something."

Leslie wanted to calm the panic she saw rising in Sara's eyes, but her mind went blank. "What would you suggest? They haven't exactly covered this in health class."

Sara brushed her hair from her cheek. "What about the cops? Do they have any idea who killed Taylor?"

Leslie shook her head. "They don't have any leads."

"I always knew Kent and his people were worthless." Sara sneered. "First Luke turns out to be a Devereaux, and now this. How much shittier can this day get?"

Leslie didn't answer. She'd learned from experience that things could always get worse in St. Benedict, and usually did.

The bell above the entrance to Mo's Diner greeted Leslie as she walked through an invisible curtain of tempting aroma. Her mouth watered when she inhaled the inviting essence of coffee blended with the succulence of freshly baked pastries.

"Are you sure Kelly wants to meet us here?" she asked as Sara walked alongside her.

"Yep. She texted not to come over." Sara eyed a few customers enjoying their treats at the counter. "I'm jonesin' for an apple fritter."

"Then why isn't she here?" Leslie asked as she walked toward a booth in the back.

Sara followed while checking out the menu above the counter. "Do you want to split one with me? Or, how about apple pie?"

Leslie stopped and faced her. "I can't believe you can eat after everything I told you. Aren't you scared?"

Sara widened her stance. "What do you want me to say? Yes, I'm scared. Someone could be decidin' which of us to pick off next. But we already know who that someone is. There's only one person who wants us out of the way."

Leslie took a step back, absorbing the blow of her comment. She scoured the diner and then dropped her voice. "You can't seriously believe Gage Devereaux had something to do with Taylor's death. He's kept his word."

Sara flipped her long hair behind her shoulder. "But we're the only ones who know what Beau did. We're a threat."

Leslie's constant churn of trepidation kicked into overdrive. She hastily pushed Sara into a nearby booth, wishing they'd never come to Mo's. "You need to think carefully about what you're saying. Gage doesn't want us dead. He wants us compliant."

Sara edged closer. "What does he do to those who aren't compliant, such as Taylor? We both know what he's capable of."

The disturbing concept flustered Leslie. "We're in too deep with Gage to back out now."

"We could leave town," Sara suggested. "Take a long road trip until things cool off." The bell above the door jingled, and she glanced back at the entrance.

"Yeah, like that wouldn't make us look guilty as hell," Leslie muttered.

Kelly stumbled in the door, white as a sheet. Her jeans and oversized shirt drowned her slim figure.

Leslie became concerned for her friend. Kelly seemed worse with every passing day. Her cheeks grew paler, her eyes duller, and her movements more sluggish.

"What's the big news?" Kelly scooted across the bench next to Sara.

Leslie waited, staring at Sara, urging her to make the announcement.

Sara rested her hands on the white table, her wide eyes pleading for Leslie to do the dirty work.

Leslie's shoulders drooped before she gave in. "Taylor didn't commit suicide. She was murdered."

Kelly calmly took a napkin from the holder and patted her face. "That doesn't surprise me. We already knew she was drawing attention to herself by digging around too much."

Her reaction confounded Leslie. She never figured Kelly to be the cool one. Maybe her instincts about people were worse than she'd imagined.

A gray-haired waitress wearing a freshly pressed Mo's uniform approached their table. Leslie recognized her former Sunday school teacher and smiled. "Hey, Mrs. V. Can we get three iced coffees?"

"Nothing for me." Kelly touched her stomach. "I can't handle anything just yet."

Leslie held up two fingers. "Two, please."

Mrs. Voss peered over her spectacles. "Why aren't you in school, Leslie Moore? Your father won't like you being here."

Leslie refrained from groaning and kept up her fake grin. "My third period class got canceled, and we wanted to check on our friend. She's not been feeling well."

Mrs. Voss inspected Kelly with keen eyes. "I suspect I know what's ailing you, dear."

"Yeah, something's been going around," Leslie commented.

Mrs. Voss glanced back at Leslie. "And you'd better head back to school after you leave here, or I'll tell your father."

Leslie remembered why she'd never skipped out in the past. Getting away with anything in a small town, where everybody knows you, was next to impossible. "Yes, Mrs. Voss."

After giving them a stern once-over and a disapproving snort, Mrs. Voss shuffled away.

"What was that about?" Sara asked. "You know that nosy bitch?"

"I know everyone in town." Leslie frowned at Kelly. "That's why we should've gone to your house."

Kelly dropped her wadded napkin on the table. "Can't. My mom is working from home today. I had to sneak out of my room to come here."

Sara motioned to Leslie. "Go on. Tell her the other thing."

A bit of color returned to Kelly's cheeks. "What other thing?"

Leslie planted her palms on the table and then began a detailed accounting of everything her father had told her about Taylor's death. She spoke softly so others in the diner couldn't hear. Once she'd finished, she sat back and waited.

Kelly remained unperturbed, worrying Leslie even more.

"We should do another séance." Kelly fidgeted, pulling at her shirt. "We can ask Taylor who killed her."

Sara's posture stiffened. "We already know who killed her. Taylor ran her mouth, and Gage must have heard about it."

Leslie didn't add her two cents. That their prime suspect was the same man who had their asses in a sling put all three of them in a precarious position.

"We should ask Taylor to make sure," Kelly insisted. "Or don't you want to talk to the dead anymore?"

The pink in Sara's cheeks darkened to deep red. "Fine. We'll go to the river and summon Taylor."

Leslie sank, letting her butt slide down the bench. "I'm not sure that would be a good idea. The river is probably crawling with police."

"The Abbey, then." Kelly removed another napkin from the holder and wiped her brow. "On Friday night, everybody will be at the river. We can slip off and do another séance."

Leslie didn't like her greenish color. "Are you sure you'll be able to go?

You look like hell."

Kelly crushed the napkin in her hand. "It's just a bug. My doctor said it will pass in a day or two."

Leslie checked out her puffy fingers. "But you've had the same bug for a while."

Sara slapped the table, drawing attention. "A séance is a waste of time. We all know what happened."

Kelly tossed the crumpled napkin at Sara. "You're just worried you can't summon Taylor. You did such a bang-up job with Dawn, after all."

Sara batted the trash away. "That wasn't my fault. If Leslie hadn't run off, we might have gotten somewhere."

Leslie tuned out the bickering and faced the window, eager to browse the shops across Main Street for a distraction. Then her gaze settled on an attractive couple coming out of one of the fancier boutiques.

The older woman wore a red dress and heels, her light auburn hair fashionably coifed. Her hand rested on the arm of the younger man, who had on dark slacks and a white dress shirt. He seemed uncomfortable with the woman's affection. The way they were together, almost awkward, intrigued Leslie.

A cougar and her cub weren't a common sight in St. Benedict. Leslie squinted, hoping to make out their faces. Then the man moved into the street, carrying shopping bags to a familiar white Mercedes.

Holy shit!

"Can we invite Luke to join us at the river Friday night?" Kelly asked.

Leslie pointed out the window. "He might have other plans."

Elizabeth enjoyed the sun's warmth as Luke took the bags to her car. The crisp air relieved her fatigue after her long night with Gage. She might not have been too enthused about bringing his bastard shopping, but Elizabeth had to admit the new clothes from Will's Haberdashery suited him. He reminded her of Gage—the way he'd been when they were first married. All he needed was a good haircut, and everybody would see the similarities between father and son.

She walked to the rear of the car and removed a loose thread from the sleeve of his new shirt. "Gage will be pleased."

He dropped the bags into the trunk. "I appreciate you taking me shopping."

"No trouble. Gage insists we keep up appearances."

He shut the lid. "This must be difficult for you. Learning about me like this so soon after losing your son."

A sting of sorrow unsettled her, but Elizabeth didn't let it show. She'd grieved the loss of her son ever since he attacked her when he was a child. The Beau she loved died the moment the monster was born.

"You're different from Beau. Gage was always pushing him. He was a star athlete, community leader, and straight-A student, but that was only on the surface."

Luke's smile brought back memories of Beau. So much of the young man reminded her of her son—the good parts she'd forgotten.

"Well, I was never a stellar student. And I ran track, but I quit the team because it interfered with my after-school job."

She liked the easy-going way he spoke about his past. "What did you do?"

Luke rubbed his hands together. "Mechanic. I love cars."

She peeked at his nails. "We might have to get you a manicure before heading to the brewery."

He backed away from her. "I couldn't sit for something like that. I'd feel weird."

"Greasy fingernails and dirty hands won't do for the son of Gage Devereaux."

He browsed the shops on Main Street. "I didn't think there would be so many expectations."

She arched a skeptical eyebrow. "What did you expect? That you could waltz into town and be his son without any conditions. From now on, everything you do will be judged by your name. You'll have to act a certain way, be courteous to everyone, generous with your time, helpful, participate in charitable works, and be a leader. Are you sure you want this?"

He watched her, his gaze traveling the length of her dress. "You sound like you want me to walk away."

"Not at all." She smoothed an unruly curl in his hair. "I want to help you. Consider me a shoulder to lean on. Gage can be demanding at times.

You'll need a friend."

She wasn't particularly enthused about his new place in the family, but he could prove useful if Gage abandoned her bed.

Elizabeth shielded her eyes as the glass doors to Mo's Diner opened. Three young women exited and stared in their direction.

She retrieved sunglasses from her expensive handbag. "Friends of yours?"

He nodded, squinting against the sun. "Yes. Sara, Kelly, and Leslie. I know them from The Bogue."

She noticed the petite blonde in the center. "Leslie Moore?"

He glanced back at her over his shoulder. "You know her?"

"Beau dated her sister." She took a step closer to Luke. "Dawn was a wonderful girl. Such a pity."

"I hear she and Beau spent a lot of time at the river."

The river. Elizabeth inwardly cringed. Beau had loved the beach along the Bogue Falaya, but the place gave her nightmares. How could kids still hang out there after all the death and destruction?

Once inside the car, she waited for him to adjust his seat belt. "Do you have a girlfriend back in Boston?"

Luke snapped his buckle into place. "No one special."

She admired the fit of his shirt and the snug cut of his slacks. Sleeping with her stepson would be the ultimate gambit against her husband and guarantee a Devereaux heir.

Elizabeth grinned and patted his thigh. "I'm sure you'll find someone very soon."

CHAPTER TWENTY-FIVE

Gage rested his arms on the folders spread across his desk. The vast pile of information, gathered by various managers, outlined the entire brewery operation to give Luke an idea of the business's scale. He peered across the desk at his son, proud of how well he'd handled his new role.

Gage had expected him to balk at the homework, but Luke had been attentive since the moment he'd stepped through his office door.

The change from Beau's whining was welcome. Getting Beau to show enthusiasm for anything other than sports or girls had frustrated Gage.

"What will you do to meet the demands of the national campaign?" Luke held an open folder in his hands. "You're distributing to two national chain grocery stores and five large liquor stores, not to mention the local businesses in several neighboring states. Can this brewery alone meet those needs?"

It was one of many astute questions Luke had asked. He had a knack for processing details and deciphering spreadsheets. "We're starting slow, limiting our supply in case we have a lukewarm reception. But I've hired architects for next year when I plan on expanding operations."

"You have the funds for this?" Luke searched the folders scattered across the desk. "Your P&L from last quarter didn't show that much of a profit margin."

Gage studied him for a moment. "Where did you learn about P&L

statements?"

Luke sat back in his chair. "The garage I worked at during school. I handled the accounts for Mr. Eldridge, the owner. He could barely read and was always sick, so when I wasn't repairing engines, I helped with the books."

Gage was impressed. "Did you manage any employees while you worked there? Hire and fire?"

Luke set his folder on the desk. "After Mr. Eldridge had a stroke, his wife let me run the garage. I had to let a few men go who weren't pulling their weight. I also hired new people to replace them and did a little advertising to attract new clients."

Gage sat back, enthralled. "Why did you leave?"

"I juggled the garage around my college classes, but Mrs. Eldridge decided to sell the place after her husband died. She wanted me to buy it, but I didn't have enough money." Luke paused as he perused the folders on the desk. "Are you going to apply for a loan for this expansion?"

Gage considered how to broach the subject of his private investors—the ones who preferred to stay off the books. He wasn't willing to share all his business with Luke just yet. "I have associates who have a keen interest in the brewery's future. We'll have all the cash we need."

Luke nodded. "That's good. This could turn out to be quite an operation."

"An operation I can't keep running alone." He stood and went around the desk. "Work with me here at the brewery, and see if this is something you feel you can do. I'd like to keep this business in the family."

Luke stood. "That's very generous, but you know nothing about me. What you're offering requires a great deal of trust."

Gage wasn't a fool. He had people watching Luke around the clock. "I'm offering you a chance, an opportunity." A thread of apprehension balled in his gut. "Be advised, though, being a Devereaux changes everything. Be wary of everyone. Many in this town are not to be trusted."

Luke glanced down at his new brown loafers. "Can I still pursue my interest in working with cars? I understand I have responsibilities to uphold, but I don't want to give that up completely."

Gage held out his hand. "We can make room for a garage in our new plans for the brewery. Some place where we both can indulge our passion. Maybe even start a collection."

Luke's face lit up. It was the first real joy Gage had seen in him.

Luke took his hand and gave it an enthusiastic shake. "I don't know what to say, Mr. Devereaux."

"Tell me you want to give this a try."

Luke looked him squarely in the eye. "Absolutely. I can think of nothing better than working with you."

The years of fights, worry, and unending sorrow Beau had given him slipped away. "Good. Connie is getting you a laptop and cell phone as we speak. When you're ready, we can submit the paperwork to change your name. If anyone asks, you're a Devereaux from this moment on."

Pink evening light streamed through the office windows as Gage pored over his spreadsheets. Last quarter's figures needed a thorough review before heading home for the night. He'd already sent Luke on his way, not wanting to push him too hard on the first day.

The reception the young man received at the brewery had been beyond his expectations. Warm, friendly, and with a savvy Beau never possessed, Luke charmed everyone he met. Gage hoped it was a sign of things to come.

His phone rang like church bells, a sound he remembered from childhood. Newfangled ringtones irritated him.

"I've got what you wanted." Kent's weary voice poured through the speaker. "It may be more than you bargained for."

Gage picked up a pen. "Let me be the judge of that."

"Well, first, he was born Lucas Alexander Cross on April 17th at Warwick Hospital in Braintree, Massachusetts. There is no name listed as the father on the birth certificate. His grandparents were appointed his legal guardians at the age of four. The documents were sealed, so I don't know why."

Gage tapped the pen against the desk. "His mother died when he was four, so it was probably a formality. What else?"

"He has no arrests, a few speeding tickets, and was a B average student. He attended an elite private school, then did four semesters at a small college in Massachusetts, majored in business, and got all A's."

Gage rested his elbows on his desk. "Women?"

Kent cleared his throat, sounding uneasy. "None of significance, except for a wealthy woman twice his age named Megan Sloan. She was the widow of a renowned psychiatrist, Larson Sloan. Luke would escort her to parties, symphony openings, fancy occasions. Rumor was he got paid for his services, but I can't confirm that. After she died, he packed up and moved here."

A nervous tic tensed his right jaw. "She died?"

"Drowned in her bathtub after taking too many sleeping pills. It was ruled accidental. The police never questioned Luke."

Gage had buried a son who was the epitome of evil. He couldn't help but suspect the worst in another. "Any problems that could follow him?"

"Nothing I've found. He had a few tough years after his grandparents died, but otherwise, he's clean."

Gage recalled the details Luke had given him about his past. "Do you know how the grandparents died?"

"Car accident when he was eighteen. He inherited their estate, which was sizable, but there wasn't much left after debts and taxes. He's got a bank account in Boston with a little over forty dollars in it. One expired credit card and an outstanding student loan for fifteen thousand dollars."

Gage scribbled another note about the student loan. He would have to take care of that. "What about employment? Any time spent in a garage?"

"Ah, yes." Kent shuffled papers. "Eldridge's Garage. He worked there during school. The business was sold. It was after that he started seeing the Sloan woman."

"What about his car? Did you run the serial number?"

"It's in his name. The plates and insurance are up to date."

Gage tapped his pen on the desk, irritated. "How far back did you go in the title search?"

"It was your car," Kent affirmed. "I found your name and your father's in the search."

Gage was confident it was his car, but he'd wanted confirmation. Satisfaction rolled through him like a good stiff shot of scotch. There were still pieces missing, but he felt confident he would learn everything in time. He had enough to keep the boy loyal and in St. Benedict. "Keep digging."

"What do you want me to look for?" Kent sighed. "What if I find something you don't want to hear?"

Gage rolled the pen between his fingers. "There's nothing I don't want to hear."

Kent's chair squeaked, irking the hell out of Gage. "Is he still at the brewery?"

Gage put his pen aside. "I had Connie drop him off at The Bogue Falaya Café a while ago. He wanted to pick up his car. It's been there since your deputies took him in for questioning."

"If I'd known he was your kid, I wouldn't have touched him."

Kent's apology fell flat. The sheriff's bumbling with the murder cases had been a godsend, but since Taylor's death, Gage debated whether Kent was the right man for the job. People in town were getting antsy, and Kent might feel he had to work harder to solve the crimes. If that happened, he would start discreetly looking for his replacement.

"I would've preferred to let everybody know about Luke in a more subtle way. You taking him in for questioning sped up my plans, but in the end, no harm was done. It provided the opportunity to get a DNA sample. Any word on that?"

"Yes, the other reason I called." Kent took a breath. "I got the preliminary results on the rush order I put in. You're right. The boy is yours. But are you sure about letting him stay with you?"

Gage nodded, taking in the confirmation. "Yes. If he does anything, I have you to arrest him." He turned to his laptop and opened his email. "I gave him a new phone. I'm sending you the information. Keep track of where he goes and who he calls."

"You do realize he's an adult," Kent argued. "You can't stop him from doing what he wants or going where he pleases. He's not even legally your son."

"Yet," Gage hastily asserted. "I'll have John Moore take care of the paperwork soon enough. If anyone in town questions it, I want to know. I won't have my authority undermined."

"You should wait and give the boy time to settle in before you thrust all that responsibility on him."

Kent's criticism incensed Gage. Maybe he shouldn't be too discreet about searching for new sheriff candidates after all.

"Call me when you get more information." Gage hung up before Kent could reply. He had all he could handle of the man for one day. There was work to do and a new son to groom.

CHAPTER TWENTY-SIX

Leslie worked her way around a group of exuberant students as they streamed through the door of The Bogue. They crammed into tables and packed the counter, eager to order. Conversations rose over the booming beat coming from the jukebox. It seemed one name was on everyone's lips—Luke Cross, a.k.a. Devereaux.

How Gage had announced finding his lost son had enthralled everybody. St. Benedict was abuzz over his college fling. The romantics painted Luke's mother as a lost love who had hidden the truth to save Gage from giving up his family empire. The realists talked about Gage's roving eye and the girl who had probably been nothing more than a one-night stand.

But Leslie had a sneaking suspicion that none of the stories were true because there was one factor no one had considered—Luke. He'd come to town already knowing he was Gage's son. All his questions about the Devereaux family and Gage meant Luke had done his homework.

"I'm gonna talk to Luke when I run into him again," a girl said while strutting by with a large drink in her hand.

"Yeah, me too," her friend added. "Imagine if one of us lands a Devereaux."

The comments reminded Leslie of when Beau had ruled the town. It was the main reason Dawn became obsessed with the biggest catch in St.

Benedict—he was a Devereaux.

"You're late," Sara said from her booth. "Kelly and I got here ages ago."

Leslie examined Kelly's pink cheeks as she drank a soda. She scooted into the booth beside her.

"Still can't believe it." Kelly pushed her drink aside. "Luke Cross is a Devereaux."

Sara pressed her lips together. "When we saw him with Mrs. Devereaux, he should've come over and said somethin'."

Carl pushed through the crowd to their table. His white apron had red stains and clung to his slight paunch. Flour brushed the top of his dark hair and along his cheek, but the mess didn't appear nearly as charming as it had on Luke.

"What can I get you girls?"

"Is Luke here?" Sara asked with a flirty grin.

Leslie wanted to slap her, but subtlety wasn't Sara's forte.

"He called this morning and quit. No notice. Nothing." Carl sliced his pen through the air. "He's working at the brewery now."

Sara rolled her eyes. "Well, his family owns the brewery."

"Everybody's talking about Luke." Carl sighed, sounding impatient. "Another Devereaux. Money sure changes people."

Kelly mimicked Sara's arrogant attitude and jutted out her chin. "That won't happen to Luke. He's a nice guy."

"I hope so. But I'm still a man short, so if you girls know of anyone looking for a job, send 'em to me." He tapped his pen against his pad. "Now, what'll it be?"

"Two large sausage, mushroom, and jalapeño pizzas," a smoky voice said behind Carl.

Leslie's heart skipped a beat as Luke stepped around Carl. She barely recognized him with his neatly trimmed hair and pressed dress shirt.

"Luke!" Sara's shout carried throughout the restaurant.

The chatter around them faded, leaving only the thump of the eighties tune coming from the jukebox. Heads turned, and then the whispering began.

Luke glanced around, nonchalantly taking in the attention. It was what Leslie would have expected from him. Gossip wasn't his thing, and those who spread it were not worth his time.

Several girls at the table across the aisle giggled, attracting his attention. He gave them one of his wicked grins and then turned back, rolling his eyes.

His reaction relieved Leslie. Despite the fancy clothes and new last name, he was still the same.

Luke held out his hand to Carl. "I hope there are no hard feelings. I would've stayed on, but Mr. Devereaux wants me at the brewery from now on."

Carl gripped his hand and shook it. "Not to worry. We'll manage. Just make sure you order lots of pies from me in the future." Carl headed back to the counter, maneuvering around several students cluttering the aisle.

Sara scooted deeper into the booth and patted the seat beside her. "Sit. Tell us every detail."

Luke eased his way into the booth, nodding to Kelly but avoiding Leslie's gaze.

Was he angry at her for calling her father to help him? Leslie twisted her hands underneath the table, analyzing the reason for his brush-off.

Sara tossed her hair over her shoulder and then cozied up next to him. "Why didn't you say somethin' before? We would have kept your secret safe."

Kelly coughed, almost choking on her soda. "Would we?"

Leslie recognized when Sara was marking her territory. She'd wanted Beau for his money and influence, and now another Devereaux was within her grasp.

Gage isn't gonna like this.

Luke moved away from Sara, putting some distance between them. "What was I supposed to do, blurt out that I'm his son as soon as I set foot in town? I was waiting for the right time. After the sheriff's men took me in, I didn't know who to call, and then I thought of him. I figured it was a test to see if he wanted me in his life."

Kelly pressed into the table. "Are you going to stay at their house?"

"Yes. It's a helluva lot better than the crappy place Carl rented me."

Sara pouted her black-painted lips. "I hope you don't think you're too good for us anymore."

He eased back in his seat. "I've only updated my address. Nothing else will change between us."

Leslie surveyed the people around them. The darting glances and tilted heads straining to eavesdrop unnerved her. Things had already changed.

"You're the new golden boy," Leslie said with a touch of sarcasm. "The town will treat you differently. Doors will open. People will act like your friend when they only want to benefit from your position or money, and you will learn to trust less and lie more."

The lines between Sara's brows deepened. "Jeez, Debbie Downer. You're gonna scare the guy right outta town."

Luke faced Leslie. "No, she's right. Mr. Devereaux warned me about the same thing. I gotta be careful from now on. I have an example to set, the family name to protect."

The way he eased his shoulders back and raised his head as he spoke alarmed Leslie. She knew firsthand how Gage's influence could become overwhelming. She would always be obligated to him and him to her. But Luke still had time to change his path, to avoid her regrets.

"Maybe you should leave," tumbled from her lips. "Refuse Gage's offer and get as far from this place as you can."

"What?" Sara screeched. "Are you crazy? Why would he give up all that money?"

Leslie felt as if every pair of eyes in the restaurant had zoomed in on her.

Luke lowered his head toward her. "Are you all right?"

"Ignore her." Sara nestled closer to Luke, demanding his attention. "Tell me you're not too good to join us at the river Friday night."

A red-faced Kelly squirmed in her seat. "You have to come. We're gonna summon Taylor to find out who killed her."

Leslie thought it weird how Kelly's interest in Luke seemed to wax and wane.

"Is that wise?" Luke arched an eyebrow, not seeming to share Kelly's exuberance. "The killer could still be out there."

"But everybody's going to the river," Kelly pleaded. "There'll be a lot of people there. No one would be stupid enough to try something then."

"That never stopped anyone before," Leslie muttered.

Sara kicked her under the table, and Leslie glowered at her.

Luke fidgeted as he retrieved something from the pocket of his dress pants. "I better go and protect you guys. I wouldn't want anything to happen to you." He tossed a phone on the table. "I need your numbers."

Sara squealed and snatched the phone.

Kelly pointed at the shiny new device while Sara keyed in her number. "When did you get that?"

"Today." Luke kept an eye on Sara as she texted her cell. "Mr. Devereaux gave it to me."

"You mean *Dad*," Sara teased with a malicious grin and handed the phone to Kelly.

Luke scratched his head, wincing. "Yeah, I'm not ready to call him that yet."

Kelly finished typing in her number and gave the cell to Leslie. "So it's settled. We'll meet here Friday night and head to the river." She looked around. "I wonder where our food is."

Leslie examined Kelly's face, amazed at her quick recovery. "You feel like eating?"

Kelly's eyes sparkled beneath the fluorescent lights. "I'm starving."

Sara set her finger under Luke's chin and turned his head to her. "Let's take your car to the river. You can protect us, and I get to ride in Pearl."

The intimate gesture perturbed Leslie. It seemed Sara had stepped up her game now that Luke was a Devereaux. She toyed with the idea of refusing the ride, but the way Luke's gaze hovered over Sara's big boobs changed her mind. Leslie prayed he wasn't stupid enough to fall for Sara's bullshit.

Chapter Twenty-Seven

Leslie climbed the stairs to the second floor of her home and slowly approached Dawn's bedroom door. She'd stayed away, afraid to relive the pain from that night, but Leslie wanted insight into her sister's inexplicable behavior. If she were lucky, sitting on Dawn's bed and staring at her pink wall collage of inspirational quotes and puppies might help abolish the never-ending numbness in her heart.

That was her constant—the vast black void. It guided her through the day and seemed to expand at night, blocking her childhood memories—the ones where she and Dawn had been friends. They were inseparable then, connected by something more than blood.

Leslie's hand shook as she reached for the door. She bit her lower lip and turned the knob, not knowing what to expect. When she flipped on the light, a warm yellow haze blanketed Dawn's pink stuffed animals and perfectly made princess bed. There were no ghosts, flashing lights, or recreation of a scene from *Poltergeist* with stuffed animals circling the room. Everything was just as she'd left it because no one dared to box her things and send them away. Leslie took a tentative step, her legs dragging as if weighted down by shackles.

With grief, everything was an effort, every movement a marathon, and every intake of breath an icy chill that hurt her throat. But she didn't dare complain. Who would understand? Half her heart had been ripped out and stomped on by Beau Devereaux, and no matter how much satisfaction Leslie took in his demise, it never lessened her constant ache. She would never be whole again. That was the hardest part of her foggy existence. How did she push through every day with only half of her left? Leslie ached to hug her sister again. Those misspent conversations saturated with anger were her greatest regret.

She cast her gaze to the frilly bed, dumbfounded by how different they had been. Dawn's affinity for pink still made her shake her head. Leslie wanted to crawl into the bed and smell her sister's chamomile shampoo. The one she swore made her hair super shiny. It didn't, but Leslie never had the heart to tell Dawn that her shampoo was overpriced bullshit. It was just another example of how she tried to protect her sister. Now, Leslie wished she'd told Dawn everything on her mind. Maybe then, she might still be alive.

Her stomach clenched when she spotted the silver-framed picture of Beau on Dawn's dresser. His chiseled features, sun-kissed hair, and bulging biceps had blinded her sister. Leslie should have fought harder to make Dawn see the psychopath lurking behind the sexy gray eyes. Another one of the mountain of regrets that kept Leslie up at night. She had waited for Dawn to see reason, but her awakening had come too late.

She flopped on the bed, wishing she could disappear. Leslie spent hours fantasizing about falling into a black hole and never returning. It would hurt less that way, and maybe she might find some peace.

The concept sucked the last ounce of air from her lungs. Was Dawn at peace?

Her fingertips caressed the silky bedspread Dawn had Shelley order when given carte blanche to redecorate her room. It was her fourteenth birthday present and a chance to allow the girls to express their individual personalities. Leslie had opted for muted tones, reflecting her growing rebellious nature, and insisted a brass day bed would make her appear smarter. Dawn had opted to unleash her inner princess.

"Are you for real?" Leslie had said the day Shelley put the finishing touches on Dawn's room. "It looks like a tampon box exploded."

Dawn had stuck out her tongue. "At least my room doesn't look like a library." She caressed her newly made pink bed. "How boring is that?"

Leslie had taken a running start and launched herself onto Dawn's bed, eager to make a big dent in her pink sheets.

Dawn had howled and tried to pull her off, but Leslie only managed to tug her sister onto the bed.

They lay like that, staring at the pink canopy and listening to their mother and father's laughter in the hall.

Dawn sighed. "When I marry, the entire church will be covered in pink silk."

Leslie propped herself on her elbows. "That's a terrifying image."

"Like you've never pictured your wedding. I bet you never want to get married."

"Maybe, eventually, but there are so many things I want to do before I get tied down. And kids?" Leslie made a sour face. "I think I'd rather repeat the eighth grade than have kids."

Dawn sat up and crossed her legs, no longer enamored with her fancy new bedspread. "How can you say that? My children will need cousins to play with. We're supposed to raise our kids together. You promised."

Leslie arched away. "When did I promise that?"

"When we were six." Dawn held up her index finger, showing Leslie the tip. "Remember, we pricked our fingers and said we would never be apart. The twin oath, you called it."

Leslie lifted her finger and could barely make out the tiny scar left from where Dawn had jabbed her with one of Mother's sewing needles. She climbed from the bed, a cold wash of fear overtaking her. Marriage and children meant leaving home, leaving her father, and spending time away from her sister. That's what happened when people grew up. They grew apart.

"You're being silly," Leslie had insisted. "When you marry your prince charming, you won't want me hanging around. You'll see."

"You can live next door." Dawn jumped from the bed, landing in front of Leslie. "That way, we can always be together."

Leslie hoped that happened. Dawn needed her. Leslie had vowed to take care of her no matter what.

But she never got the chance to tell Dawn that. Her father had crashed through Dawn's door and taken them both to the floor for one of his famous tickling sessions. Leslie had been happy at that moment, and the future was a bright place filled with pink silk weddings and side-by-side homes.

Her sister's empty bedroom replaced the happy images. Tears clouded her vision, and she wiped them away, wishing the lump in her throat would dissolve.

Leslie hated remembering. It made her weak, but lately, it was all she seemed to do. She was the strong sister and fought to keep her emotions from everyone, but sometimes the bite of sorrow would overwhelm and dissolve her control.

Then the glint of the silver frame on the dresser distracted her. There he was—the asshole.

Leslie climbed from the bed and charged the dresser, wanting to fling Beau's picture across the room. Her extended hand touched the tip of the frame and then remembered how much the photo meant to Dawn. This was her room, her sanctuary, and no matter how much Leslie wanted to take a razor to Beau's smirking face, she didn't have the heart. It wasn't her place.

Instead, she tipped the frame, letting it smack against the wooden dresser, hiding Beau's mug. But instead of settling, the frame bounced and toppled to the floor.

"Shit! Figures."

Leslie sighed and stooped to retrieve the picture. Something tucked away beneath the dresser caught her eye. She squinted at an object shoved under the thick mahogany furniture. Leslie got on her knees and stuck her head closer to the gap between the dresser's base and the floor. She reached into the dark space and worked the item forward, scooting it along the carpet.

A book with gilded edges and a pink cover containing glitter slid out. *Diary* was spelled out in gold across the front. Leslie sat back, staring at the small book complete with a combination lock.

"Since when did you keep a diary?"

That Dawn had put pen to paper shocked her. Her twin equated writing English essays to medieval torture.

Leslie caressed the surface of the journal, afraid to look inside. Leslie couldn't cope if all she had left of her twin were angry passages about their last months together.

But it wasn't all bad. Remember?

Images of the time spent in their cramped bedroom at the lake filled her head. Dawn had been different, then. They had found some common ground, bonded as sisters, and even laughed as friends.

Leslie had returned home hoping she'd gotten through to Dawn and that Beau's influence had faded.

The diary called to her. The secrets locked away could comfort and help her understand those last days. Why Dawn had pretended to be her still ate at Leslie, leaving a hole in the center of her being that she feared might never go away.

Her courage returning, Leslie tapped the combination lock, wondering what three numbers her sister would have favored to protect her thoughts. It couldn't be complicated, considering Dawn forgot her locker combination more than a dozen times.

Leslie closed her eyes, struggling to recall any mention of favorite numbers or a series Dawn had remained partial to.

She tried their birthday—May 7th. Nope.

Leslie put in their mother's birthday, followed by their father's. The lock remained secure.

Then the frame on the floor stoked a memory. Leslie stood outside the school, watching Coach Brewer trotting toward the football field for after-school practice, a player at his side. The coach patted the player's shoulder and smiled. The number four on the back of the jersey sent a shudder through her.

Beau's number.

Leslie rotated the wheels until they read four, four, four. She tried the lock, and the click of the clasp sent her heart racing.

Her mouth went dry. There might be entries she shouldn't read. Then again, the journal might contain the answers she desperately needed.

Her fingers trembled as she opened the book.

Not ready to read it all, she flipped through the pages looking for the last entry.

A picture tumbled out. It was from the St. Benedict High Spring Dance. Dawn, swathed in pink, wore her hair up with their mother's pearl necklace dangling from her slender neck. Leslie remembered the fight she had that night with her mother about why Dawn got to wear the treasured keepsake. A corsage of pink roses added to Dawn's radiant smile. Everything seemed perfect. In a black suit and tie, Beau's malicious grin reached out to Leslie, adding to the sinking feeling in her stomach. She always suspected evil lived inside of Beau, but he kept the depth of his depravity and cruelty well-hidden.

She returned the picture to the journal, making a note to cut Beau out of the photo. He didn't deserve to be among Dawn's possessions.

Leslie discovered a rose Beau had given her sister pressed between the pages. There were articles about Beau's winning football games clipped from the *St. Benedict Herald*.

She turned to the last entry, and her breath hitched. It was dated the day before Dawn died.

> *October 30th—Zoe told me she thinks Beau overheard her talking to Leslie about meeting Derek at the cells before the Halloween party at the river. He even knows what she's wearing and that she's bringing champagne. He has something planned for her. Something bad. I just know it. I have to make this right. I have to go in her place. Leelee always tried to tell me what a monster Beau is, and I didn't want to listen. Now whatever he's planning is all my fault. I should have gotten away from him months ago.*
>
> *I brought the monster into our lives. It's me who needs to pay in my sister's place—whatever the price.*
>
> *He avoided Taylor and Kelly after he raped them. I just have to fight him and pretend it's my first time. I know he wants Leelee's virginity. Maybe after he thinks he gets it, he'll leave her be. I've done it before. I can do it again.*
>
> *I can't tell Leelee any of this. She'll try and stop me, but I have a plan to get away and keep her at the house to make sure she's safe. It's my turn to protect my sister. After Halloween, we'll both be free of Beau Devereaux forever.*

Leslie curled up on her side, clutching the diary to her chest. Her sobs filled the bedroom, and then she turned her face to the carpet, not wanting her parents to hear her.

If only Dawn had told her, her sister would still be alive, and Beau would be ...

Where would Beau be? Enjoying the same privilege he'd reveled in before raping Taylor and Kelly? Gage wouldn't have gotten rid of his son over that.

Leslie considered how Gage remained a master of his emotions no matter how trying the situation. Hell, the man never shed a tear for his son. Maybe it was time to follow his example and stop letting her feelings guide her. The more in control she remained, the greater her advantage. It was clear the grip of the Devereaux's had to end. Leslie's growing certainty about her future blunted the sharp edge of her grief. She would turn the tables on Gage and carve out a new purpose. From now on, Leslie Moore wouldn't try to destroy the Devereaux dynasty—she would control it.

Chapter Twenty-Eight

Branches of red buckeye bushes scratched the window next to Leslie. She relaxed her grip on her seat belt, grateful to finally arrive at the river. Sara had beguiled Luke on the ride over from The Bogue, stroking his thigh and running her fingers through his hair. Leslie couldn't wait to bolt from the Mustang.

The number of cars in the parking lot surprised her. The area had just been the site of a crime scene, but that was of little consequence to the students of St. Benedict High. On Friday nights, only the party mattered.

Luke parked Pearl close to the entrance. He'd just turned off the engine when a blue pickup slid in next to them.

"Is that …?" Kelly peered out the window.

Leslie scoured the familiar dents in the old truck, and her stomach knotted into a tight ball.

You have got to be kidding me.

After squirming her way out of the back seat, Leslie stepped out onto the shell-covered lot and heard a lively beat. The festivities were in full swing. Dancing light from a blazing bonfire filtered through the brush along the path.

Derek got out of the truck, still dressed in the slacks and long-sleeved shirt he wore to his after-school job. He stopped in front of her, his cheeks flushed. "What are you doing here?"

Leslie's frustration skyrocketed and she folded her arms, trying to contain her irritation. "I could ask you the same thing. Are you following me again?"

Derek glared at Luke before he spoke. "I heard about who he is, and it scared the hell out of me. It should scare you, too."

His comment disappointed her. "He's not a killer." She instantly regretted her words. *Idiot!*

Derek closed the distance between them with one long stride. "I never said he was. What are you talking about?"

Panic constricted Leslie's chest. She took two steps back, bumping into Luke's car. Derek had always been able to read her, know her thoughts before she shared them. If she interacted with him, no matter how infrequently, she risked letting her horrid story slip.

Sara leaned against the Mustang's door and smirked at Derek. "Well, well, just like old times."

"But it's not, is it?" Derek gestured to the path leading to the beach. "None of you should be here. It isn't safe."

Kelly hurried from the back seat and hooked her arm around Sara. "We want to make things right for Taylor. We're going to The Abbey for a séance."

Leslie closed her eyes, wishing Kelly hadn't said that. Derek would be impossible now.

"What about Beau?" Luke asked, walking around his car. "Doesn't he deserve to have his murder solved?"

Derek balled his fist. "That son of a bitch got what he deserved. So if I were you, I'd watch my back."

Luke slipped his keys and phone into his jeans pocket. "Is that a threat?"

Derek stuck out his chest as he stood before Luke. "Just a friendly warning."

Luke arched his back, looking like a predator about to close in for the kill. His eyes flickered, and his fingers twitched. The Luke she knew didn't have a temper. It was as if the affable guy had turned into a stranger.

Just like Beau.

She couldn't let Derek fight another Devereaux—Beau had bested him too many times—and Leslie wasn't about to let history repeat itself. She was about to step between the two when Sara held her back.

"Not yet," Sara whispered. "It's about to get good."

Disgusted, Leslie shirked off Sara's grip and stepped toward Luke.

Looking into Leslie's eyes, Luke softened and offered Derek a strained smile.

The gesture should have reassured her. He'd regained control. Still, his metamorphosis into something all too familiar frightened her.

A mellowed Luke faced Kelly and Sara. "We should leave them to talk."

Sara slipped her arm around Luke's waist. "Ah, yeah. Let's go and check out the party before we start the séance.

Kelly watched Sara and Luke walk away before she glowered at Leslie. "You better not leave me alone with them," she muttered before joining the couple.

Sara was almost to the path leading to the beach when she called out, "Hurry up. The spirits won't wait forever."

Leslie held her breath as the three disappeared behind the brush, leaving her and Derek alone. The music echoed across the empty parking lot, and then her uncertainty returned. It was as if a vast chasm had opened between them, and she'd never be able to broach the distance.

"What is wrong with you?" She struggled to keep her voice down. "You practically challenged the guy to a fight."

"I'm sorry. But when I found out who he is, I couldn't leave you alone with him. I'm afraid for you." Derek leaned against the Mustang's trunk, hanging his head. "What else was I supposed to do? You've completely shut me out."

She longed to run from the parking lot, especially knowing it was where Taylor had died. "I can't do this here. I've got to go."

He stepped in front of her, blocking her escape. "I'm going with you."

"You can follow us if you want," she brusquely told him. "I won't stop you."

Derek moved to her side. "You can act like you don't care, but I know you do. We need to figure things out. We can't go on like this."

She was about to tell him to leave when the temperature plunged, and she started shivering. Leslie studied the dark edges surrounding the lot, hoping to find an explanation for the sudden change. She didn't like this.

Derek took advantage of her distraction and drew closer. "Tell me one thing. Do you still love me?"

His words brushed away weeks of fog clouding Leslie's judgment. After Dawn's death, and her deal with the devil, every thought was an avalanche of misgivings, or a reminder of what was at stake. Would he still feel the same if he knew the truth?

"You don't want me. I'm not the girl I was." Her secret burned like fire, but she didn't give in to the raging battle between her heart and her head. Leslie sucked in a painful breath, ready to walk away.

Behind Derek, traces of moonlight landed on a shimmering figure moving through the trees. It wore a white cloak that bent and twisted as if caught in an ethereal breeze. The fabric outlined a feminine shape with a hood pulled low over her head, casting her face in shadows. She hovered silently above the ground, the hem of her garment leaving the twigs beneath her undisturbed. Her eerie glow didn't disappear as she moved beneath branches and almost seemed to pass through trees. The apparition reached the edge of the lot where the white shells met a blanket of brown pine needles. She paused, and a beam of moonlight landed on her cloak. The cloth pulsated, its vibrant shine intensifying.

Leslie's mouth opened in a silent scream. The terror cementing her feet crept up her legs.

"Leslie?"

Derek sounded far away. She registered his touch, but instead of warmth, there was only ice.

Derek gripped her arms. "What's wrong?"

Leslie tried to point, to give him some warning, but her body would not follow her commands. Her heart chugged like a runaway locomotive as she gaped at the undulating specter. Soon, black spots appeared before her eyes.

Is this how death feels?

The ghost, gleaming against the darkened woods, tilted her head ever so slightly, enough to dislodge the folds of her hood. The covering fell to her shoulders, revealing a woman's face. Her skin, translucent and glistening, highlighted her full, ashen lips. Strands of pale hair cascaded around her face before settling against her sharply cut cheekbones. Then she raised her head and stared directly at Leslie.

Her captivating eyes held a bitter sadness in their depths. Leslie became transfixed, but then a shadowy figure, small and diminutive, peeked out from behind the woman's shimmering cloak. It reminded Leslie of a child hiding amid her mother's skirts, but then baggy clothes and the thin face of an adult emerged from the murky darkness.

The slender figure shifted and changed, moving out from the cover of the billowing apparition. The features of the slight spirit became clearer, and Leslie spotted strands of brown hair and eyes brimming with sorrow. An icy rush overtook her as she recognized the features of the frightened girl who had once looked at her with the same lost gaze.

Taylor.

Leslie wanted to run to her friend and demand to know what had happened, but then Taylor's aura dimmed, and her outline quickly blended into the black woods behind her. In an instant, she had vanished, and Leslie's renewed sense of loss siphoned the strength from her wobbly legs.

No. No. No.

Leslie took a step toward the ghostly image of the woman, wanting to know where her friend had gone. Her pale lips parted, and a breathy voice filled the parking lot, drowning out all other noise.

"*Leave here.*"

The scream Leslie had been holding in rose upward, building steam as it shot from her lips. She trembled as her gaze stayed locked on the lady in white.

Derek spun around and froze when he spotted the otherworldly figure at the edge of the lot.

Time stood still as Leslie waited for Derek to move or shout while the phantom floated a short distance away. The music and laughter coming from the beach was all around them, but the noise gave Leslie little comfort. She was too frightened to run.

A long, eerie howl came from the woods, drowning out the sounds of the party.

Leslie's knees finally buckled, but Derek caught her before she fell. Picking her up, he held her tight against his chest and headed for the beach.

Derek's heart pounded through his shirt as she clung to him. Leslie feared what might be following them to the beach, but before Derek reached the path, she found her courage and peeked behind them.

Nothing was there—only cars and tall trees swaying in the breeze.

The moment Derek staggered down the path, the music stopped, and everyone grew ominously quiet.

Luke was the first to meet them as Derek struggled to stay upright with Leslie in his arms.

"What is it? What's wrong?" Luke demanded.

Others gathered around, wearing the same slack-jawed expressions.

"We saw something in the parking lot," was all Derek offered.

Someone touched Leslie's shoulder. Sara was there with Kelly. Their pallid faces reminded her of the ghostly vision.

Derek lowered her feet to the sand. Many of the partygoers quickly gathered up their things and doused the bonfires.

"They heard the howling," Kelly explained. "Everyone's scared."

Leslie choked back the vile taste in her mouth. She was grateful for Derek's support as he held on to her waist.

Sara eased closer, a curious twinkle in her eyes. "What did you see?"

"The lady in white," Leslie managed to get out through trembling lips. "And Taylor," she said only loud enough for Sara to hear.

Sara grabbed Luke's arm, pulling him toward the path. "We need to leave."

Her reaction surprised Leslie. What kind of medium wants to run away when spirits appear? She gripped Sara's wrist. "You said you could contact her." She pointed at the path, heading toward the parking lot. "So go contact her."

Sara shook off her hand. "No. I can't."

"I don't get it. If you're the one who talks to the dead, then why did I see her?" Leslie's eyebrows drew together.

Sara backed away. "I don't know. She shouldn't be here at all. She shouldn't have come back, and ..." Her words evaporated.

Leslie's instincts sparked to life. This wasn't Sara's usual bravado. She was terrified. She got in Sara's face. "You know something. What is it?"

"Back off." Luke put his arm in front of Sara. "You need to settle down."

Luke's protective gesture disappointed her. Were he and Sara already a couple? When had that happened?

"Let's get out of here," Derek murmured, coaxing her back toward the path.

Leslie held her ground, refusing to return to the parking lot. Then she saw students with dour faces going around her and Derek.

"It will be all right." Derek encouraged her forward. "Everyone's leaving. The parking lot will be filled with people and cars and noise. She won't be there."

"You did see her, didn't you? Taylor?"

Derek's eyebrows shot up. "No. I only saw the lady in white."

Leslie wrung her hands, wondering if she imagined her friend. "Did you hear her speak?"

He shook his head. "What did she say?"

That revelation deflated her confidence. "'Leave here.'"

Derek urged Leslie up the path. "I don't get it. Why didn't I hear her?" He pulled her close as they trudged up the incline.

"Maybe the lady in white wanted to warn me. She spoke, and then the dog howled. You know what that means."

They arrived at the parking lot to a cacophony of revving engines and screeching tires.

Leslie slowly turned toward the spot where she'd seen the ghostly figures. Nothing. Just trees and darkness. "I think she was giving me a message."

Derek waited by her side. "Which is what?"

She took his hand. "Someone else is going to die."

CHAPTER TWENTY-NINE

Gage sat behind his desk, irritation gnawing at his insides. The single lamp cast distorted shadows across the ash paneling while he listened to the groans and creaks of the old plantation home, waiting for the rumble of the Mustang's return.

Kent had tracked Luke's phone to the river, and Gage feared people would talk if he spent too much time there. He'd ignored the stories about Beau, but he wouldn't make the same mistake twice. He would squash any hints of trouble with Luke.

His father had lived by a strict code of conduct and taught Gage the rules. He ignored Edward's advice for years until he discovered the beast of which his old man had warned—the Devereaux curse.

Gage had laughed when he first heard the term, but he'd learned the hard way that *curse* was indeed an accurate way to describe the repercussions.

When Gage had returned home from Boston, he'd followed his father's instructions to the letter. He finished college at Tulane, worked hard at the brewery, and married the girl his father had chosen.

Then, Beau came along and inherited the same curse.

A muffled throaty roar disturbed the stillness in his office. The sound brought back memories of his youth, when the car had meant everything to him. Well, almost everything—Carol had meant more.

With his elbows on the desk, Gage tented his fingers and waited. He heard the slight thump of the mudroom door closing. The gentle creak of the peacock doors, and then the groan of footfalls across the hardwood.

The steps led right to the open office door. Luke moved into the light of the desk lamp, carrying his loafers. A classic mistake. Shoes never gave anyone away in the old home. Their weight on the floorboards did. He would probably master the right places to step to avoid detection, just like Beau had.

Luke stumbled backward when he spotted Gage. "You're up."

"How was the river?"

Luke eased inside. "How did you know?"

Gage coyly raised one side of his mouth. "Experience."

Luke eased closer to the leather chairs in front of the desk. "Is that a problem?"

Gage shifted forward, summoning his patience. "You're my son. You're free to come and go as you like, but there are some places you shouldn't go. The river is at the top of that list."

"Is that because of everything that's happened there?"

Gage's frustrated sigh fluttered a few papers on his desk. "It's a bad place. Please don't go there again."

Luke sat in the burgundy leather chair across the desk from Gage. "Is this where you're going to go over the house rules? Tell me what I can and can't do as your son?"

The sand on Luke's brown loafers fell onto the leather seat. An ugly memory of his father, haggard with sand trickling from his dark suit, crossed Gage's mind.

Gage refocused his attention on Luke. "People in St. Benedict have certain expectations of us. They want to be helped, supported—led. To do that, we must keep them at arm's length. You can't conduct business, hold town council meetings, and hire and fire friends. You can only form deeper relationships with the people you can trust—which is your family."

"You mean you." Luke pointed at the ceiling. "Not your wife."

"Your stepmother," Gage corrected.

Luke cocked his head and grimaced. "I'm pretty sure she doesn't want me calling her that."

Luke had a touch of Beau's insolence, which would have to be dealt with quickly. "I know there'll be trying weeks ahead. You're living under a new roof with new rules and expectations. But I encourage you to think before you act. Use self-control in all things. When dealing with people, remember that you're a Devereaux. You can't get angry, lose your temper, or waste your time at the river."

Luke's chuckle circled the room. "Oh, I'm a master of self-control. I've learned how to keep it all inside over the years. I was patient with ignorant people who asked why my grandparents had to raise me. I discovered how to ignore the inquiries about my mother, the quips about not having a father, and learned how to survive without asking anyone for help. I've kissed ass to snobs, put up with finger-pointing and whispering, and all the while I held my head high, knowing one day I'd show them. I'm good at hiding who I am from people. I've been doing it all my life."

Gage picked up on his disgruntled tone. Luke appeared to have a short fuse simmering below the surface. "That's all behind you now." Gage went around to the front of the desk. "This is where you're meant to be."

Luke stood. "As long as you don't try and make me like you, we'll be fine."

"What's wrong with being like me?" Gage crossed his arms.

Luke moved in front of him. They were the same height, the same build, and he even had Edward Devereaux's slight dimple in his chin.

"I'm not you." Luke offered him a wry smile.

"I don't want you to be me," Gage countered with a hint of assertiveness. "I want you to be a Devereaux." He motioned to the door. "We've got an early start tomorrow at the brewery. I want you to begin prepping for the campaign launch party I'm hosting in two weeks. I plan to announce you as my heir, so practice your public speaking. You'll be doing a lot of it as a Devereaux."

The impertinent glint in Luke's eyes let Gage know the discussion was far from over.

After Luke closed the office door behind him, Gage returned to his desk, his mind a sea of troubles.

This better not turn into another colossal fuckup.

CHAPTER THIRTY

Elizabeth's darkly tinted glasses did little to reduce the glaring rays streaming through the windshield. The two cups of black coffee and four aspirin she'd downed earlier had hardly touched her splitting headache. A few months ago, she could have written off the pain to the booze, but that wasn't why she felt like hell. She still wasn't pregnant. The appearance of her period made that abundantly clear.

The brewery road curved to the right, putting the sun directly in her face. She groaned and slapped the visor down. Elizabeth turned into the parking lot outside the administration building. There were dozens of cars and no place to park. *Damn.*

Why Gage wanted to use the brewery's large meeting room for Benedict Beer's national debut party was beyond her. She'd suggested an upper-end restaurant in town, but as usual, he'd shot her down. Gage considered the brewery his business, not hers. Her only job was to play the dutiful wife and stand by his side.

Elizabeth left her Mercedes across the street, outside the delivery center, next to a green Benedict Beer delivery truck. She walked across the parking lot.

I hate this place.

Gage had insisted they live in the wasteland of St. Benedict—something Elizabeth regretted every single day. She'd learned to make do with the inferior shops and lack of social events, but it was the people to whom she'd never warmed. Their small-town minds and limited education drove her insane. When she had her baby, she'd insist on moving back to New Orleans. Anything to get out of St. Benedict.

At the main door to the administration building, Elizabeth removed her sunglasses and breathed in the chilly air, reviving herself.

God, give me strength.

Elizabeth slogged along a hall cluttered with posters of Benedict Beer. The murmur of conversation peppered with laughter wafted her way. She stopped at the open door to the meeting room, and the harsh fluorescent lights ramped up her headache.

She quickly assessed the crowd. Employees had gathered with their families, and the few city council members present were all devoted to Gage. The consummate businessman had kept anyone with a dissenting opinion far away from the press.

Elizabeth found Gage at a buffet table filled with processed foods and an array of soft drink bottles. There wasn't a fruit or vegetable tray in sight.

Typical.

He gave her his usual disdainful nod—the one she got whenever he was displeased. A lecture was sure to follow. Gage would let her know just how disappointed he was that she was late.

Luke stood next to him, smiling and chatting with a few employees still clad in their green overalls—standard uniform for everyone working in the processing plant.

Gage smiled at his staff and shook their hands as he worked his way around the room. His pleasant countenance disappeared when he stepped in front of Elizabeth. "You're late." His voice was dark and dismal—classic Gage.

"I wasn't feeling well this morning, so it took me longer to get ready."

He looked her up and down. "What's wrong with you?"

She raised her head, holding in her emotions. "I got my period."

There was a brief hint of disappointment in his eyes, and then it was gone. "We've only been trying for a little over two months. Give it time."

His words were meant to offer some consolation but felt derogatory, like everything else he said to her.

He took her arm and led her deeper into the room. "You're to stand next to Luke and me when I announce the expansion. We need to put on a united family front for the employees and the press."

Elizabeth wanted to laugh, but decided against it.

"Go around the room and thank people for coming." He put his lips to hers, feigning a kiss, and whispered, "Do your job."

He let her go and briskly walked away, heading back to his son.

The disregard she'd dealt with for years twisted her gut. Elizabeth had tried to love Gage in the beginning, but after Beau attacked her, she'd pulled away. Why did she stay?

Humiliation was a strong deterrent. But years of hiding from Beau and his tantrums, putting up with Gage's mistresses, and enduring the spiteful gazes of everybody in town had broken her. She just wanted another baby and to be left alone.

"Elizabeth." John Moore offered her a friendly peck on the cheek.

"John. So glad you could come."

He slipped in next to her while browsing the crowded room. "Gage asked me to, and as his lawyer and part of the team who made this national debut possible, how could I refuse?"

She politely chuckled, as did he. "Did anyone come with you?"

He motioned to a pale, slender young woman who chatted with a tall redhead—both girls she instantly recognized.

"You brought Leslie. How sweet."

"Yes, she came with her friends to support Luke."

Elizabeth eyed the redhead and noticed how her gaze frequently went to Luke. "Is that Kelly Norton?"

John nodded. "Yes, she and Leslie have become quite close."

Elizabeth peeked behind John. "Is Shelley here?"

He dropped his head. "No. She's still not feeling well."

Elizabeth wanted to offer encouragement, but remembered she was in mourning, too. Her grief wasn't Shelley's. Had Beau been normal, maybe she would've been as incapacitated as the Moore family.

"Luke is impressive." John directed his attention to the young man and Gage as they approached a podium in the corner. "I sat in on a meeting with him yesterday, and he was quite well-versed on the business. Gage seems pleased."

"Gage is happy to have Luke on board." She watched her stepson adjust his tie, appearing nervous. "He has another chance to be a father."

Gage nodded to her, and she acknowledged him with a sarcastic smile.

"If you will excuse me, John. My husband needs me." She headed toward the podium. Gage had always warned her to say little to the family attorney, especially when Beau was alive.

With an impatient frown, Gage pointed behind him.

She dutifully stepped in the back. The two tall men dwarfed her, so no one would even notice she was there. It was just how Gage liked his women—compliant and out of the way.

"Ladies and gentlemen," her husband began.

The murmuring around the room quieted. Everyone turned toward the podium.

Gage flexed his shoulders. "Thank you for coming out on this beautiful Saturday and sharing in Benedict Brewery's success."

Flashes from a camera temporarily blinded Elizabeth. To spare herself a resurgence of her headache, she dropped her eyes.

She studied the curve of the men's butts, surprised at how similar they were. Elizabeth wondered if Luke's would feel like Gage's.

"The early numbers are in for Benedict Beer's first foray onto the national scene," Gage announced. "And we've surpassed all the projections. Offers are pouring in from national chain stores to put Benedict Beer on their shelves."

Loud cheers added to her misery. Elizabeth applauded, just not as enthusiastically as the others.

"I want to thank each one of you for your efforts. This is our brewery, our business, our future. We all make Benedict Brewery what it is, and I'm grateful to be a part of our wonderful family."

Another round of exuberant applause carried throughout the room, but Elizabeth didn't join in. Gage's words were just an act. The brewery belonged to the Devereaux family and no one else. Those listening knew it, too.

"This is great news for the brewery, and I have decided to step up our expansion plans." Gage put his arm around Luke. "My son, Luke, will be working closely with me in overseeing our efforts. He'll be learning the ropes. I count on all of you to show him how we do things at Benedict Brewery."

The camera flashed again, and Elizabeth closed her eyes.

"We've all been through a great deal over the past few months, myself and my wife included." He glanced back at her.

Elizabeth jumped into position and put on her best fake smile. She wasn't surprised he used their grief to garner the backing of his employees. He was like a politician, milking the public for the sympathy vote.

He's just like his father.

She gritted her teeth when another bright flare of light went off in her face.

"We will persevere and get through difficult times together." Gage motioned to a wall behind the podium. A green drape with 'Benedict Brewery' across it hung from the support beam above.

"Without further ado, I want to show you what we have planned for our brewery." Gage handed Luke a gold cord attached to the drape and nodded.

Elizabeth watched the interaction, amazed by the likeness of their profiles. They shared the same rugged good looks, thick hair, square jaws, and straight noses. They were a magnetic team, sure to attract a lot of attention on the national stage.

Luke tugged the cord, and the green drape slid aside.

Oohs and *ahs* filled the room.

Elizabeth stared in wonder at a map of the brewery that took up almost the entire wall. Their plantation home was at the top, with new buildings added in several places currently occupied by green space. The administration building was four stories instead of two, and the processing plant had doubled in size. Alongside the delivery center were fifty Benedict Brewery trucks replacing the two dozen in current use.

While her husband pointed out features to the audience, she went to straighten Luke's crooked tie. "You've made quite the impression."

"I'm just following orders," he mumbled.

Gage smiled and patted Luke on the back.

Elizabeth noted how Luke's stare seemed to burn into Gage. She wasn't the only one annoyed by the dog and pony show. They might have more in common than she'd initially surmised.

Gage kept his arm around Luke as the photographer snapped more pictures, and Elizabeth took the opportunity to slip away. She'd only moved a few feet when someone touched her arm.

Gage stood behind her, scowling. "Where are you going? We have more press photos to take."

"You don't need me. You have Luke." She removed his hand.

"And it's your duty to support him. You're my wife."

She wanted to balk at his definition of wife. "No one will notice me. They never do."

"Whose fault is that?"

Elizabeth held her head high. "You never could stand anyone stealing your thunder."

A buxom blonde dressed in black rushed toward the podium. She tossed her arms around Luke's neck.

"You were fantastic," she shouted.

Elizabeth's anger stirred. "Who's that girl with Luke?"

Gage's irritated hiss took her by surprise. "Sara Bissell. Her father works for me."

Elizabeth chuckled. "Since when do you know the names of your employees' children?"

He kept his focus glued on Sara as she clung to Luke. "She was a friend of Beau's. You would've met her if you'd gone to Dawn Moore's funeral like I asked."

Elizabeth shook off his rebuke, remembering what Gage had told her about Beau's female *friends*—the ones whose silence he'd paid for.

Sara's loud giggling ignited her ire. "You'd better keep your eye on Luke around that one. We don't need another Beau on our hands."

Gage grumbled something she couldn't hear and headed straight for the podium.

Her duty complete, Elizabeth navigated her way through the room. She was about to make her escape when Kelly eased in front of her, barring her way.

"Mrs. Devereaux, I was wondering if we could talk."

The request was odd. Elizabeth had never exchanged more than a few words with Kelly.

"Of course." She offered the girl a concerned smile, hoping to put her at ease.

"Not here. Not with my mom around." Tears welled in Kelly's eyes. "Can we go outside?"

Intrigued, Elizabeth nodded. "What's this about?"

Kelly wiped her cheek. "It's about Beau. There's something you should know."

Chapter Thirty-One

Gage sat at his office desk, peering over the rim of his glass at Luke. He'd expected the young man to be nervous at the presentation, but he wasn't. It said a lot about his character and ability to handle the brewery one day.

Luke slipped his tie from around his neck. "I never liked these things."

"Neither do I." Gage put his scotch down on the desk and poured one for Luke. "I only wear them when absolutely necessary."

Luke grabbed his drink. "Are functions like that the norm around here?"

"I like to make the employees feel special. We have several parties throughout the year, which you will be required to attend."

"Everyone was very nice today," Luke said. "I thought I'd get a chilly reception."

Gage opened a drawer. "We have some families who've worked here for three generations. They want to make sure the brewery continues." He removed a credit card and a set of car keys and tossed them on the desk. "These are for you. You can buy whatever you need from now on. Just don't go crazy."

Luke touched the keys, and the blue and white BMW logo glistened in the light.

"It's a lease." Gage shut the drawer. "You can avoid putting too many miles on your Mustang."

"This is very generous, considering I'm practically a stranger."

"You're not a stranger." Gage sipped his drink. The bite of the scotch felt good. "You're a Devereaux."

Luke sat back, studying Gage. "Most people would have me checked out before accepting me into their family."

Gage swirled the last of his scotch. "I'm not most people, but I did check you out."

Luke stiffened. "And?"

Gage set his glass aside. "Who was the older woman? I got the impression she took care of you, financially."

Luke lowered his head and smiled. "She did, for a while. Megan Sloan was her name. Widowed and part of a wealthy, well-connected family, she wasn't like the other rich snobs she hung out with. She was fun."

Gage liked the way he spoke with affection for the woman. "How did you meet her?"

Luke looked him squarely in the eye. "Her car broke down, and I stopped to help. We chatted and hit it off. I never set out to get involved with an older woman—it just happened. I liked her, but she had a drug problem, sort of like my mother. Drugs killed her in the end."

"What do you have going with Sara Bissell?" Gage analyzed Luke's reaction. "I saw her flirting with you at the party."

Luke squeezed the back of his neck, grimacing. "I was hoping you didn't see that. She's just a friend. Nothing more."

Gage considered the best way to phrase his warning. The last thing he needed was Sara getting close to Luke and him finding out about their arrangement. "Women around here see the Devereaux name as a ticket to a better life. I wanted to marry a local girl, but my father was the one who advised against it. In the end, he was right."

"Who was the local girl?"

Gage's right hand twitched. "Her name is Carol Foster. She used to work—"

"Derek's mother?"

Gage had underestimated him. He seemed to know more people in town than he'd realized. "How do you know Derek?"

"He used to date Leslie Moore. Leslie told me it was over, but Derek sure doesn't act like it."

Gage tensed. "You and Leslie sound close."

Luke stared into his drink, avoiding Gage. "She's become a good friend. I got to know her, Sara, Taylor, and Kelly when I first arrived."

Gage's paranoia flared. That Luke had consorted with those girls seemed too coincidental. He didn't want to believe he'd intentionally set out to get to know Beau's victims, but until he had proof of his guilt or innocence, Gage decided to keep Luke busy. The less time he had for friends, the better.

"I want you to help oversee the new construction at the brewery."

Luke lowered the glass from his lips. "You're joking."

Gage kept up his somber demeanor to better instill confidence. "No, I'm not. I have the national campaign and daily operations to look after. I believe you have what it takes to ensure everything runs smoothly."

Luke straightened and squared his shoulders.

His reaction was just what Gage had expected. Men with a lot of responsibility thrown on them either rise to the challenge or fall apart. Luke didn't strike him as a failure.

"I'd love to tackle that project." Luke's chest expanded. "Thank you."

Gage stood, ready to drop his next bomb. "And I'd like you to enroll at the local university in Hammond. Southeastern is a good school. There, you can finish your business degree. You'll need it." He walked around to the front of the desk. "Once you have your bachelor's, I'll send you to Tulane in New Orleans for your MBA."

Luke set his empty glass down. "You have this all mapped out."

Gage leaned against the edge of his desk and folded his arms. "I don't like to leave anything to chance. I can have someone help get you registered and your credits transferred when you're ready."

Luke stood, keeping his chin raised. "I'm ready now."

Gage held out his hand, quieting his apprehension. "Then I'll set the wheels in motion first thing in the morning."

"Thank you." Luke shook his hand, beaming.

Church bells clanged from his desk, and Gage snapped up his phone. When he saw Kent's name, he hesitated.

Now what?

"It's late, Kent." Gage went back around to his desk chair. "Is there a problem?"

"Gage, can you come to the station? There's something I need to show you." Kent paused. "It's about Beau's case."

"Hold on a second." Gage nodded to Luke. "Why don't you head home? Look in on Elizabeth. She wasn't feeling well today."

Luke collected his credit card and new car keys from the desk. "I'm not sure she'll want me checking on her."

Gage would have a stern word with Elizabeth later that night. "Give her time. I want you to be friends."

Luke nodded and then walked toward the office door.

The moment Gage heard the click of the lock, he returned to Kent. "What is it? What have you found?"

Kent's heavy breath sounded dire. "I can't explain on the phone. I need you to come and see this for yourself."

Pissed at the sheriff, Gage hung up, but he had too much at stake to ignore the summons. The main thing eating at him was what he'd have to do if Kent found more than he should have about Beau's death.

He grabbed his keys, picturing Kent's head on a plate. "This better be nothing. I'd hate to have to start looking for a new sheriff so soon."

Gage gritted his teeth the moment he stepped into the bright lights and musty air of the sheriff's department. The gnawing in his stomach grew as he predicted what Kent had discovered. Maybe his pesky ass had cracked his son's case.

He'd expected to see Amy behind the front desk, but instead, Kent waited for him. He stood with his legs slightly apart, shoulders back, and his mouth set in a grim line. It wasn't his usual warm greeting, which only magnified Gage's apprehension.

Gage slowed as he approached, weighing his pensive expression. "Is there a problem?"

Kent motioned to the glass doors by the front desk. "Let's talk inside."

They walked down a hallway reeking of stale coffee. When they passed Kent's office, Gage's fears about the sheriff digging too deep into Beau's death shook his confidence.

They arrived at the last door on the right—the interrogation area.

Gage hesitated before he turned to Kent. "What the hell is going on?"

Kent opened the door. "This is official business. I've got to ask you some difficult questions."

The tension in his shoulders and back snapped. Gage wanted to punch something or someone. He had to find a way to turn whatever this was to his advantage. No one, including the burnt-out cop he'd hired, would get the better of him.

Gage strolled into the room, repeating his mantra—the one he'd pounded into Beau—*never let anyone see who you really are.*

He went to one of the wooden chairs set up at the rectangular table and took a seat, noting every sound around him—the hum of conversation from the hall, the hiss of the air blowing through the vent above.

Gage relaxed in his chair, his stalled confidence reenergizing. He had planned his son's murder, leaving nothing to chance. The men he dealt with had assured him there was no evidence left behind, especially since the wild dogs had committed the crime. If Kent had uncovered anything, it was a minor detail and easily challenged.

Kent took the chair opposite him and retrieved a manila folder set to the side. The bags under his eyes were more noticeable, and when he spoke, his voice sounded raspy and tired.

"Thank you for coming. I wanted to wait until after your event at the brewery to discuss what we found."

Gage eyed the white cinderblock walls and the harsh lights, carefully planning his words. "Is this a formal interrogation? If so, I should have John with me."

Kent opened the file, and his hardened exterior cracked as a half-grin crept across his chapped lips. "Hardly. I'd never do that to you. What I have is a problem, and we won't be overheard here."

The knots in Gage's back relaxed, and he put his hands on the table.

Kent removed a single sheet, featuring colorful graphs and numerical calculations, and set it in front of Gage. "This is the DNA test I finally got back on that Jane Doe we found at the river." He selected another sheet from the file with identical graphs. "I had the lab run a match to see if her DNA connected with anyone in our system. I got one hit—Beau." He looked at Gage. "I need you to tell me why our dead girl and Beau are related."

Gage gleaned each of the reports. "I don't understand."

Kent sat back and locked his hands behind his head. "She's a

Devereaux, and I'm convinced you know who she is."

Gage clenched his jaw, not sure of what to say. Whatever lies he proposed would never hold up against scientific evidence.

"I can't cover this up for long," Kent told him. "I'm the only one who knows, but soon others will find out. You have to tell me who she is before this blows up."

Gage kept up his stoic countenance as he unbuttoned his jacket, bracing for the inevitable. The sins of his past had caught up with him. There was nowhere to hide.

Chapter Thirty-Two

Summer 1990

The ceiling lights shone down on Edward Devereaux's commendations and certificates of merit from the Louisiana State Legislature, making Gage feel like an inept teenager.

He hated the impersonal red leather furniture and the ugly red rug. When he finally got to run Benedict Brewery, he would change the office. Make it warm and inviting. He'd ask Carol to do it. She always had the best ideas.

"I want to talk to you about that girl," Edward Devereaux said in his harsh, bearish tone.

Gage waited until his father looked up from scribbling in one of the numerous folders that cluttered his desk. He flinched when his father's dark eyes met his. Gage approached the desk, waving away the cigar smoke. "Her name is Carol Keppard, not *that girl*."

Edward lifted his pale hand, urging quiet. "She's not Devereaux material. Get rid of her. You're going to college in Boston. I have connections up there. It's all arranged."

"Boston?" Gage's jaw muscle quivered. "I can't leave. I love Carol, and I'm going to marry her."

Edward slammed his fist against the desk. The thud resonated around the office. "No, you're not. You'll do as I say, or I'll cut you off without a cent."

"I don't want your money." Heartache fueled Gage's anger. "I don't need you or this damn family."

"Yes, you do." Edward stood. "You will do as I say. You're not going to humiliate this family by marrying some Creole tramp. Disobey me, and you'll never see her again. Do you understand what I'm saying, boy?" Edward leveled a chilling glare at Gage.

He swallowed hard, knowing what his father implied. Edward never issued threats without every intention of backing them up. Gage had listened at the study door when Edward spoke on the phone to his dodgy friends. He knew how his father got rid of problems. He would do the same to Carol unless Gage obeyed.

He clasped his hands behind his back and lowered his head. "I'll go to Boston for one year if you promise not to touch her."

Edward flopped into his chair. "One year, then. Time apart might cool your fascination with the silly girl."

A century could pass, and he wouldn't love Carol any less. How could he tell his old man that Carol kept him sane, cooled his anger, and gave him peace? "I'll never stop loving her."

"Yes, you will." Edward reached for another folder from his pile. "You'll marry who I choose for you, and it will never be that girl."

Gage held in the flurry of expletives he wanted to spew. One day the Devereaux wealth would be his to do with as he pleased. He would be different from his father, kinder to the people of St. Benedict, and he would love who he wanted and raise his children with respect.

"Get out of my sight, boy. We're done."

His father's harsh command rattled him. Gage fled from the room and hurried past his mother. Amelia, decked out in her usual designer label finery, appeared ready to attend some charity function or luncheon with her friends.

"Darling, are you all right?" she asked, sounding concerned.

He halted and debated what to say. Her sweet voice had been his only comfort throughout his prison sentence in the dismal plantation house.

"Everything's fine, Mother. I'm going for a drive." He scrambled for the peacock doors at the end of the main hallway, anxious to get into his Mustang and head for the only place he'd ever found solace—the river.

~

Still agitated, Gage eased his car into a spot close to the path that led to the beach. He just needed some time alone to consider how to get his father to change his mind about Carol. He had to have her in his life. Without the woman he loved, he was nothing.

He turned off the engine and punched the steering wheel as hard as he could. Gage instantly regretted the violence against his prized dark green Mustang GT.

He got out of his car and heard the rhythmic buzzing of katydids in the woods. Over the treetops, he saw the two tall white spires of The Abbey cutting into the evening sky. The beauty of the old building never ceased to amaze him. He was sorry to see it fall into disrepair. He'd bugged his father for years to buy back the land and rebuild the church to its former glory, but Edward had refused. It was another item on the long list of things Gage would do as head of the Devereaux family.

He slapped at the branches that were in his way as he trudged along the dirt path to the beach. Preoccupied with his thoughts, he didn't notice the girl at first.

She stood at the water's edge, staring into the gentle waves. A blue-checkered sundress highlighted her long, lean legs while ringlets of strawberry blonde hair flowed down her back. With a pert nose and full lips, she was very pretty, but he doubted she was kind like Carol. Most pretty girls were bitchy.

"Hello," he said, wanting to let her know he was there. He expected her to flinch or scream, but she remained still, staring into the water.

"Hello," she sweetly replied.

"Is everything okay?"

She turned to him. The light in her eyes, unruly and almost wild, appealed to him. "I'm fine. I came here to get away."

He stuffed his hands into the pockets of his jeans, suddenly nervous. "Yeah, me too."

"Who are you getting away from?"

He glanced back up the path. "My father. He's an asshole and a control freak."

Her airy laugh danced around him, reminding him of a songbird. "So is mine. Why are they always like that?"

He shrugged, wishing he could hear her laugh again. "Who knows. It's like he has my whole life planned out."

A few seconds ticked by. Gage wanted to say something suave, but all he could think of was small talk. "You're not from around here."

She shook her head. "I'm just passing through. I've been driving around Southeast Louisiana on sort of a holiday before I head back to college."

She was older than him. Gage smiled. "Where do you go to college?"

"A small private art college in Boston. You've probably never heard of it."

He kicked the sand, wishing he'd listened to his mother's pleas for him to obtain some culture. "Yeah, I'm not into art."

She tilted her head, her long hair cascading around her shoulders. "What are you into?"

"Cars." He attempted to find something else to make him sound more interesting. "And football. I was the quarterback on our high school team."

Her smile was slight but devastating. "Quarterback, huh? I bet you had all the girls after you."

His cheeks burned. "Nah."

She edged closer. "What's your name?"

"Gage Devereaux."

She held out her small, delicate hand. "Pleased to meet you, Mr. Devereaux. My name is Lila Price."

A howl carried through the air.

Lila spun around, checking the bushes and trees. Her face paled, and Gage could see her pulse through the veins in her sleek throat.

"What was that?"

He struggled to remain calm, but on the inside, he was as shaken as Lila. "The wild dogs who live on The Abbey grounds. It's said that when the dogs appear, death is near."

Her pink lips turned downward. "Are you trying to scare me on purpose?"

"No, not at all. It's a local legend." He motioned to a path near the thick brush. "The Abbey is still standing, as are the cells behind it. It's a creepy place at night, but the building is beautiful."

Her eyes danced with a mischievous light. "You'll have to show me sometime."

Gage studied her, wondering why the woman appealed to him. Maybe he should figure out what he found so damn alluring. "Sure."

Lila dipped her hand into the water, dancing her fingers along the surface. "What do you and your friends do for fun around here?"

Gage tried to think of something he could say to make himself sound cool. "Mostly, we hang out here or at Mo's Diner. They've got good strawberry cheesecake."

She caught the tip of her tongue between her teeth as if suppressing a giggle. "Cheesecake, huh? I'll have to check that out." She left the river's edge, flicking water from her fingers. "What else does this town have to offer?" Lila unexpectedly placed a wet hand on his chest.

The heat of her touch through his shirt damned near knocked him to his knees. "Um." His confidence floundered. "Depends on what you like to do."

She took a step back, displaying a sly grin. "I like what all girls like to do. Shop." She covered her mouth when she laughed, muffling the airy sound.

Gage looked at her pretty dress. "We've got some nice shops in town. Dottie's Boutique on Main Street is the most popular. My mom shops there sometimes."

She casually swept her long hair over her shoulder, exposing the soft white flesh of her neck. "Tell me more. I want to hear all about your little town."

Gage reminisced about the place where he'd grown up—the good and the bad—surprised at how easily he could share things with Lila. She listened to stories about his friends and their escapades at the river. She even enjoyed his descriptions of the characters he knew, especially old Sheriff Will Guidry and his love of chewing tobacco.

The sun had almost disappeared from the sky when he realized he hadn't stopped talking since they sat down in the sand. Suddenly, he became tongue-tied.

Lila stood, wiping the sand from her dress, and looked at him. "It's getting late. I'm sure you need to get home."

He hurried to his feet, wanting to steal a few more minutes together. "I'd prefer to stay here with you."

She dragged her fingers across his chest as she swept past him. "Your father will wonder where you are."

The way she moved, the swing of her hips, hypnotized Gage. "How do you know that?"

Lila stopped before heading up the pine-needle-strewn path to the parking lot and faced him, wearing a beguiling smile. "Controlling fathers always want to know where their children are."

His heart pounded as she turned to go. "Hey, can I see you again?"

Lila glanced at him over her shoulder. "Tomorrow, I'll meet you here before sundown." She nodded to the beach. "Then you can show me The Abbey."

Gage tingled with excitement. "I'll be here."

"It's a date."

Time stood still as a pair of fireflies danced around Lila's face. Then she ran up the path before he could tell her goodbye.

Gage returned to the water's edge, fighting the urge to follow her. He didn't want to appear too desperate and had to play it cool for now. He closed his eyes as the evening breeze off the water doused the fire radiating over his skin.

He breathed in the humid air and thought about seeing Lila again.

Next time, I won't let her walk away.

The fading rays of the sun filtered through the trees along the river, creating a kaleidoscope of shadowy images atop the sand. Gage rechecked his watch, hoping Lila didn't stand him up.

He remained thankful for the intense summer heat, as it kept everybody from flocking to the river. He didn't want to explain Lila to his friends, especially Carol. Gage wanted a few uninterrupted hours with her to explore why he felt so drawn to the captivating creature.

The patter of feet on the path behind him quickened his breath. Gage spun around, hoping for Lila and dreading anyone else.

The lithe, strawberry blonde in a yellow sundress hurried toward him and flung her arms around his neck. The kiss she planted on his cheek was unexpected but welcome.

She let him go and stepped back. "I wondered if you would come."

He grinned, afraid to tell her he'd felt the same way. "I told you I would. I always keep my word."

Lila took his arm. "I'm glad to hear you're not the sort to break your promises. Not a lot of people are like that these days."

He escorted her along the beach. "My father would agree with you. He's always going on about how people let him down."

"No one lets you down more than family," she whispered

He studied her for a moment. "You sound like you have some experience with that."

"A little." Lila tipped her head, letting her hair tumble over her shoulder. "I've noticed the Devereaux name all over St. Benedict. Your family seems pretty powerful."

Gage bristled at the mention of his family. "My father is the one who wields the power. Not me. When I take the reins of the family business, I plan to do things differently."

"That's good. I can think of nothing worse than growing up and becoming your parents." Lila drifted closer. "Now, where's this abbey you promised to show me?"

Gage pointed at a swathe of bushes ahead on the left. "We're almost there."

She halted and let go of his arm. "Oh, what about those wild dogs you mentioned? Is it safe?"

He took her hand. "I promise nothing will hurt you."

"Then, I'm all yours."

He guided her as they climbed the embankment. Her hand remained in his, giving him confidence. Gage forgot about his father and Carol. His only thoughts were of the strange beauty and how she made him feel invincible.

They encountered a rusted iron gate with a *No Trespassing* sign. Gage held it open for her as various summer bugs darted around them. A breeze washed away the humid heaviness in the warm air. When they stepped onto The Abbey grounds, he waited as she raised her head and peered at the imposing structure.

The two spires rose upward, commanding attention as they touched the last traces of light in the sky. The red brick and limestone building had dense green vines growing wild along one wall, while a tangle of trees leaned lazily against a few boarded windows.

"Wow. What a place." She let go of his hand and set out across the thick, high grass.

He enjoyed how the breeze molded her yellow dress to her curves. Her body aroused his appetite and the way she moved, like a graceful dancer, set off a host of fantasies.

"The Abbey dates back to the 1800s, when my family built it as a private chapel." He followed her across the neglected grounds. "One of my ancestors gave the property to the Benedictine monks and the Catholic Church, probably hoping to buy forgiveness for a multitude of sins."

She swept her hand over the thigh-high weeds. "Where did they go?"

He caught up to her and glanced at the empty belfry atop one of the square-shaped spires. "The monks who ran the seminary school abandoned it and went to New Orleans. It's been falling apart for years."

"That's sad." She stared off in the distance, seemingly entranced by the triple-tiered fountain topped with an angel raising its arms to the heavens. "How could they walk away from so much beauty?"

Gage scanned the trees along the edge of the field, keeping a sharp eye out for the dogs. "I wish I knew." He took her to the granite steps partially hidden by overgrown grass. Twigs and dead leaves rustled as the wind picked up.

Plywood covered the windows on both sides of the entrance while a cracked stone arch rose above two large doors carved with crosses. A chain with a padlock barred their way inside.

Lila tugged on the chain. "How do we get in?"

"Through here." He pushed on one of the doors. It gave way, creating a gap big enough to crawl through.

She looked through the opening. "Do a lot of people go inside?"

Gage motioned to the cloisters behind The Abbey. "They go to the cells behind the church. But we won't visit there. It's in bad shape. I'm sure someone will board the place up completely one day."

She glanced back at him. "Is it haunted?"

He liked the way Lila bit her lower lip, appearing nervous. "A lady in white is said to wander the grounds wearing a cloak. I've heard she comes out when the moon is full or during storms."

She checked out the sky. "The moon is supposed to be full tonight."

Gardenia-scented perfume wafted off her skin, tempting him. "Are you scared we'll see her?"

Lila raised her chin. "Have you ever seen this lady in white?"

She was so close Gage could kiss her, and part of him wanted to, but he didn't. This woman was a stranger. He had Carol to consider. Cheating on her would break both their hearts.

"Not yet, but if she shows up ..." He lowered his head to hers and waited a few seconds before whispering, "Run."

Lila squealed and darted into the gap. He lost her in the darkness. With one last look out over the weed-covered grounds, Gage ducked inside.

Slivers of the last traces of light trickled through several small holes in the roof. The eerie radiance landed on a central portion of the cracked stone floor where a fallen ceiling beam lay gathering dust. A few birds, nesting in the pillared archways, fluttered their wings while their cooing resonated throughout the church.

A flickering flame floated toward him.

"Good thing I keep this on me for emergencies." Lila held up a lighter.

Pretty and resourceful. Impressive.

Gage took her hand. "There's a lot of trash on the floor, so follow me."

The faint illumination revealed dozens of rotted pews, leaves, twigs, and piles of crumbled plaster.

"This is gross." She lowered the lighter to a rat's skeleton. "What do you come here for?"

"Guys like to bring girls here so they can be alone."

Her airy laugh returned, blotting out the echo of their footfalls. "Ever hear of a motel?"

He raised his attention to carvings of men and angels on the walls and atop the arches. "This is St. Benedict. We only have a bed and breakfast owned by Mrs. Hewitt. She knows the name of every guy under twenty-one in town."

Lila gazed up at the painting of Adam and Eve, barely visible on the ceiling along the central aisle. "Don't you feel funny making out with them watching you?" She pointed at a rendering of Moses carrying the Ten Commandments, his eyes blazing like fire.

He chuckled. "I said guys bring girls here. I didn't mean me."

She walked ahead, taking the light to the archway marking the entrance to the altar. The orange of the lighter's flame shone on the granite above where the altar once stood.

"You've never been here with a girl?" Lila walked behind the altar to the apse and looked at the boarded windows. "Have you even done it?"

Her question dented his pride. Gage didn't want her to think he had no experience with women.

He slowly walked toward the granite block. "I've got a girl—a great girl I plan to marry. We don't need to come here. We have other places we go to be alone."

Lila tossed her long hair over her shoulder. "Ah, a man of experience." She let the lighter go out. "Does your girlfriend please you?"

The sudden darkness unnerved him. He couldn't see her in the shadows. Then, she drifted into a fading ray of light.

Gage waited for her to return, excitement surging through him. "She pleases me just fine."

Her hand settled on his shoulder. He shouldn't give her any encouragement, but her supple body, and the way she moved, intrigued him. Gage tried to picture Carol and remember all the reasons he wanted to stay faithful, but like Adam pictured in the fresco above, he felt helpless against the temptation that was Lila.

"A satisfied man wouldn't be here alone with me." Lila's lips hovered close to his ear. "I bet something's missing. A craving you can't explain, a need you can't satisfy. You're a man with special tastes. You want more than to make love to a woman. You want to let go."

Gage closed his eyes, turned on by her silky voice—and her words. He'd fantasized about doing different things to Carol. Painful things. But he'd refused to indulge his impulses, fearing he might frighten her away.

"How would you know what I want?" Gage shook as he grappled with restraint.

Lila skidded a hand across his chest. "I know what's in your blood."

Gage had spent so much time repressing his dark desires that hearing someone else say they knew what he wanted scared the shit out of him. If he gave in, he might never be able to keep those impulses under control.

He glanced at the entrance. "We should head back."

She trailed her hand down his chest to his belt. "Tell me what you want. What do you fantasize about?"

The floral essence of her skin was everywhere. Gage couldn't escape it. He yearned for the musty smell of the church, the scent of decay—anything but her.

Lila kissed his neck, and fire ran to his groin. He tightened his grip on her arm, imploring her to stop. Her warm mouth inched upward until her teeth clamped down on his lower lip. Gage longed to pull away, but couldn't.

"Don't be afraid," she whispered. "I can take anything you want to do, be whoever you need me to be."

His resistance ebbed as he caressed her soft skin. The urges, the dreams he'd fought to conquer, stirred to life. Gage clasped her throat. "I don't want to be gentle."

Lila didn't try to wiggle free, but pressed against him. "Then don't."

Her permission unleashed a torrent of cravings. Gage spun her around, pushing her into the wall.

She laughed as he raised the hem of her dress. His fingers skimmed the inside of her thigh.

Lila endeavored to undo the button fly on his jeans, but he didn't want her participating—he wanted her compliant and submissive.

Gage gripped the ridged outline of her windpipe and bit the back of her neck.

She gasped. "More."

He lost all self-control and sent her into the wall, slamming her cheek against the plaster. He held her with one hand as he reached between her legs and spread her flesh apart. Gage rammed into her, no longer caring about her needs, only his. He took out pent-up emotions on her pliable body, driving deeper with every thrust. The louder she moaned, the more he wanted to cause her pain.

When his depravity reached its zenith, a delicious tingle rose along his back, tightening the muscles along the way. He finally let go, spilling into her, but it wasn't Lila he saw before him—it was Carol. A tidal wave of guilt overwhelmed him. He pulled out of her and slammed his hand against the wall.

What have I done?

CHAPTER THIRTY-THREE

Summer 1990

By the time the height of the summer heat blanketed the river, Lila had become everything to Gage. He couldn't concentrate on work at the brewery, couldn't stand to be home or focus at the gym, and he'd skipped several dates with Carol, claiming he was busy. All he could think about was being alone with Lila.

He hated himself for it and tried like hell to curb his desire. Every day he practiced the speech he would give her the next time they met, ending it for good, but when he saw her naked, his determination melted.

Their weeks together had changed him. Gage became paranoid, angry, insensitive, and, at times, he'd swear he'd turned into his father. The only person who seemed to soothe him was Carol.

"I'll wait for you," she'd promised the day he told her about Boston. "We can survive a year."

Carol was his savior. She would be devastated if she ever learned about Lila, so he vowed never to tell her.

One day, while preparing to leave for college, he found a note from Lila on his windshield. She asked him to come to The Abbey.

She'd never contacted him like this before. Their meetings had been planned on the phone, never by paper that others could read. The brazen summons was a wake-up call. Gage was ready to end it for good this time.

Pink ribbons like cotton candy crossed the sky when he pulled his car onto the shelled lot. The heat and humidity clung to his skin, and beads of sweat broke out on his brow as he set out for The Abbey. There were no other cars, and he was glad. They would be alone.

The breeze off the river cooled his skin as he headed down the dirt path. He'd carefully practiced what he would say to Lila, hoping she would walk away without a fight. They had never professed to love each other. All they had shared was sex.

He'd come to the end of the path when a woman's sharp taunts brought him to an abrupt halt. He couldn't hear what she said, but he recognized Lila's husky tone.

Gage rushed ahead, eager to find out who she was with, and then someone else shouted—a man.

The stranger's surly manner raised the hairs on the back of his neck.

What the hell is my father doing here?

Terror filled his mouth with an acrid taste. Edward had found out about her.

Gage ran onto the beach, his feet sinking into the sand. His father had gone too far. Lila was none of his business. He raced along the water's edge to confront Edward.

Lila wore a pretty red sundress, but her stiff body language shouted impertinence and defiance—qualities his father abhorred.

She spotted him and her rigid posture relaxed, and then a seductive smile washed away the look of contempt on her face. "Come here, Gage. Join us."

His father wheeled around and saw him. "Go home, now!"

Gage moved closer, not about to leave her with the bloodthirsty asshole. Whatever Edward had planned to get rid of her, Gage had to stop. He wouldn't let her suffer for his summer of fun.

"No, he needs to join us." Sarcasm rolled off Lila's tongue with such ease. "He has to learn the truth about the Devereaux family."

"Eva, don't do this," Edward ordered. "Whatever quarrel you have, it's with me. Leave my son out of it."

Eva? Gage couldn't move. He hadn't heard that name since he was a child, but he remembered it well.

It can't be.

"Your son?" She recoiled from Edward. "Really, Daddy. Can't you at least acknowledge I'm part of your family, too?"

Gage put his hand over his mouth, suddenly sick to his stomach.

"Aw, what's the matter, baby brother," she teased. "Cat got your tongue? Don't you have anything to say to your long-lost sister?"

Edward slapped her hard across the face.

Her hair whipped around and covered her reaction, but as Eva raised her head, she grinned. "Your son is so much better at that."

Gage stumbled back, almost falling into the sand. He sucked in air as black spots crowded his vision. "You can't be Eva. She died when I was six."

"Died?" Eva scowled at her father. "Is that what you told him?"

She laughed, but this time it wasn't the fascinating sound he'd relished. It was dark and menacing, just like her eyes.

"I was nine when Mommy and Daddy shipped me off to an institution in the backwaters of Louisiana. Locked me away so I could never bother them again." She held out her hands, flourishing them like an actor on stage. "But I'm back, and boy do I have a story to tell the world."

"I will not have this!" Edward held a fist to her face. "I sent you away because you were sick. Every year you got worse. Killing pets, torturing the servants, attacking others in school. We had to do something before you ruined our good name."

Gage couldn't believe it. All the stories they'd told him about his sister had been a lie. Her funeral, the sealed bedroom he could never visit, and the playground her father had built in her memory, all had been part of an elaborate scheme.

"Why didn't you tell me?" he shouted. "I was devastated when I thought Eva died. She was my sister. I had—" Gage fell silent, remembering the things they had done.

"She's a disease," Edward spat out. "She had to be locked away."

"He almost got away with it." Eva crept closer to Gage. "I spent years planning my revenge on this family, and thanks to a friend at the institution where Daddy put me, I got my chance to see it through." She rubbed her belly. "What would hurt the precious Devereaux name more than the ultimate scandal? The disgusting tale of a brother and sister having *carnal knowledge* of each other," she said in an overly pronounced drawl. "And the birth of their ungodly, pure Devereaux child. Where will our precious family name be then?"

Edward grabbed Eva's arm. He spun her around to face him, his cheeks crimson.

"You will not destroy everything I've worked for. I will not allow it. I don't believe you're pregnant. And if you are, it doesn't belong to Gage. Probably the bastard of some unsuspecting fool you seduced to help you get what you want."

She fought against him, scratching his arms. "It's Gage's baby. Ask him. Ask him about the nights I met him at The Abbey behind the altar. Ask him about all the depraved things he did to me."

Edward slapped her again, leaving a trickle of blood on her lower lip.

Gage lunged to defend her, but his father thwarted his advance with a stiff arm.

"Go home. I'll take care of her. You're not to involve yourself in this."

Gage wanted to argue, to defend her, but Carol's angelic face popped into his mind. What would she think of him if she knew the truth? His father was right. He had to let him handle the situation. Gage knew nothing about dealing with a woman filled with vengeance.

He ran back to the path and up the embankment, a firestorm of grief and humiliation blinding him. Disgust hastened Gage's pace to the car. The vile images of the things he'd done to Lila—to his sister—flooded his thoughts. He weaved as he made his way, then dropped to his knees and vomited.

When he finally reached his car, he fumbled to get his keys from his pocket. They tumbled from his hand. He clawed at the shells covering the lot while tears stained his cheeks. The pain, the overwhelming constricting ache that pressed in from all sides, petrified him.

What if she was pregnant? What if she carried out her threats?

Then a robust voice awakened in his head, brimming with a certainty he'd never possessed.

You're a Devereaux. No one can stand in your way, ever.

Slowly, he found the strength to stand.

Gage got in and started the car, convinced Eva would not ruin his life.

"I know what's in your blood," she had said to him that first night in The Abbey.

Gage floored the gas and peeled out of the lot, Eva's words ringing in his head. He would never allow another woman to have such mastery over him. Not Carol, not anyone. From now on, he would be the master of his destiny, and no one—no matter who they were—would ever threaten him or his family name again.

The brilliance of the dining room chandelier did little to hide the scowling, condescending faces of the Devereaux men who stared back at Gage. Eerie shadows cast by the strange light seemed to bring the portraits of his dead relatives to life. Gage's anxiety escalated as he took in the men who had come before him. He could almost hear them screaming, demanding to know how he could have sunk so low.

Gage had downed half the bottle of scotch he'd stolen from his father's office, but it hadn't alleviated his shaking. He struggled to keep a grip on the glass, and his fingers ached from the effort. He drank, paced, and talked to his ancestors, begging for their forgiveness. Gage didn't know what else to do while waiting for Edward to return home.

It was almost midnight when he heard the door to the mudroom slam.

He tensed, waiting for his father and the real argument to begin.

Footsteps approached, echoing through the first floor of the historic home.

When Gage saw his father in the dining room doorway, his shame turned his resolve to mush.

His hair disheveled, pasty face haggard, and suit rumpled, Edward Devereaux had aged overnight. Sand that trickled from his right jacket shoulder caught in the glint from the chandelier.

Gage could see how devastating his incestuous relationship with Lila had been to his father.

"She won't bother us anymore." Edward sounded defeated. "I've paid her off."

Gage set his glass on the dining table. "What about the baby?"

Edward rested his shoulder against the doorframe. "There was no baby. She only said those things to upset me."

Gage furrowed his brow. "You believe her?"

Edward pushed away from the door. "She will never see you again. And we will never speak of this, ever. She's gone, for good." He walked away, setting off the hall's various creaks and groans.

After his father climbed the grand staircase, Gage rocked his head against the back of the dining room chair and closed his eyes.

That Eva had survived only to live such a heinous life locked away reopened old wounds. Images of the affectionate, doting, playful, and cheeky sister he'd adored besieged him. They had spent many a night staying up late and talking—vowing to stay close no matter where they ended up in the world.

Tears stung his cheeks. Gage grieved for the family he could never have and the sister he would never see again.

Chapter Thirty-Four

Present Day

Gage raised his head to the fluorescent lights in the interrogation room as the past slipped away. The story still sounded unreal, but there it was, out for the world to know and for others to judge. He sucked in the stale air, desperately wanting a stiff drink.

"Your father killed her." Kent sat across from him, his face a mask of stone.

Gage's fingertips brushed the gouges in the table. "I wasn't positive until you found her body. I'd always hoped she'd taken the money and left, but for my father, that would never have been enough."

"What happened to you after that night?"

"Knowing the truth about Eva, and all the things we'd done, almost destroyed me. I went to Boston willingly, desperate to bury my shame and memories. But I never did, not really." Gage paused.

"Go on." Kent motioned.

Gage clasped his hands together. "A pretty freshman with long, strawberry blonde hair like Eva's struck up a conversation with me at a fraternity party. Her name was Pamela Cross. She had the same grace and smile—the same sensuality. I got very drunk and used her to get Eva out of my system. Luke was the result."

Kent methodically tapped a single finger against the table. "You ever find out where Eva was kept? Get in touch with them about her time there?"

"After my father died of a heart attack, I found the bills for Broadmoor Psychiatric Institution in Sabine Parish among my father's papers. I never contacted them."

Kent scratched his head. "Did you question your mother about it?"

"I tried, but my mother, Amelia, refused to tell me anything. Not long after, she packed her things and returned to her ancestral home in England. We haven't spoken since."

Kent edged forward in his chair, hunching over the table. "You said she involved a friend at the facility to help carry out her plans. Was it an employee? Another patient?" Kent's voice rose.

Gage rocked back against his chair, completely drained. "It doesn't matter anymore. She died at the river. My father buried her there so no one would know."

Kent glanced at the papers on the table. "I'm sorry to put you through this, but I had to find out the truth."

A bead of sweat trickled down Gage's temple. "What will you do now that you know?"

Kent returned the paperwork to his folder. "If anyone asks, she's a Jane Doe. Edward's dead and can't be brought to justice. Enough lives have been ruined already. I can't see a reason to ruin any more."

"And the body?" Gage asked, stunned by his compassion. "What happens to her?"

"What do you want me to do?" Kent asked with a blank expression.

Gage briefly considered the question. "Release her to me. I'll make sure she has a proper burial on our property. She should come home to rest."

Kent picked up the folder and stood. "I'll make the arrangements."

Gage was pleased they had come to an agreement on Eva. Kent had won a reprieve. There would be more problems down the road, but, for now, the family name remained protected. Gage hoped the sins of the past were behind him.

The mouthwatering aroma of butter and salt wafting through the kitchen teased Leslie as she waited for her popcorn to finish in the microwave. It still felt strange to enjoy anything without Dawn around. Her sister would always steal big handfuls of her snacks, irritating her. Now, she'd give anything to have that happen again. But time marched on, and Leslie learned to come to terms with her grief. She didn't accept it—she never would—but realized it would always be as much a part of her as breathing.

She headed to her room with her popcorn, ready to tackle her tiresome paper on *Hamlet*.

If Shakespeare only knew how much high school kids hate him.

Leslie was halfway up the stairs when the doorbell rang. She set her bowl on the bottom step and went to the front door.

She flinched when she spied the familiar Stetson of the town sheriff through her peephole.

What the hell is he doing here?

Her shaking fingers fumbled with the deadbolt. Had one of the girls talked? Leslie's breath hitched as she opened the door. "Sheriff Davis, can I help you?"

"Hey, Leslie." Kent removed his hat. "I'm sorry to stop by so late, but your father's expecting me."

That didn't make her feel any better.

She opened the door all the way. "Come on in."

He walked inside and then raised his nose in the air. "Popcorn. Smells good."

She shut the door. "Yeah, I was just heading upstairs with dinner to do homework."

He tapped his hat against his thigh. "Popcorn for dinner?"

She tucked a lock of hair behind her ear, heat rising in her cheeks. "Yeah, ah, Mom doesn't cook much these days. She hasn't been feeling well."

The downturn of his features added to her embarrassment. "I can only imagine how tough it's been for all of you."

"Kent?" John rounded the stairs and turned into the small entryway. "I thought I heard your voice."

Kent shook her father's hand. "Thanks for seeing me."

"Not at all." Her father gave her a don't-even-ask look, then motioned to the stairs. "Thank you for showing him in, Leelee."

Her father never curtly dismissed anyone unless something was wrong. Leslie's curiosity went into overdrive. Why had the sheriff come to their home at such an hour to speak with her father? Was it about her? Beau's case? Taylor's case? The possibilities were endless.

John showed Kent to his office and Leslie peeked around the stairs, observing the two men. Kent fidgeted with his Stetson as he casually inspected photos while walking through the family room.

Is the sheriff nervous? About what?

The soft *thud* of her father's office door shutting spurred Leslie into action. She listened at the base of the stairs to make sure Shelley was in her bedroom, and then tiptoed across the brick floor of the family room.

Leslie briefly chastised herself for eavesdropping, but she wouldn't sleep if she didn't find out why the sheriff was there. She leaned in, remembering every scene she'd watched in movies of characters doing the same thing and getting caught. She needed to make sure that didn't happen. Leslie could never explain her actions to her father. If he knew the mess she was in, he'd be devastated.

She put her ear near the door but couldn't hear a thing, so she pressed against the wood. Suddenly, the faulty lock clicked and the door popped open.

Her mouth went dry. *Oh shit!*

"It was the most disturbing story I've ever heard." Kent's frantic voice floated through the crack. "I know the Devereaux family holds a lot of credibility in this town, but Gage would be ruined if this ever got out."

The lure of getting any information on Gage Devereaux encouraged her to stay put.

"A lot of jobs would go up in smoke in the bargain," John said, sounding grim.

"I told Gage I'd keep the girl as a Jane Doe, but what if someone starts digging?" Kent paused and then sighed. "It wouldn't be hard to find out Gage had a sister and Edward institutionalized her. I checked the place online—Broadmoor is still in Sabine Parish. Anyone there could easily trace Eva Devereaux back to St. Benedict."

Leslie almost dropped to her knees. Taylor had found out about Eva and the Devereaux family history of mental illness. But she hadn't uncovered that his sister had been institutionalized. Or had she?

"If I hadn't asked the lab to run a DNA match and stumbled on her relationship to Beau, Eva Devereaux would have remained a Jane Doe.

What if someone requests what I've found—"

"Then make sure they never get the information you collected," John angrily cut in. "Destroy the file, make it go missing. No one can ever know that Edward Devereaux killed his own daughter and buried her at the river."

Leslie covered her mouth, stifling a gasp. This family was more screwed up than she'd imagined. This could be a motive for murder. Gage wanted Taylor silenced. Leslie had proof to take to Sara and Kelly.

Common sense implored Leslie to sneak away, but she couldn't because of something her father said. Why had he urged Kent Davis to hide the evidence and destroy the files? John Moore was an honorable man, beyond reproach, but this made him the same as her—a pawn in Gage Devereaux's game of lies.

"We've got another problem," Kent grumbled. "Preliminary reports have come back from the Taylor Haskins's murder. There's a DNA match to someone who was at Beau's murder scene. It's a female, but there's no record of her in our system."

Beads of sweat broke out on Leslie's forehead. *Are you kidding me?*

"Could it be contaminated samples?" John asked. "A lot of people move through that area of the river where Beau was found."

"That could be argued in court. You're the lawyer, not me. But I have to look into the possibility of a woman being at both crime scenes, no matter how remote the chance of actually finding her."

Leslie stepped away from the door, shaking all over. They knew a woman had been at the scene of Beau's death, but there were four of them. So, who killed Taylor? It wasn't her. So that left only two possibilities—Sara and Kelly. How could one of them turn on Taylor?

Leslie fled to the stairs.

She gripped the railing on the staircase, and then a wave of nausea overwhelmed her. Taylor had been one of them, privy to Beau Devereaux's crimes.

I've got to find the killer before someone else ends up dead.

Chapter Thirty-Five

Rain battered the cracked and buckling blacktop as Leslie pulled into the parking lot at St. Benedict High. Cars were everywhere, and a few had even parked on the quad—something Madbriar would hand out detentions for. When she arrived at her usual spot, she found another vehicle parked there, a big black truck.

"Damn it, Sara." She slapped her steering wheel.

It took ten minutes for her to find another space, far away from the school's entrance. She lugged her heavy book bag across the lot as fat raindrops fell on her face.

Leslie was almost to the top of the front steps when the last bell rang.

Shit.

She would be late for English lit. Her paper on the depressed Dane still wasn't done. Her day seemed to be going from bad to worse.

"Girl, you're late." Zoe snuck in next to Leslie as she walked through the school doors. "You're never late."

The pretty girl with the button nose and hazel eyes had on her white St. Benedict cheerleading uniform. The sight of the red dragon on Zoe's chest gave her pause.

Leslie massaged her temples, fighting off a headache. "I'm screwed. I didn't finish my *Hamlet* paper."

"I guess you haven't heard the big news, then." Zoe kept up with Leslie as they headed for class.

Nothing Zoe said was ever *big* news. A well-known school gossip, the busybody cheerleader had kept her distance since Dawn's death.

"Heard what? Did one of the cheerleaders get caught under the bleachers with the track team? Or did one of the freshman girls hook up with another senior?" She stopped, her irritation getting the better of her. "Don't you have anything better to do than spread rumors?"

Zoe thrust her shoulders back and tilted her head. "What's up your ass?"

Leslie should have tried harder to hide her frustration, but she wasn't in the mood today. "There's a long list of things up my ass, but I'm not about to discuss them right now."

She turned to hurry to class when Zoe called out. "Do you know about Kelly Norton?"

Leslie stiffened, swallowed her indignation, and turned around. "What about her?"

Zoe grinned, looking pleased. "She disappeared over the weekend. Some think she found a guy and skipped town. I'm surprised her mom hasn't called you yet."

Leslie didn't stop to ask for more information. She took off in the direction of the nearest ladies' room, recalling the last time she'd seen Kelly at the brewery party on Saturday. She'd walked out of the celebration with Mrs. Devereaux and hadn't come back. Leslie's texts had gone unanswered since that night.

No, no, no!

After she rushed through the restroom door and quickly checked all the stalls to make sure she was alone, Leslie set her book bag on one of the sinks and rummaged through a side pocket for her phone.

She wanted to scream when she found her ringer switched off. There was a single missed call. But it wasn't Kelly on the panicked message.

"Leslie, this is Beth Norton, Kelly's mom. I need you to call me right away. I can't find my daughter. She never came home after the party at the brewery. Please call me."

A bleak cold hugged Leslie. There had been four girls who had a hand in Beau's demise. One was dead, the other missing. That only left one suspect—Sara.

Leslie tapped Sara's name in her contact list and waited as the phone rang.

"Hey. You hear about Kelly?" Sara asked with her usual acerbity.

Leslie's hand trembled. "Where are you?"

"I skipped class. I'm in the library finishing my stupid English lit paper."

Leslie tried to keep her cool as she spoke. "I'm coming to meet you. Stay there."

"What's wrong? Have you heard somethin'?"

Leslie hung up and grabbed her book bag. Sara might not be so different from Beau—a monster pretending to be a friend.

The halls were practically empty as she worked her way toward the library entrance. All worries about her unfinished paper forgotten, she pictured Kelly in a ditch on the side of the road with a bullet in her head. Her practical nature scoffed at such an outcome, but Leslie had been tangled in a web of deceit for months and had learned to ignore her rational mind. Since her sister's death, instinct had driven her, and now that uncanny sense screamed her life was in danger.

Leslie raced through the library entrance and scanned the room. When she spotted Sara's platinum hair, she made a beeline for her.

Sara looked up from her laptop and rolled her eyes. "Let me guess, Kelly's mom called you."

Leslie dropped her bag and grabbed the nearest chair. She scoured the nearby tables, anxious to see if they were alone. She positioned her chair right next to Sara. "What did you do?"

Sara recoiled, wearing a sullen frown. "Shouldn't you be askin' Kelly that question? She's the one who ran away."

Leslie's insides twisted tighter. "But you had something to do with it."

Sara held up her hands in a sign of surrender. "Hey, I didn't knock her up."

Leslie slumped forward, winded like she'd taken a blow to the gut. "Pregnant? What are you talking about?"

Sara appeared pleased with herself. "You really are dense. Didn't you see it? All the bouts of sickness, the inability to eat, the aversion to greasy foods, and she was so emotional. Come on. Even I could tell she was preggers."

"But how? She hasn't been with anyone since ..." Leslie closed her eyes, counting back the months since Beau had raped Kelly.

Sara smacked her lips, and the sound broke the silence between them. "Yeah, I did the math, too. It's his."

Leslie berated herself for not seeing the signs. She could have helped her friend and saved her from such an extreme course of action. "She has to be at least six months along. How could she not know? And if she did, why not say something to me?"

"Kelly probably couldn't accept she'd gotten knocked up by that asshole." Sara snorted. "I bet she planned to use the kid to get ahead. The baby is a Devereaux, after all."

Leslie shook with rage. "How can you say something like that? Kelly's our friend."

"Is she?" A smug smile spread across Sara's black-painted lips. "Or are we just four people thrown together by one sick-ass man?"

"Only you would think that." Leslie could almost feel her outrage dripping from her fingertips. "The rest of us have considered what we share as a close bond."

"That's the problem. None of you think like me. Never have." Her chin thrust forward, and her eyes glowed with a fiendish fire. "We've got a sweet deal here, and you're all gonna blow it. You've had money all your life, but I haven't. I don't want to jeopardize our little golden goose."

The girl had a spiteful streak. Leslie always knew it, but Sara's animosity seemed more intense than ever. She had to come up with a way to quash Sara's resentment before the greedy little idiot did something they would all regret. "What do you think Gage will do when he finds out about the child?" Leslie demanded in a loud whisper. "He'll think we lied to him. Set him up. He'll claim Kelly slept with Beau to get her hands on the Devereaux fortune, and we'll be the next ones they find buried at the river."

Sara tossed her long hair around her shoulder, not appearing too concerned about their predicament. "Maybe Gage already took care of Kelly. We both saw her leave the party with Elizabeth Devereaux. Kelly could've spilled the baby beans, and Lizzy went straight to her husband."

Leslie rubbed her face, fed up with all the second-guessing. "That doesn't explain Taylor."

"Taylor?" Sara's cruel snicker sent a tremor through Leslie. "That stupid little bitch was a tickin' time bomb." She turned to her laptop. "I'm glad she's gone. One less problem to worry about."

Sara's contempt raised the hair on Leslie's arms. Sara was a heartless bitch at times, but Leslie had never heard her spew such venom, except when it came to Beau. She'd sounded the same right before the four of them agreed to take part in his humiliating downfall. Her hate seemed tangible then, just like it was now.

Leslie reappraised her friend, her instincts once again screaming for attention. "Is there something you're not telling me about Taylor's death?"

Sara slammed her laptop closed. "Me? What would I know? She killed herself, and that's the story we're stickin' to. Better to let everyone think the nutjob offed herself. It will only help us in the end."

The comment poured gasoline over Leslie's dread. "How will it help us?"

Sara picked up her book bag from the floor. "With Gage, of course. He'll know we can be trusted and keep payin' to keep us quiet."

Leslie dragged her nails along the leg of her jeans as she remembered what Sara once said to Taylor.

"*If you screw this up for us, I'll kill you.*"

That another vicious murderer could exist right under Leslie's nose sent an explosion of icicles through her veins. She'd thought Beau was the worst person she'd ever meet. She was wrong.

Leslie tilted her chair closer. "Did you kill Taylor?" On the inside, chaos ran roughshod through Leslie as she waited for Sara's answer. Why did she sound so at ease when confronting a possible killer?

Sara didn't shout or adamantly defend her innocence. She put her laptop in her bag, keeping up a cocksure smile.

"Well, aren't you the little Nancy Drew. What makes you think I got rid of the dweeb? Gage Devereaux had a lot more motive than me. For fuck's sake, she was the one carrying around that video and picture of Beau on her phone. Talk about a smoking gun."

Leslie wanted to strangle Sara, but the dozen other students in the library kept her from it.

"I overheard Sheriff Davis telling my father they have a woman's DNA from Beau's crime scene, as well as Taylor's, and they match. Taylor is dead. Kelly is missing. That leaves you and me."

"How do I know it wasn't you?" Sara coolly appraised her. "You had more to lose than any of us if Taylor talked."

Leslie's muscles tensed. "What could Taylor have said to hurt me?"

Sara picked up a pen. "That night, after we left Beau tied up in The

Abbey, you dropped me, Kelly, and Taylor off at school. But then you disappeared. No calls, no texts. We all wondered where you went in such a hurry. After you said Gage wanted to take care of us because of what Beau did, Taylor was the first to put it together. You and Gage got rid of him."

Leslie's shoulders arched as she thought of strangling the shit out of Sara. Despite the new ride and clothes she had arranged for her, Sara would never be loyal to anyone but herself.

She put her bitterness aside and refocused, keenly aware that their game of chess was far from over. "I didn't kill Beau," Leslie argued, a hard edge in her voice. "The wild dogs got him."

Sara pointed her pen at Leslie. "You said, 'wild animals don't attack unless provoked.' So, who provoked them? That makes you an accessory to murder."

Leslie's fight disintegrated. Sara might be right. Someone had set the dogs on Beau, and Gage knew who that someone was.

"I'd rather be an accessory than accused of killing Taylor." Leslie's jaw dropped. "That's why you didn't want to do the séance and were hell-bent on getting away from the river that night after I saw Taylor in the parking lot. You were afraid she'd tell everybody what you did." Leslie got to her feet and stood over Sara. "Why did you kill her?"

Sara never took her gaze off Leslie as she tossed the pen aside. "Because she wasn't gonna stop. All she wanted was to dig up more dirt on the Devereaux family. So, I lured her to the river with some bullshit about Gage that I had to share in person. It was too easy. Then all I had to do was make it look like a suicide."

"She was our friend," Leslie said through bared teeth.

Sara thrust out her chin, adding to her defiance. "A friend wouldn't try and fuck up my meal ticket. Now, there's Luke to consider. If I play my cards right, I might end up in that fancy house with him."

Bile rose in Leslie's throat. "You won't get away with this. I'm going to the sheriff."

Sara's response was the same cruel laugh Beau had tormented her with.

"Who do you think he'll arrest first? You, me, or Gage Devereaux?" Sara asked, sounding smug. "You talk to the cops, and I'll make sure you're the one who goes down for Beau and Taylor. You had the motive. You were obsessed with Beau. You wanted him, but your sister got him. Everyone knew you didn't get along." Sara's eyes narrowed. "I'll even say you killed Dawn."

Leslie got within inches of Sara's face. "You wouldn't dare."

"Heifer, please. All I have to say is Beau found out what you did and threatened to tell, so you killed him and left him for the dogs. Taylor found out, and you silenced her, too. It'll wrap up a lot of questions the cops have about the murders. I'm sure Gage Devereaux will be so pleased with my performance that he'll pay whatever price I ask."

Leslie clenched her fists. "Nobody will believe it. I was at home when my sister died. And when Taylor died."

"So what?" Sara stood. "You know as well as I do, counselor, that evidence can be twisted to fit any circumstance, no matter the alibi. I'm sure I can supply the sheriff with enough damning testimony to make them doubt anything you say."

"You're a sick bitch."

Sara put her finger to her lips. "Shhh. If you want to stay out of prison, keep your mouth shut."

Leslie considered the shame she'd bring on her parents after all they'd been through. She would never give in to Sara's blackmail, but this wasn't the time or place to deal with her. "What about Kelly?"

Sara wrapped a platinum strand around her index finger. "What about her? Who cares."

"I care." Guilt plagued Leslie. Had she doomed both Taylor and Kelly? Leslie had involved her friends in the plan to get revenge on Beau. It was her fault they were in this situation. She grabbed her bag and backed away. She had to fix this.

Leslie recalled her meeting with Gage. It was right after Halloween when she'd walked into his office and shut the door. The silence that had greeted Leslie almost shattered her courage. He'd been at his desk, self-confident and commanding respect, when she marched up to him and calmly recited what she knew.

"*Your son killed my sister. He's assaulted and raped girls at the river. I'm not here for money, Mr. Devereaux. I just want your word that Beau will never harm anyone ever again.*"

His no-nonsense manner had permeated the room, and when he'd spoken to her, not acting shocked or devastated by the news, she knew Beau would be stopped.

Pretending to be the lady in white that night had been her idea, and Gage had procured a cloak for the occasion.

The onslaught of emotion felt like losing Dawn all over again. Guilt, sorrow, and unrelenting anger seared through her, but she hated the helplessness most of all. That unbearable inability to save a loved one from pain and suffering.

Leslie grabbed her bag and bolted through the library doors. She sprinted down the corridor, her mind racing. Before she could stop, she plowed into someone. She stumbled, but then a hand grabbed her and kept her from falling.

"Leslie?" Derek helped steady her. "What's wrong? Didn't you see me? I was standing there, calling your name, and you still ran into me."

She didn't remember any of that. All Leslie knew was that he was there. She tossed her arms around his neck, holding on to him as if her very life depended on it. She reveled in his warmth and strength. Leslie had missed that since breaking up. He'd supported her, and without him, she was rudderless.

Derek embraced Leslie, then moved to search her face. "What is it?"

"I'm so sorry," she whispered. "Please forgive me for being a fool. I shouldn't have pushed you away."

He held her. "You're trembling."

Leslie realized she couldn't lie anymore. She'd believed hiding the truth would protect Derek, but all she'd done was endanger the ones she loved.

"I have done something you may never understand and never forgive me for, but I need your help. Someone wants to kill me."

"Kill you?" He browsed the empty hall. "No one wants to—"

"It's Sara," she muttered while twisting her hands together. "She murdered Taylor. I think she got rid of Kelly, too, and I know I'm next."

Derek appeared more confused than concerned. "Why would she hurt you? You're her friend."

She drew a deep breath and looked around, panicked about being overheard. "Sara knows what I did to Beau."

Derek took a step back, his face etched with lines of disbelief. "Let's get out of here." His arm went around her shoulders. "Tell me everything, and don't you dare leave anything out."

Chapter Thirty-Six

Streetlamps sent shafts of light through Gage's windshield as he sped toward the massive black gates to the Devereaux estate. His heart hammered against his chest while he gripped the steering wheel. He glanced at the white envelope on the seat next to him, knowing he had to do something—and quickly.

Gage had found the note when he'd left his office at the brewery. He'd guessed it was another extortion letter and wasn't surprised when he read the demands.

> *I want one hundred thousand dollars, or I will tell everyone about Eva.*
>
> *I have kept quiet for twenty-five years but won't much longer.*
>
> *I will be in touch.*

He waited as the gates slowly opened, a muscle twitching in his jaw. Gage's misgivings about Taylor had been unfounded. The mention of twenty-five years was a clue about the blackmailer's identity. The timing couldn't be worse. He was more vulnerable now than ever, with the national campaign in full swing. Gage couldn't dare tell anyone and risk opening a Pandora's box about his family and Beau. He'd handle this problem alone.

He drove along the winding road to his ancestral home. The comfort of the bright lights reaching through the trees reminded Gage of who he was and how much he'd overcome. He would conquer this foe like he had many others.

He formulated a list of associates and friends he'd known for over two decades, but none of them knew about Eva. His parents had squelched any rumors by sticking to the story that she'd died as a child.

When the smooth pillars of his home bathed in white light appeared, a memory surfaced.

On the beach that fateful night, Eva had bragged about someone helping her at the institution. Gage never gambled, but he would bet money it was the same person. How could he know for sure?

You must finish this.

Edward Devereaux's gruff voice in his head told him he had no choice. Soon, he had to go to Sabine Parish and find out how Eva had escaped the psychiatric facility—and who helped her. A former employee or disgruntled worker would talk, if paid enough. It wasn't the best time to leave town, but it was a small price to pay for protecting the Devereaux name.

Inside his five-car garage, he looked for Luke's BMW. The car was there, giving him one less worry. He wasn't out partying at the river.

He stuffed the note into his pants pocket as he walked inside. He would destroy it once he was alone.

Gage eased the mudroom door closed, going over what he would tell his wife. Elizabeth had never cared when he went away on business, but with her in the grips of baby fever, he suspected there would be questions about when he would return.

Gage strolled the main hallway, keeping an eye out for his wife. He'd almost made it to his office door when he spotted her coming down the stairs.

She wore a wine-red dress that dipped low and hugged her slim waist. The sexy outfit had been purchased with one intention—seducing him.

He liked Elizabeth in red. It highlighted her creamy skin. He would have taken her upstairs had it not been for the note in his pocket.

"I was hoping you would come home early. It would be nice to have an evening together."

"Where's Luke?"

She raised her eyes to the white plaster ceiling dotted with roses and thorny vines. "Playing with the computer you gave him."

Gage chuckled. "I hope he's not watching porn."

She eased closer and placed her hand on his chest. "Would that be such a bad thing?"

He took a step back. "I have work to do."

She lowered her gaze to his crotch. "After you finish, then."

He straightened his shirt sleeve, his temper edging higher. "I have to go out of town."

"What for?" She sounded disappointed.

He kept a measure of irritation in his voice, hoping to persuade Elizabeth to buy his lie. "A new company wants to discuss the distribution of Benedict Beer. They've invited me to tour their facilities. I've decided to take them up on their offer, so I'll be gone for a while."

She nodded, but her lips remained pressed together—something she did when angry. "I see."

He wanted to tell her not to pout, but there would be no point. Elizabeth's childlike behavior had initially endeared her to him, but like most things with his wife, Gage eventually grew bored with it.

"Look after Luke while I'm away."

Her sulking ceased, and she put on a resplendent smile. "I'll take good care of him. I promise."

He lowered his head, attempting to read the change he saw in her. "I'm counting on you. If you're a bitch while I'm away, I'll hear of it."

He turned for his office door, not interested in her reaction.

Time away from her would do them both some good. He'd grown weary of her moods and her growing demands.

Elizabeth proceeded up the stairs, grinning as she ran her hand along the smooth banister. Her stomach fluttered. Gage's trip out of town would give her a few days alone with her new stepson. That would be plenty of time to get what she wanted.

She peered down the burgundy carpet running along the second floor and caught a glimpse of Beau's locked bedroom door. She quickly looked away, wanting to avoid rekindling the difficult emotions her son had left in her. Elizabeth approached Luke's bedroom. She'd been trying to run into him as often as possible to break the ice, but Luke had much of his father in him.

She stopped outside his half-open door, listening for activity. Voices floated into the hall, followed by some very intense music.

She stuck her head inside. He was on the bed, his face glued to his computer screen.

"What are you watching?"

He gave her an empty grin, reminding her of Gage. "An old detective movie."

She eased into the room. "Any good?"

Luke shrugged, appearing noncommittal. "Okay, I guess."

She sat on the edge of the bed, debating what to do next. She smoothed out her dress, hoping he would notice her.

"Gage is going out of town, so it will be just you and me for a few days. Maybe we can get to know one another."

His intrusive gaze set Elizabeth's teeth on edge. Why did she feel like a mare at auction?

Luke pushed the computer aside, the drama paused on the screen. "Let's go out to dinner. Gage wants me to get acquainted with more people in town, and you can help me. What's the best restaurant in St. Benedict?"

"Marillo's. Joyce Davidson owns it. Best Italian food anywhere. I'll make a reservation."

His smile wasn't empty this time, but full and amiable. "Perfect."

Elizabeth stood. This might turn out to be easier than she thought. "I look forward to it."

On her way out of the room, she noticed red mud on his loafers by the door—the ones she'd bought him. She turned back to the bed. "How did you get that mud on your shoes?"

He got to his feet and strolled toward her. "I met some friends at the river earlier."

The mention of the river brought on a brief bout of shivering. Elizabeth struggled to keep her curiosity in check. "Did you meet Sara Bissell there?"

"What if I did?" He stood over her, appearing as intimidating as Gage. "Are you going to tell me to stay away from her, too?"

A familiar dull pang went down her side—something she got whenever Gage hovered, demanding she do as he wanted.

"Gage told me she was all over you at the party. You need to be careful with girls like her."

"I'm not interested in girls." His gaze traveled the length of her dress. "I've never had much in common with younger women." Luke moved back to the bed. "I went to the river to see some friends. They're worried about Kelly Norton. She's missing."

"Girls like that are always chasing after something. I'm sure Kelly will be back soon." She picked up his muddy shoes. "I'll get these cleaned for you."

Luke settled back, gazing up at her. "I hope while Gage is gone, we can become friends."

"Me, too." She hurried out of the room and closed the door.

In the hall, Elizabeth bit her lower lip but couldn't suppress a smile. *We'll be very good friends by the time he gets back. I promise.*

Chapter Thirty-Seven

Excruciating pain roused Kelly from a fitful sleep. She woke on a rickety metal bed and peered around the room. Candlelight flickered on roughhewn walls with one small window overlooking the dark woods. It reminded her of a prison in a scary movie. Her jacket and a few towels were on a chair beside the bed, but there was no sign of her purse.

Kelly attempted to pull herself up, but a long silver chain secured to her wrist kept her from getting out of bed. She cast aside the blanket and saw a shackle around her left ankle. Kelly yanked at the chains. "No, no, what is this? What's going on," she cried.

Kelly's heart felt like it would explode. A debilitating wave of dizziness overtook her, and she crumpled back on the lumpy mattress. Kelly's entire body hurt. Her stomach was as hard as a rock, and she had no strength.

"You shouldn't sit up." The woman's voice came from the darkened doorway. "The drugs in your system will weaken you, but they'll do the job."

Freezing panic went up her spine. The last thing she could remember was the party and telling Mrs. Devereaux about the baby. She'd run outside to the parking lot after Beau's mother had scoffed at her claim and called her a worthless slut. In the cold night air, tears had stung her cheeks. Then a funny pain had cropped up on her neck. She thought it was a bug bite, but not long after, she'd gotten woozy and then blacked out.

"What am I doing here?" Kelly's demanded in a raspy voice.

A figure in a brown cloak entered the room. The hood hid her face while the dim light cast an ethereal glow.

"Who the hell are you?" Tales of monks and the haunted abbey raced through her muddled mind.

A hand emerged from the sleeve of the cloak. Pale and graceful, it wasn't ghostly, but human.

"Now, now. I've been looking after you for a while." The stranger moved closer. "You and your baby will be safe."

A searing pain shot through Kelly's stomach. She raised her knees, and the chain connecting her to the bed rattled as she moved.

"You know I'm pregnant? How?"

The woman beneath the cloak laughed.

"Oh, I've been watching you and your friends for quite a while at The Abbey." She pushed her hood back, revealing sharp cheekbones, fiery eyes, and pale skin. Her strawberry blonde hair curled around her shoulder in a long braid. "I know all about your local legends, the wild dogs, the monks, the lady in white." She paused and eerily grinned. "I've seen her, you know, on nights when the moon is full."

The barking dogs outside her window sent Kelly retreating to a corner of the bed.

"My children are hungry," her captor told her. "I should feed them."

The dogs, the monk robe—Kelly's terror intensified. "Why? What do you want?"

Her captor's smile was almost motherly. "I have to protect my son. He must take his rightful place beside his father. It's what I've sacrificed everything for."

Throbbing flared in Kelly's forehead, and her wooziness returned. She concentrated on what was happening to her, trying to comprehend why anyone would do this. "I don't understand. Who is your son?"

The woman's smile vanished, and a dark, malevolent shadow washed over her delicate features.

"You know, I've seen you with him. Your eyes give away your affection. But that's not his child in your belly. It's Beau's."

Kelly put a protective arm over her midriff. "How could you know that?"

The dogs barked again, and the woman glanced out the window. "I saw Beau take you to the cells that night. I know what he did to you and the others. But rest assured, I gave him the end he deserved."

Kelly's hands trembled. "Wait. Are you saying you killed Beau?"

The woman gazed into Kelly's eyes. "I saw him running through the woods near the river that night, and I set my pack on him. His screams did go on, until I ordered my children to end him." She cocked her head. "Just before he died, he called me Leslie."

Bitter disbelief rippled through Kelly. The area teemed with crowds of rowdy teenagers, families tubing the river, and hunters searching for game. How had this woman lived in the woods without a soul knowing she was there?

"Who are you?"

"My name is Pamela Cross." She scowled. "I believe you know my son, Luke."

Kelly stared vacantly at her. "What?" Another hard pain shot through Kelly's stomach, bending her over in bed, and she screamed. Sweat poured from her face as she gripped the blanket. The chain attached to her ankle jingled as her body shook.

Kelly sucked in air, trying to clear her head. It didn't work. Her skin was on fire, and no matter how she turned in the bed, her discomfort never ceased.

"What did you give me?" she spit out between gritted teeth.

The woman who snatched her from the brewery stood over her, a hand on Kelly's swollen abdomen. Her scary eyes glinted in the light from the kerosene lamp. "Just a little something to speed things along. You're baby's almost here. Time to wake up and push."

"No. I need to go to the hospital," Kelly begged in a quivering voice.

Pamela wiped Kelly's brow with a rag. "Now, now. This is how it's supposed to be. I felt as you do when I had my son. Just when you think you're gonna die, a miracle happens."

An unending cramp sent Kelly falling back on the bed. A shriek erupted from her lips. The dogs outside her window howled as if sharing her anguish.

A gush of fluid poured from between her legs, saturating the sheets.

Panic surged through her. *What's that?* Kelly raised her head, fighting the urge to vomit as she glimpsed the blood-tinged liquid beneath her.

Something cold touched her inner thigh. She might have recoiled at the violation if it weren't for the agony raging through her.

"I can feel the head," Pamela announced in a triumphant tone.

Kelly wanted to fight back against the psychotic woman, but the resistance siphoned out of her as another contraction hit. She wanted to draw her knees up and curl into a ball until her suffering went away.

She screamed again, and then something hard was shoved into her mouth.

"Bite down on that and push with all your might." Pamela positioned herself on the bed, spreading Kelly's knees apart. "Let's get this baby out of you."

Kelly thought of her mother and how much she wanted her there. She wished she'd told her about the baby. Things might have been different, and she wouldn't have ended up in the woods being tended to by a crazy woman with wild dogs.

The burning in her groin raced along her spine, knotting every muscle in her lower back, making her feel as if she were about to split apart. Kelly had never known such unbearable pain.

"Help me," she mumbled over the object in her mouth.

Pamela seemed uninterested in what she endured. It wasn't until she saw the knife in the woman's hand that Kelly's efforts to push out her baby floundered.

Kelly ripped the wooden block from her mouth. "What's that for?"

Pamela sat perched between Kelly's legs. "To cut the cord. Now, give me another big push. If you don't get this baby out, you'll both die, and I can't have that."

Kelly became overwhelmed by another incapacitating spasm. She closed her eyes and concentrated on bearing down, using every ounce of strength to help her baby.

Please let everything be all right.

Her silent prayer set off a flurry of worries. She'd read about the importance of prenatal care, being monitored by a doctor, and a healthy diet to help a child—all the things she'd never done. Images of her baby deformed or dead plagued her as the last of the forceful contractions ignited another throaty wail.

"There, that's it," Pamela encouraged. "Keep going."

Kelly tucked her chin into her chest and gave one last tortuous push. An inferno exploded between her legs. Then she felt the tear of flesh and a rush of more warm liquid spilling out of her.

She rocked back on the bed, unable to go on. Thankfully, the incapacitating contractions ended, and relief coursed through her.

Kelly sucked in the stifling air, grateful for the end to her ordeal. Then, as silence surrounded her, she anxiously looked for her child.

She glanced up to see Pamela grabbing for towels on the chair.

"Is my baby okay?" Kelly asked, on the verge of hysteria.

Pamela said nothing as she wrapped something in the swath of towels.

Kelly propped herself on her elbows, wincing at the movement. Her groin throbbed, and her body ached. "What is it? What's wrong?"

A weak cry, like the high-pitched call of a bird, filled the room.

Pamela stood, cooing and smiling at the bundle in her arms. "She's perfect."

"She?" Tears blurred Kelly's vision. "I have a daughter?"

Pamela never answered. She appeared too intent on the tiny human she cradled.

A well of numbing jealousy rose in Kelly. Why should the crazy cow get those first precious moments with her child? "Give her to me," Kelly demanded.

Pamela didn't look at her as she said, "You rest, girl."

"No. I want to see her," Kelly argued, her strength returning.

Pamela headed to the entrance of the suffocating bedroom, carrying the baby.

Kelly couldn't stand watching her child in the arms of another. She ached to hold her, to see her face. It didn't matter who the father was or how she came to be, all she wanted was her daughter and a fresh start.

"Bring her to me," Kelly called out, working her way to the edge of the bed.

Pamela stopped at the doorway and faced Kelly, a malicious grin on her lips. "I'll take care of her. Don't you worry. I've got big plans for this one."

Chapter Thirty-Eight

The soothing tap of rain on the windshield eased Leslie's trembling as they sat in the parking lot of Mo's Diner. The warm cup of coffee Derek had bought helped, too. His quiet, nonjudgmental way of listening calmed her most of all. It was cathartic, telling him what they had done to Beau, the pact the girls had forged, the agreement she'd made with Gage, and the conversation between her father and the sheriff—even her disclosure about Sara's confession had rolled off her tongue without reservation.

"I knew something was wrong, but I don't get why you didn't want to tell me any of this," Derek said after a long pause.

"I was wrong to keep things from you," she whispered. "But I had to protect you. I couldn't drag you into my mess. What I did, I did for my sister, and it's me who must suffer if we get caught. Not you."

He clasped her hand and squeezed it. "Don't you get it? Anything that happens to you happens to me. No matter where this goes, there can be no more secrets. Do you hear me?"

His support bolstered her. Come what may, she could weather the storm better with Derek than without him.

"I don't care about what you did to Beau." Derek let go of her hand. "That prick deserved what he got. But how Gage wrangled you and the others in, buying everyone off with clothes and cars—"

"Sara was into the clothes, not the rest of us," she admitted as shame cracked her voice. "He didn't buy us off. He gave our parents bonuses to provide us with what we wanted. Looking back, he probably planned it that way to make sure he was protected. He could never say it was a bribe as long as it was given to our parents."

Derek wiped away a thin film of sweat from his forehead "How can you believe anything Sara told you? Especially accusing you of killing Dawn. No one will trust a word out of her mouth."

Leslie turned down the heat. "I know, but Sara can make up any story she likes and drag my name through the mud. My father will spend months defending me, and what if he learns the truth about what I did? I can't let that happen. Then there's the problem of the DNA Sheriff Davis found at Taylor's crime scene. It belongs to a woman—a woman who was at Beau's murder scene. If it wasn't mine or Kelly's, that only leaves Sara. I have to find something on her."

Derek leaned across the central console. "No, you have to go to the cops and tell them everything."

She set her coffee in the cup rest. "I can't risk Sara turning on me. Besides, Sheriff Davis knows Gage's father killed his sister, Eva. He's going to cover it up for him. What chance do I have of the police listening to anything I have to say about Taylor, Beau, or even Kelly? They need a scapegoat. I can't be that."

"Then what about confronting Gage?" Derek asked.

"No way." She emphatically shook her head. "I can't go to him until I know for sure about Kelly and Taylor, or at least have something to protect myself."

"Then what do we do?"

Everything she knew about the Devereaux family rolled around in her head like eggs in a basket. Mainly what the sheriff told her father about Eva. "Maybe we start with Gage's sister—the woman they found at the river. If we can learn more about her, that'll be something we can use to make people listen to us, believe us. It would be worth checking her out. The problem is that the only place I know to look is in Sabine Parish."

He scratched his head. "Sabine Parish? What's there?"

"Broadmoor Institution. The facility where Eva was kept. I looked it up online. Maybe we could find someone who knew her." She turned to him, more compelled by her idea with every passing second. "If Gage's family covered up his sister's death, what else are they hiding? I'm sure we'll find some answers there."

A wary gleam sprang to life in his eyes. "Are you sure you don't want Luke to go with you? I know you two are—"

"We're friends. Nothing more," she insisted, cutting him off. "He's a Devereaux."

"And if he wasn't a Devereaux?"

An avalanche of self-doubt swept through her. She stared at the droplets spattering the windshield, searching for something to appease Derek. "Sara is the one chasing him. Not me. He's not my type. You know that."

He studied her, silent for a moment. "Okay, then. So, we drive to Sabine Parish and check out this Eva. But when do you propose we do this? People will want to know where we're going."

An idea popped into her head. Leslie grabbed her book bag and scrounged for her phone. When she was able to pull up her school app, she showed Derek the calendar on her screen. "We've got graduation coming up. We can go after that and do some snooping."

He combed his hand through his hair. "What do we tell your parents? My mother? And anyone else who asks. We need a plausible story for the trip."

She put her phone in her bag, her plan brewing. "We're heading to LSU to visit the campus. My father will be thrilled. He'll probably even pay for the trip."

Derek's mouth opened in silent surprise. "I had no idea you were this calculating."

"I prefer the term creative." Leslie smirked. "Dad likes us together. He trusts you. And it's the only way I can think he'll let me out of his sight for more than a few days."

"But your mother won't like it," he countered in a defeated tone. "She'll stop us from going anywhere. There must be another way. Maybe we can do some investigating online."

"No." She shook her head, determined. "We have to go to Sabine Parish. Since my sister died, I feel like I've been watching life pass me by. This is my chance to set things right. I thought I was avenging Dawn's death, but there's no avenging anyone's loss. This will allow me to do something bigger than all of us. I can expose a corrupt family and everybody will see what they truly are—a sick and twisted lie."

Derek sat back in his seat, grinning. "'*The impact of their demise will resonate like a dying star throughout the heavens. But beware their wrath. Such a fate can fashion the monsters men come to fear.*'"

"*The Dust of Giants.*" She smiled, remembering his favorite book. "The story about the Greek Titans."

"I've got a feeling we're going to see a battle of the titans played out firsthand." His features darkened as he surveyed the parking lot. "I'm sticking close to you from now on. Are you sure you're okay with that?"

She glowed on the inside, ecstatic to have him back in her life. Derek took away every bit of cold that had haunted her for months. "I'm counting on it."

"Glad we're agreed." He pulled her into his arms and kissed her head. "From now on, where you go, I go."

She curled into his chest, comforted by his presence. Derek gave her clarity. With him, she felt like herself again.

What about Luke? Have you forgotten how he makes you feel?

The disconcerting inner voice belonged to Dawn. Her sister wouldn't have cast the newly crowned son of Gage Devereaux aside so quickly—but she wasn't her twin. Or was she?

Grief was a slippery slope. It could take away identities, friends, family, and lovers, if allowed. For Leslie, it had opened a door. Before losing her sister, she'd shied away from adventure, opportunities, and men, wanting to stay the course she'd set for herself. Now she longed to shed her rigid mindset and go wherever life took her.

She could almost hear Dawn cheering. Reason enough to keep her options open.

EPILOGUE

Kent's chair groaned as he eased back. His neck ached after spending the day behind the wheel of his patrol car. He tossed his Stetson on his desk and sighed at the stack of files needing his signature. This was a small town, supposedly filled with small-town crimes. Murder cases had never figured into his plans in St. Benedict. But here he was, back in the thick of it like his NOPD days, buried in autopsy reports and crime investigation records.

He picked up his favorite coffee mug and frowned. "Noreen, we got any fresh coffee?"

A plump woman with graying brown hair piled atop her head and secured with two pencils stood in his doorway. "I can put a fresh pot on. Give me a sec."

Kent was grateful his secretary had stuck with him for the years he'd been sheriff. "Thanks, I'm gonna need it."

Noreen peered at him over her glasses. "You get that situation straightened out with Harold's dogs?"

Kent winced as he shifted in his chair. "You wanna tell me why I'm the one who has to deal with Harold Pinter every time his coonhounds get out?"

Noreen chuckled. "Because Harold won't listen to anyone but the sheriff. He'd probably shoot one of your deputies if they showed up at his farm. You know how onery he is." She walked up to his desk and eyed the paperwork. "When you're done with those, Gage sent over some new figures for next year's department budget. He needs you to okay them."

Kent closed his eyes, wishing his boss wasn't the father of one of his murder victims. "Yeah. I'll take a look at that later."

Doreen rested her hand on her hip. "Not too much later. You know how he is if you keep him waiting."

He pounded the space bar on his keyboard to wake up his computer. "You don't need to remind me."

Doreen repositioned a pencil stuffed in her lopsided bun. "And Wayne from IT said you gotta empty your spam folder. It's full again, and he's sick of doing it for you."

Kent briefly pictured shooting a bullet into the ass of the young, gangly IT guy who annoyed him. Especially his habit of popping bubble gum as he worked. "Yeah, yeah. I'll put that on my list."

Noreen chuckled. "I'd better call Emma and tell her you'll be late for dinner." His secretary left his cubicle of an office.

Kent grumbled under his breath. There were days he hated his job, but the people of St. Benedict kept him wearing his sheriff's badge. He hated abandoning them, especially when they needed him most.

Except for Harold Pinter. He's an asshole.

When Kent solved the murders troubling his town, he might think of hanging up his hat. He wanted to catch the son of a bitch who had left dead bodies in his wake. Nobody deserved the horrid endings he'd witnessed. Someone had to pay for those crimes.

Kent squinted at his computer screen, searching for the email icon. He needed reading glasses but hated feeling old. The moment the long list of spam emails popped up, he slouched in his chair. Kent hated technology. It made people lazy and stupid—or stupider, in some cases.

The tedious task of looking through the emails distracted him for a while. He had to make sure he didn't miss something important. Cases could fall apart if a detective missed evidence in something as simple as an email. Diligence was the key. Well, diligence and coffee.

The aroma of the percolating coffee drifted in his door, and he grabbed his mug. Kent was about to leave his desk when he noticed a familiar name in his spam folder—TaylorHaskinsLAgirl@gmail.com.

Kent set his cup aside. *Taylor? It can't be.*

He clicked on the email and held his breath.

If you are reading this, I am dead.
You might find the attachments interesting.
Taylor

Kent reread the message twice. One picture and one video waited in a side window for viewing. He debated whether this was a prank to download a virus onto his computer. It wouldn't be the first time, but someone sending an email with Taylor's name made him willing to take the chance.

Kent started with the video. It appeared to be a poorly lit sex tape of a man and woman in a small room. The shaky quality made it difficult to recognize the faces, but then something caught his eye, and he paused the tape. Beau Devereaux had his hands around a woman's neck, but the dark-haired female on the cot was hard to make out.

A slow burn erupted in Kent's chest. He remembered Andrea Harrison, the naked girl who'd washed up at the river with a broken neck.

"Son of a bitch." Kent slapped his palm against his desk. The tape incriminated Beau in her death. "I always knew you were a sick little shit." A dark photo filled the screen. A man bound to a chair that had toppled over took shape. Candles surrounded him, with some scattered across the floor. The grainy image was hard to make out, but he took a sharp breath as the face became clear. It was Beau Devereaux.

"You gotta be kidding me." Kent closely examined the picture. Zip ties secured Beau's wrists and ankles to the chair. It wasn't until Kent spotted a fallen charred beam that the significance of the picture resonated with him. It must have been taken on the last night of Beau's life.

He was murdered. I knew it.

Kent checked the date of Taylor's email. It was sent the day after she was found dead. She must have scheduled it to send later. But why? "If Taylor went to the river that night to meet someone and thought she might not make it back, this was her last message," he mumbled, tapping his computer screen. "That means Taylor Haskins knew her killer."

Kent rocked back, his mind a whirlwind of questions, the biggest of which was why Taylor Haskins had possessed such a photo. Kent's right hand closed into a fist as he slowly put the pieces together.

Fuck me.

ALEXANDREA WEIS · LUCAS ASTOR

RIVER OF GHOSTS

Bonus Chapter: River of Ghosts ~Book III~

Chapter One

Work lamps set up along the cordoned off beach blazed through the darkness, illuminating the dark water of the Bogue Falaya River. The chill in the air settled into Sheriff Kent Davis's bones as he listened to the hum of the police generator. Red and blue lights flashed in the distance from the parking lot. Kent hated the early morning calls that woke him from a dead sleep. They were always bad news, but this was worse than he could have imagined.

Kent kicked the sand off his cowboy boots and nudged his Stetson back. Around him, deputies in blue sheriff's department uniforms swept the brightly lit area, searching the picnic benches and trash cans for any clues. He feared the repercussions of the latest grim discovery along the Louisiana river when news reached the residents of St. Benedict.

There's gonna be hell to pay.

A black body bag waited by the remains of the young woman he'd known only by name—Kelly Norton. A blue tarp covered her wet, naked body, but he could still picture the wide, ugly tear in her throat that exposed her spine. Her head was so unstable, hanging only by sinew, he feared when the technicians moved the body, they might decapitate her.

Dr. Bill Broussard turned from the victim and ambled toward him. The pear-shaped man with thick, black-framed glasses raised the crime scene tape and awkwardly ducked under it.

"Don't take this the wrong way, Kent, but I'm sick of meeting you at the river." The St. Tammany Parish Coroner took a deep breath, looking grim. "This is getting old."

"She was reported missing by her mother a few weeks ago. We thought she might be a runaway, but I never expected she'd end up like—"

"Beau Devereaux? She's even chewed up like him. Identical dog bite radius, too. And this is close to where he died. It's almost like someone is taunting us." He pressed his meaty lips together. "By the looks of her perineum and the heavy amount of bloody discharge, my guess is she was killed soon after giving birth."

Kent's insides burned. How was he going to break this news to her mother? "I'll get my people on the phone to local hospitals to see if they have any record of someone fitting Kelly Norton's description who recently had a baby."

"She didn't give birth in a hospital," the coroner said, his eyes bereft of light. "The ligature bruising on her wrist and ankle looks fresh. She was tied up while she had her baby. After that, they set the dogs on her."

Kent swallowed back bile. He removed his hat and combed his hand through his hair. "What was the damn point of doing that? Did they want her baby? Or are we gonna find a newborn along the river, too." Kent fought to control his shaky voice. "This makes no sense."

Bill waved men in white hazmat suits forward. "I gave up looking for sense in anything the day after I took this job."

Kent watched as Bill's technicians lifted the tarp covering Kelly's body. He wanted to turn away to respect her remains, but the detective in him wouldn't allow it. Every picture Kent's mind took would help him get one step closer to the killer. And he was determined to find the son of a bitch who'd done this.

Kelly Norton was left naked on the beach, with jagged tears surrounded by patches of black dried blood marring her arms, chest, legs, and neck. Her long, red hair fanned out behind her—positioned by the killer, no doubt. Her arms remained tucked at her sides, but her legs were splayed.

"I wonder how she got here." Kent said. "We didn't see any drag marks."

Bill took a tablet from one of his technicians. "I'll know more after the autopsy." He scribbled his name on the pad with his finger. "When are you going to tell her family?"

The churn in Kent's stomach sent a wave of nausea through him. "I'll go see her mother after I leave here. She's worked for Gage Devereaux for years."

Bill handed the tablet back. "Did you wake Gage with the news?"

Kent observed the men in hazmat suits carefully shifting Kelly's remains onto the black bag. "He's out of town on business. I'll tell him when he gets home."

"I'm glad I don't have your job." Bill patted his shoulder. "I do better with the dead than the living."

Kent understood Bill's trepidation. He'd visited too many homes and watched too many parents crumble when told of their child's death. The only person who had not fallen apart was Gage. He remembered how stonelike the patriarch of St. Benedict remained when he broke the news of his son's demise. He didn't make a sound, didn't flinch, and his face never twitched. The blood in Gage's veins had to be cold as ice.

Bill wiped beads of sweat from his upper lip. "The girl's mother is going to ask about the baby. What're you gonna say?"

Kent tapped his hat against his thigh, dreading that meeting. "Her mother never mentioned the girl was pregnant when she filed the missing persons report. I have a feeling she didn't know."

"Holy Mary, Mother of God." Bill lowered his head, accentuating the bulge of his double chin. "I don't envy you having to tell her. And people are gonna shit when they hear about another body."

Kent straightened his back, readying himself for the mass hysteria about to grip the small town. "I'll tell everyone the same thing. This is a high-priority case, and we'll do everything in our power to find the killer."

The purr of the zipper slowly locking away Kelly's remains set Kent's teeth on edge. He'd heard the same noise too many times to count in his career, but lately, the finality of sealing someone into a body bag disturbed him more. St. Benedict had offered a haven from the non-stop assembly line of murder cases he'd worked in New Orleans, and he wished he could shut off his emotions like he had when at the NOPD.

Kent turned to Bill as the technicians lifted Kelly's body from the sand. "You know the drill. Get me the autopsy report as soon as you can. If you find anything unusual, call me right away."

"What do you define as unusual?" Bill pushed his glasses back up on his nose. "Every case has been unusual."

Kent thumbed the brim of his Stetson. "You can say that again."

Bill let out a long sigh, sounding exasperated. "Any luck finding me a dog big enough to bite like that?"

"Not yet. And as you pointed out, this is more than a dog attack." Kent clenched his jaw. "Someone kidnapped her, stood by as she gave birth, and then let the dogs have her. I need something I can use here. We're running out of time."

"I'll do my best." Bill hesitated, giving Kent a once over with his beady gaze. "By the way, where's the case of scotch you owe me for helping out on that Jane Doe?"

Kent sagged his shoulders as he remembered his debt. He hated owing people, but in his line of work, favors helped solve crimes. "I'll make sure you get it before the week is out." Kent offered his friend a half-hearted smile. "I appreciate what you did. You eliminated a lot of headaches with that Jane Doe. If her cause of death remained a homicide, I couldn't get her a decent burial."

"Tell me you found a place to put her." Bill cocked an eyebrow. "I'd sure like her out of my freezer."

Kent scratched the stubble on his chin. "Gage Deveraux is handling it. We should have her out of your hair after processing the paperwork in another day or two."

"Glad to hear it." Bill glanced at the technicians carrying the black bag across the beach. "Because my little morgue is getting crowded."

Kent put his hat on and nodded before turning to go. Reaching the narrow path covered in pine needles, his thoughts shifted to the wave of panic sure to spread through St. Benedict when news of Kelly Norton's death broke.

But what Kent dreaded most was confronting the frigid, stern gaze of his boss, Gage Devereaux. What would he tell the man when he demanded answers for why another body had turned up at the river?

Kent didn't have one fucking clue.

About the Authors

Alexandrea Weis, RN-CS, PhD, is a multi-award-winning author, advanced practice registered nurse, and historian who was born and raised in the French Quarter. She has taught at major universities and worked in nursing for thirty years, dealing with victims of sexual assault, abuse, and mental illness in a clinical setting at New Orleans area hospitals.

Raised in the motion picture industry as the daughter of a director, Weis learned to tell stories from a different perspective. She grew up on movie sets from *Live and Let Die* with Roger Moore to *My Name is Nobody* starring Henry Fonda. The first person to give her writing advice was Tennessee Williams, a family friend.

A permitted/certified wildlife rehabber with Louisiana Wildlife and Fisheries, Weis rescues orphaned and injured animals. She lives with her husband and pets outside of New Orleans.

Weis is a member of the International Thriller Writers (ITW) and the Horror Writers Association (HWA).

www.AlexandreaWeis.com

Lucas Astor is an award-winning author and poet with a penchant for telling stories that delve into the dark side of the human psyche. He likes to explore the evil that exists not just in the world, but right next door, behind a smiling face.

Astor is from New York, has resided in Central America and the Middle East, and traveled throughout Europe. He currently lives outside of Nashville, TN.

www.LucasAstor.com